Where the Heart Is by Sally Lai...
After marrying the man of ...
whisked away from Laurelwoo...
and taken hundreds of miles a... ...ism. Nothing her
husband Blake has said about life at a lumber mill prepares her for
what she finds. Blake is gone almost every waking hour, and Leah
faces a loneliness she has never known. Will she ever find happiness in this wilderness?

New Beginnings by DiAnn Mills
Betsy Malone is living a lie. Married to her childhood sweetheart, Nicholas, Betsy tries desperately to hide her horrible
secret: She no longer loves him, if she ever did. Always percep-
tive, Nicholas can't be fooled for long, and Betsy fears what will
happen when he discovers the truth.

Turbulent Times by Andrea Boeshaar
A fractured family. That's all the century-old painting passed
down in his family has ever meant to college student Nick
Malone. A senior at Kent State University and an active pro-
tester against the Vietnam War, Nick wants to provide a real
family for his unborn child. But his girlfriend Raine's parents
disown her when she insists on marrying Nick, and they soon
realize that they need more than love to build a strong home.
Will they find real answers in the midst of turbulent times?

Going Home Again by Yvonne Lehman
Thomas Wolfe once said, "You can't go home again," and Nick
Malone is certain that statement is true. He's tried it, and it
hasn't worked. Nor can he change the past, as much as he wants
to. It's over. Done. As unchangeable as the family painting that
haunts his memory. Will the truth set him free, or in going home
again, will he bring untold harm to people he loves?

her dreams, Leah Somerville is
her beloved childhood home.
way to Wrangan Valley

The Painting

A Timeless Treasure of Four All-New Novellas

Andrea Boeshaar
Sally Laity
Yvonne Lehman
DiAnn Mills

BARBOUR
PUBLISHING, INC.
Uhrichsville, Ohio

Where the Heart Is © MCMXCVI by Sally Laity.
New Beginnings © MCMXCVI by DiAnn Mills.
Turbulent Times © MCMXCVI by Andrea Boeshaar.
Going Home Again © MCMXCVI by Yvonne Lehman.

Illustrations by Mari Goering

ISBN 1-57748-640-4

All Scripture quotations are taken from the King James Version of the Bible.

Published by Barbour Publishing, Inc., P.O. Box 719, Uhrichsville, Ohio 44683 http://www.barbourbooks.com

Member of the
Evangelical Christian
Publishers Association

Printed in the United States of America.

The Painting

Where the Heart Is

by Sally Laity

To Don, forever home of my heart

Special thanks to
Dianna, Gloria, and Andrea. . .
World–Class critique buddies

Chapter 1

Pennsylvania, 1860

L eah Somerville paused in taking down the wash and breathed deeply of the moist, late winter breeze. Above her head, huge clouds scudded across the heavens, their pristine puffs of white a stark contrast against the cerulean blue sky. And all around, rivulets of water trickled from leftover mounds of dull snow, forming puddles while more and more patches of winter-barren ground appeared beneath the March sunlight. Proof of spring's imminence.

She smiled at the fresh scent of the sheets as she folded and put them into the basket. They'd be crisp and clean on Daddy's bed tomorrow, just the way he liked them. Not that anything was really the way Daddy liked anymore, since a massive stroke left him paralyzed on one side and hardly able to speak. Purposely turning her thoughts away from the unpleasant matter, Leah tucked the last clothespin into her coat pocket and bent to pick up the laundry.

The back door banged open just then, and her lanky,

dark-haired younger brother, Willis, burst out, leaping down the three porch steps and bounding toward her, his work boots thudding over the half-frozen ground. "It's mine!" The obvious excitement that made his voice crack added a spark to the chestnut-brown eyes so prominent in the Somerville family.

"What's yours?" she had to ask.

"This. Everything. Mom says it's my place now." He flung his muscled arms wide and spun in a circle, not even attempting to harness his joy.

"Wait a minute, Will." Leah set down her burden to brush aside a pesky strand of sable hair the wind feathered across her face. "What are you talking about?"

He grinned, and a broad sweep of even white teeth added boyish charm to features growing more manly and appealing by the day. "Mom says the place is too big for her to manage, now that Dad's confined to his bed. She wants me to get married and take over. I'm gonna go tell Marty we don't have to wait any longer."

With that, he whirled around and took off down the muddy lane toward the road, his long legs quickly covering the mile-and-a-half distance to the Sands' farm.

Gaping after him, Leah reminded herself to close her mouth as a heaviness settled over her spirit. Laurelwood, Will's already? He was the only son, and inside she'd always known the property would pass to him one day. But he was still just a kid. He wouldn't be eighteen for three more months. At twenty-two, and almost five years older than he, Leah had worked longer and harder than either of her two younger siblings to help make the orchards profitable. Somehow she'd hoped Will wouldn't want the place, that her parents would decide she'd earned it. How could she have been so stupid? So naive?

She turned and let her gaze roam the large, homey house her paternal grandfather had built for his bride—two stories of white clapboard with the broad front porch and weathered roof, set in the lush green Back Mountain area of northeastern Pennsylvania, in Huntsville. Leah, twenty-year-old Nancy, and Willis had all been born here, as had their father before them. She couldn't even imagine living anywhere else. But soon her kid brother would marry her own very best friend, Martha Sands, and the two would raise a new brood of little ones who would grow up roaming the rolling hills around the Somerville Orchards. She knew she should have seen this coming, but she hadn't. Not even after Nancy married last summer and moved into town with her schoolteacher husband, Tim Grogan. Now it hurt to dwell on her own inevitable departure. With a sigh, she retrieved the laundry basket and trudged back into the house.

Her mother, Alice, turned from the big coal stove, where she'd been boiling water to brew Daddy's afternoon tea. One hand rested on her hip, and she stretched that shoulder, as if to relieve a kink. "They've dried already?"

Leah nodded and hung her coat on the rack of wall pegs just inside the door. "It's really quite mild today. I can smell spring in the air."

"Wouldn't that be a treat, an early spring. These old bones never ache so much once winter is finally over."

"You're not old, Mom," Leah chided, assessing her mother's trim frame and straight posture in the maroon calico day gown and protective apron. Except for the hours she spent lately sitting with Daddy, she never seemed to stop fussing about the house, keeping it tidy or baking things to satisfy the appetites of her hungry family. "Your hair might be a touch gray, but you're still strong and healthy. Why, there aren't half as many wrinkles in your face as there are in Opal Spalding's, and she's the same age as you."

"That may very well be," she said with a droll smile, tucking some loose hairs into the salt-and-pepper bun at her neck, "but I don't feel much like a young filly anymore. We all considered your dad hale and hearty, too, but look what happened to him. Struck down in his prime— and scarcely two years older than I. It gives a person pause for thought."

"I suppose."

Her mother's sparse brows drew into a frown, revealing new lines of strain around her azure eyes—the only different-colored ones in the family. "Is something troubling you, daughter?"

Debating whether to confess her disappointment, Leah opted not to. She shook her head. Will's announcement had been so recent and unexpected, she needed time to think about things. Time to pray. Even to start planning for a future elsewhere. Obviously their parents thought they were doing the right thing.

But was it the best thing? Leah knew Will and his shortcomings better than anybody, except perhaps Martha Sands. Undoubtedly the prettiest young woman within a ten-mile radius, Marty could have had her pick of any eligible bachelor, until Willis set his cap for her and turned on the charm.

Oh well, Leah told herself as she gathered a stack of linens to put away in the hall closet. Will could do worse than wed Marty. The girl's few years' advantage in age and maturity would help settle him down. It would be a good match. And to her credit, she did love Laurelwood.

"Come have tea with us, dear," her mother said in passing as Leah placed the clean sheets and towels neatly in their spots on the shelves. "I've an extra cup here."

"Sounds lovely. I'll be right there."

Moments later, she joined her parents in the sickroom. The master bedroom hadn't had that qualification for years, not since Grandmother Somerville's final lingering illness. Now despite the pretty floral wallpaper, the hand-stitched quilt, and other needlework accessories that always gave it such a welcoming air, it had that same stuffy odor again, all closed up from winter. Leah softly approached the walnut four-poster and gave her father a thin smile. "Daddy."

Graham Somerville's dark eyes glistened in recognition, and he attempted as much of a smile as he could manage from his propped-up position on half a dozen pillows. His pallor was nearly the same hue as his thinning gray hair. And he appeared so frail now, so. . .small.

Sitting on the bed next to him, Mother offered him spoonfuls of tea. "He's looking better, don't you think?" she asked a little too brightly. "Any day now he'll be jumping up and dancing a jig, wait and see."

"You do look well, Daddy," Leah said dutifully, turning to pour herself a cup of the hot brew and moving to the window. "It's lovely outside today. Like spring, almost. The orchards will soon be filled with apple blossoms."

But even as she passed along the cheerful news, she sensed that his recovery, if the Lord so willed, would be a long, hard one. Doc Fredericks was skeptical there would be much improvement.

Mother glanced her way. "I suppose Will told you his big news."

"Yes, just before I came inside. He certainly seemed thrilled." *To say the least. Unlike me, he was smart enough to have expected it.* It was all Leah could do to suppress her innermost feelings. Switching her attention to the lace curtain panels, she gazed through them as she sipped some of her drink.

"Well, actually," Mother went on, "your father and I discussed the idea some time ago. Of course, we were thinking of the future, but that's of no consequence. It's time Will took on more responsibility. And getting married goes a long way in bringing about that end. Martha will make a fine wife. She's been practically a fixture around here since you girls were in pigtails making mud pies for your dolls."

"She'll feel right at home," Leah said, surprised that she'd spoken aloud. "Well, no doubt Willis will be bringing her back with him for supper. I'd best see about starting the meal. Keep resting, Daddy. Get strong." Setting her empty cup on the tray, she smiled at her mother and left the room.

As she expected, Willis had Marty by the hand when he came home. The pair disposed of their coats, slipped off their boots at the boot tray, then padded into the kitchen.

"Well, Sis, here she is," Will said proudly. "My soon-to-be bride." He drew out a chair and seated her. "Think I'll go tell Mom and Dad the good news. Be right back."

And like that, he was gone, his cheery whistle indicating his progress up the stairs.

"Were you shocked?" Martha asked in the sudden quiet, her heart-shaped face serious as she met Leah's gaze.

"A little." Leah rinsed the potato she'd been peeling and quartered it before adding it to the stew simmering in the big pot. "Not that you're marrying my brother, but that it's going to be so soon."

Marty toyed with a strand of fair hair, a wistful expression making her dainty features all the more beautiful. "Well, I certainly was surprised. I'm still reeling from the fact that I love Willis in the first place. Especially since you and I vowed neither of us would marry until we were at least thirty."

"Perhaps we thought nothing would change as long as we didn't take that step," Leah replied. "Funny, the things one believes when it seems life will last forever." She dried her hands on her apron and eased herself down onto the seat across from Martha. "But you'll be good for Will. You've always been able to curb that reckless streak in him. He acts older when you're around."

"Thanks. I think." A dry smile curved her lips. "You make it sound as if I'm robbing the cradle."

"You know what I mean. You bring out my brother's best qualities. You always have, really. Even when he was a lad, sneaking up on us to toss a frog down our pinafores. One smile from you, and he would forget the mischief and all but sprout a halo."

Marty sputtered into a giggle, and Leah joined in.

"What's all this about mischief?" her brother's voice interrupted as he strode into the room. "A fellow leaves for one minute, and suddenly there's secrets being bandied about behind his back." With an adoring grin, he slid into the chair beside his fiancée's and clasped her fingers in his.

"Oh, nothing, sweetheart," she answered coyly. "Just girl talk. You needn't be concerned about it."

"All I'm concerned about is supper. When's it gonna be done?"

"Hold your horses, little brother," Leah chided. "Everything's cooking. Soon as *my best friend* and I set the table, it'll be nearly finished." She eyed him keenly. "So when is the big day to be, anyway?"

He and Marty exchanged heart-stopping smiles. "We're going to try for the end of April," she answered breathlessly.

But that's only a month away! Leah almost blurted out. Instead, she drew a slow breath and quieted her voice. "Will that give you enough time to arrange everything?"

"What's to arrange?" Her brother flicked a crumb from the tablecloth with his fingernail. "All we need's a preacher and a church."

"And a gown, flowers, relatives and friends, and food to feed them," Martha added. She gazed up at Leah. "You will help with my gown, won't you? You're so good at beading. We'll work on yours, too, of course."

"Wouldn't miss it," Leah said. "We'll make the most special bridal dress the world has ever seen."

"Women!" Will said in derision. "If it were up to you to run the world, everything would have to be a big production."

She and Martha traded pitying glances. "You know getting married is an important step in a girl's life," Leah reminded him. "It should be a day she'll always look back on with joy."

A rosy flush crested the honey blonde's fine cheekbones. "I can't believe this is happening already," she said softly. "Everything's suddenly being set into motion."

"Which brings us back to the subject of your gown," Leah said, reaching over the table to pat her friend's hand. "Maybe tomorrow we can impose on my handsome brother to drive us into town so we can choose the fabrics we'll need. Satin or taffeta or silk, perhaps. What color would you like me to wear, Marty?"

"I hadn't even thought about it yet. Let's wait until we see what's available."

"Speaking of available, Sis," Will cut in, "isn't it about time you start thinking of encouraging some of the interested males at church who've been after me to put in a good word for them? Or are you planning on staying here forever? We could use a good cook and washerwoman, I guess. It would give the two of us more time for. . .other more enjoyable pastimes." He jabbed Marty in the ribs, and she turned beet red.

Leah didn't dignify his remark with a response. She merely got up to check on the stew and found it ready to eat. "Mind helping set the table?" she asked Martha. "And Will, go tell Mother supper's ready."

"Sure, sure. What I need is one more female here to keep me in my place," he said with a good-natured grin. But he sprang to his feet and did as bidden.

"That was ungallant of him," Martha commented, taking bowls out of the cupboard. "Suggesting you'll be in the way here. I hope you don't feel that to be true." She crossed to the table and set them out before going back for silverware.

Leah gave a silent huff. "Oh, he's just being the tactless brother, as always. But I've no intention of remaining underfoot around here after you two marry."

Marty paused, cup in hand, and looked up. "But where would you go?"

With a shrug, Leah unwrapped a loaf of bread and sliced several generous hunks, then stacked them on a small plate. She brought them to the table, along with salt and pepper shakers. "I haven't decided that yet. But there's really no point in my staying here, is there? Think about it. You and Will deserve a chance to start your life together without the interference of an older sister. An old maid one, at that," she added with a smirk.

"You wouldn't be an old maid for long," Marty said gently, "if you'd show Curtis Randall or Steve Henderson the slightest encouragement. You could be mistress of your own home then."

Leah turned. "Couldn't you just picture me married to Curt and those pigs of his? Hmph. And Steve. Now there's a prize catch for you. I'd have to put up with Mother Henderson always elaborating on my deficiencies and how much better a wife Marietta Perkins would have been, if she hadn't up and run away with that railroad conductor." Her voice gentled. "Besides, the only man I ever really wanted chose someone else, if you recall."

But her friend wasn't easily put off. "Well, there are other eligible males in the area, you know. And as far as I'm concerned, you don't have any deficiencies. You're the dearest, kindest, sweetest—"

"Talkin' about me again, are you?" Willis said teasingly as he reentered the kitchen. "I do like to hear my gal talk about me that way." Coming up behind his fiancée, he slid his arms around her slim waist and nuzzled her earlobe.

Leah was in no mood to watch the display of affection. With a pained grimace, she presented her back and went to bring the stew pot to the table.

But after supper, when the house was quiet again and she was alone in her room, she had plenty of time to think about weddings. And being available. About the eligible bachelors she had known all her life, and how far short of her dreams they all seemed. She just couldn't picture herself married to any of them.

And she thought about how quickly her world had turned upside down.

Laurelwood was the house she had always wanted to be mistress of. It was the only home she had ever known. But it could never, ever be hers.

With a ragged sigh, she went to her bureau and opened the bottom drawer, where she kept her sketches. Flipping through the collection, she couldn't help noticing how many were of Laurelwood. Even when she had focused on the lilac bush or the orchards or the summer roses, the house was always visible somehow. It was the very heart of all her drawings.

Perhaps she'd find the time to do a real likeness, in oils. A portrait of Laurelwood that would go with her wherever she went. She'd work on it whenever she had a spare minute. At least no one would be able to take that from her.

Chapter 2

Blake Malone shifted in the hard chair, watching Hayden Lane, attorney-at-law, shuffle through a raft of legal documents in the rather small office, its confines made even closer by the blue haze of cigar smoke.

"So, I take it you have no interest in returning to Lehman permanently, setting up residence in your late grandfather's house." Drumming stubby fingers atop the cluttered desk, the bespectacled lawyer glanced up, the flickering overhead lights glinting over his bald pate as he looked at Blake.

His attention momentarily on the numerous leather-bound volumes lining floor to ceiling bookshelves directly behind the man, Blake met the shrewd gaze straight on. "None whatsoever. It's bad enough I had to leave Wisconsin at all, right now. I can't afford to hang around Pennsylvania indefinitely. The lumber mill's too much for my brother to handle on his own."

"Nevertheless, the will did stipulate that you see to the disposing of the property personally. I've a friend who happens to be a land agent. Perhaps he's already received a few inquiries from interested people. Once the sale is completed and you sign the proper forms to that effect, you'll be free to get back to your. . .uh. . .enterprise." He stood and reached out his fleshy hand.

Getting up to return the polite gesture, Blake couldn't help but notice how unnaturally soft those pudgy fingers were as he clasped them in his own calloused ones. "Thank you, sir. If you need me, you can contact me at Harvey's Lake, at the Lake House."

"Fine, Mr. Malone. I'll be in touch." With a nod of dismissal, the lawyer settled his bulky frame into his desk chair once more.

Outside air had never smelled more refreshing. Blake filled his lungs and expelled the breath in an attempt to rid himself of the last remnants of the rank odor. Why had his grandfather inserted that particular condition in his will? Certainly the old man knew he was welcome to come to live in Wisconsin at any time. Blake and his younger brother, Matthew, had invited him more than once. Handy as the old gent was, he might have been an asset to them in the shingle mill, if not in the regular lumber camp, and they could have looked after him, been there for him when the end came.

But Blake surmised that more likely his grandfather's intent was for him to return to his Pennsylvania roots for awhile. . .hopefully long enough to feel compelled to stay for good. "Too bad, Gramps," he muttered, climbing aboard the rented buggy and taking the reins. "It ain't gonna work."

Clouds hung low in the sky, but even with the possibility of rain, there was no time like the present for driving past the old place, to see what condition it was in. No doubt it would appear as well kept as ever. Except for the unexpected heart attack which had claimed him, the old man had never known a sick day in his life.

Taking the hilly cutoff which led from the road to the house where he and Matthew had grown up, Blake recognized some of the rocky outcroppings and groves the two of them had designated as forts in their boyhood. He couldn't recall a single unpleasant memory until their parents perished in a storm during a voyage to Europe. Only fourteen at the time, Blake grew up a lot that summer. Gone were the carefree days of childhood, replaced by the conviction that he'd go after his dreams while there was still time to do so.

The horse emerged into the clearing just then, and Blake drew in on the reins and stopped. Not a footprint or wheel track marred the melting snow on the rolling land before him. The sprawling one-story stone house still crowned the gentle knoll, tall pines and maples still bracketing it on either side. The whole place appeared like a scene from a picture book. He'd almost forgotten how breathtaking it was. He urged the bay slowly forward once more, feeling somehow reluctant to make unnecessary noise.

Blake found everything as Gramps had left it, even inside, where his breath came out in little clouds of vapor. Glancing around the spacious parlor with its comfortable furnishings and an ample supply of chopped wood waiting to be added to a roaring fire in the hearth, he felt a twinge of sadness. If not for the death notice the lawyer had shown him, Blake could almost have expected to glance up at any second and see the familiar form striding toward him, hear the booming voice, wince at the stout clap on his shoulder. What a shame he and Matt had missed out on the old man's affection and encouragement these last few years since they'd invested their inheritance in the fledgling lumbering business in northern Wisconsin. But nothing could have dissuaded them from venturing off to worlds unknown, trying their wings, seeing if they had what it took to succeed.

He made a swift tour of the rest of the house, then at the first patters of rain on the roof, returned to the buggy and headed toward Harvey's Lake. He did not regret deciding to book a room at a hotel. It would have been hard to remain here without Gramps around.

When Sunday came, he followed the inclination to attend the service at the small church his grandfather had helped establish. The man had never gone after his own dearest dreams—of enrolling in theological school and becoming a minister—so he'd done the next best thing by becoming one of the most faithful members of the little flock at Grace Church and teaching Bible study classes. He never missed a scheduled service for any reason. Blake knew it would probably seem strange to walk into the house of worship and not be able to spot white-haired Gramps occupying the second pew, right on the aisle. For that reason, he purposely arrived a few minutes late so he wouldn't have to talk to anyone beforehand.

Already the strains of "Rock of Ages" drifted toward him as he mounted the steps of the little white country church in the hollow bordering the township of Huntsville. He chose a space as far back as he could. A young man in the same pew offered him an open hymnal. Blake nodded his thanks and followed the words without singing.

That is, until a curious pause followed the second verse.

"Well, well," jovial Pastor Milton Burgess said, his hand upraised. "I do believe I see a former member visiting us today. Blake Malone, stand up, so everyone can see you."

His neck warming under his collar and vest, Blake stood and gave an off-handed wave, recognizing several individuals he'd known, friends of his grandfather's, plus some new faces. "Greetings, folks," he muttered. "A privilege to be here again."

"We were just about to sing the third verse," the bristling-haired minister went on, his broad sideburns widening with his grin. "How about you doing us that honor instead? It's been ages since we've been treated to that powerful voice of yours."

"Oh, please," Blake hedged, but to no avail. A few too many heads were nodding in agreement. Suppressing an inward sigh of resignation, he decided to get it over with and walked to the front. He took the place the preacher had vacated, then gave a nod to the attractive dark-haired lass at the organ, and the music began again.

"Nothing in my hand I bring; simply to thy cross I cling. . . ." The well-known words touched his own heart as he sang, but it still came as a relief when everyone joined in on the last stanza and he retook his seat. The entire atmosphere of the place seemed noticeably warmer after that, and Blake met and returned numerous friendly smiles.

"I'm sure the congregation joins me in thanking you, son," Pastor Burgess said with a measure of chagrin. "I shouldn't have imposed on your good nature. I trust you won't hold it against me, as it did happen to go right along with my sermon this morning: Taking Advantage of a Friend. We're going to examine some instances in the Bible where people took advantage of a friendship. Sometimes for good, sometimes for bad. Turn with me, if you will, to the eleventh chapter of Luke's Gospel, verse five.

Blake shook his head slightly in disbelief as he flipped open his frayed Bible to a passage he had read so often he'd all but committed it to memory.

Leah felt her sister's elbow stab her in the ribs when after leaving the organ she came to sit with Nancy and her bookish husband, Tim Grogan, who grinned at her through wire-rimmed eyeglasses.

"Ever hear such a voice?" Nancy whispered under the cover of fluttering pages as people turned to the announced Scripture. "But then, with that face. . ."

Leah frowned at her. They'd only recently started attending this church after the church in the opposite direction from home had burned to the ground when a nearby tree had been struck by lightning. But in dire need of an organist, this congregation had welcomed her whole family with open arms. Now it felt as if they'd always been a part of this flock. Still, the last thing Leah wanted was to have her sister obvious in her attempts to shove her toward some available young man. And in this case, a total stranger.

He was more than a little handsome, she allowed, with sun-streaked fair hair and eyes that rivaled the summer sky. Straight teeth flashed in his embarrassed grin, along with an endearing set of dimples. When he'd first come forward, she'd found herself playing from habit rather than paying attention to the written notes, as her eyes focused on that strong profile and the broad manly shoulders that tapered down to a trim waist on his tall, confident frame. Blake Malone. Must be the grandson of old Hiram Malone who'd been such a mainstay here until his sudden death scarcely a month ago. People mentioned a pair of grandsons who were his only living relatives. Likely the two would have attended school in Lehman. Huntsville was so sparsely settled it didn't have a school of its own, so Leah and her siblings had attended classes a few miles away in the larger town of Dallas, where they also did any needed shopping.

Pastor Burgess's voice droned into her consciousness then, and Leah gave herself a mental shake and reminded herself to pay attention.

"So you see, dear friends," he was saying, "our guest could easily have refused my request to sing for us earlier. I was taking rather bad advantage of our prior relationship. But knowing Hiram's grandson the way I do, I counted on the fact that he'd acquiesce and give us that special blessing. I doubt he'll hold it against me. Remember in your dealings with your own acquaintances not to take unfair advantage of others. Let us pray."

Leah returned to the pump organ once more and wheezed out the closing hymn and the postlude. She preferred playing music to useless chatter, so she always remained where she was until most everyone had taken their leave. When she stood to gather her music together, she heard only two voices still in the church. They grew stronger as the speakers neared the organ.

The pastor's voice she knew well. "So you won't mind singing a special for us next week, Blake?"

Leah's heart did a flip-flop. She couldn't keep from glancing over her shoulder. Sure enough, her eyes locked onto a slightly amused pair of the clearest blue eyes she had ever seen.

"This is our little accompanist," the minister told him needlessly. "Leah Somerville. I'm sure she wouldn't mind staying a few moments longer while the two of you choose a solo number for next Sunday. Would you, Leah?" The man finally sought her approval.

"Well, my family—"

"I assured Willis we'd see that you got home in short order."

"Oh. Well then, I suppose I can stay," she said on a doubtful note. She did her best to appear completely at ease, all the while knowing beyond the shadow of a doubt that once Nancy got wind of this, she'd howl with glee.

"My pleasure, Miss Somerville," Blake said, his gaze somehow assessing more than just her face as he tipped his golden head.

"Mr. Malone," she said politely. "Have you a particular hymn in mind?"

"I thought perhaps 'Jesus, Lover of My Soul' might go along with the pastor's upcoming sermon topic. If you know that one, of course."

She nodded and lowered herself to the organ stool, arranging her jade velvet skirt comfortably about her while the minister retreated to the pews, tidying up hymnals and the like. After checking her own book's contents, she opened to the specified page.

Blake Malone rested his elbow atop the organ, his gaze still centered on her.

"Do you not have a copy of the lyrics?" she asked.

"No need. I've always known this one."

"Indeed. Well, then." And without further ado, Leah placed her fingers on the correct keys, gave a few priming pumps to the pedals with her feet, and then began the introduction.

His rich baritone joined in at the first word, and his expression turned pensive as if caught up in the true meaning of each line.

Leah tried not to watch him, but turned slightly away from her the way he was, she could not help but look up to Blake often as she played. She adjusted one of the stops to blend more with his tone and was pleased by the improvement. Particularly when those compelling eyes of his turned to her, a smile tipping up the corners of his lips. It was the first time in her life Leah ever actually listened to the beautiful words penned by Charles Wesley. She was disappointed when it ended.

"Magnificent," Pastor Burgess said, coming to the organ. "That will fit perfectly with next week's service. Thanks to both of you."

"P—perhaps we should go through it once more," Leah heard herself say and cringed as a silly flush warmed her cheeks.

"Splendid idea," Blake said casually. . .and bestowed another breath-stealing smile on her that curled her toes.

Afterward, she was slightly mortified when ever-so-helpful Pastor Burgess suggested their visitor see her home. "You'll find the lad to be a perfect gentlemen," he assured her. "I've known him all his life."

In no position to refuse, Leah accepted the young man's assistance into her warm cloak and then up to the seat of his buggy. She knew she wouldn't think of a single thing to say the entire ride. "I feel guilty that you have to go out of your way like this," she finally managed.

"I don't mind in the least, Miss Somerville. It gives me something to do. It would seem I'm on an extended vacation, whether I like it or not."

She nodded. "I'm terribly sorry, about your grandfather's passing. I can't think of a soul who wasn't fond of him."

"He was one of a kind. My brother Matt and I will miss him. We tried several times to entice him to join us in Wisconsin. I think he'd have liked it there."

"You have just the one brother?" Something about his tone, his easy way of speaking, put Leah at ease. She relaxed against the seat's cushioned back as the gelding plodded along over the rutted road.

He nodded. "The two of us run a lumber mill in northern Wisconsin. Of course, once winter sets in, we switch our efforts to a shingle mill. Keeps us busy all year. Matt up and got married a couple years ago. Took a fancy to a little gal who did most of our camp cooking, she and her aunt, that is, until the lady took sick and died. Now Julie does it all. She's a fine cook, if I do say so myself. They have one little one and another on the way."

"Do you have many workers at your lumber camp?" Leah asked, more to keep conversation going than anything. She did relish the rich timbre of his voice.

"During our busy season we hire on three or four others. Otherwise, we handle most of the work ourselves. It's useless to try to compete with some of the huge lumber conglomerates in the area, but we manage to hold our own."

"That's our lane coming up on the right." Leah indicated a road just ahead.

"Well, that didn't take long, miss. Looks like your family chose a real pretty spot, too."

"We like it." She smiled as the first glimpse of Laurelwood came into view.

"Charming house," he responded. "Those orchards?"

She nodded again. "Apple. My grandfather planted them when he first built the house. Then my father took over. He's ill at the moment."

"Oh. Sorry to hear that. I'll pray for him this evening."

"Thank you. And thank you for the ride home, Mr. Malone. It was very kind of you."

"No trouble at all. Helped fill an otherwise empty day, actually."

Leah picked up on the lament in his tone. Despite herself, she turned to him. "I don't suppose you'd be interested in staying for dinner. My mother is an excellent cook."

He brightened considerably, and those appealing dimples emerged again with his smile. "Say, that sounds delightful. Anything beats hotel food." Halting the horse, he hopped out and helped Leah alight.

His hand was cool beneath the fingers she'd withdrawn from her muff. But there was nothing at all cool about his gaze. Leah shivered deliciously as they strolled side by side up the path to the house. No doubt her family would be surprised at the unexpected visitor, but after all, she was merely repaying a young man for his kindness.

Or so she told herself as she smiled into those friendly blue eyes.

Chapter 3

More than a little pleased at the turn of events, Blake went inside with the willowy, fetching accompanist. His stomach growled when enticing aromas met them at the door—a combination of roast beef, potatoes and gravy, perhaps flaky biscuits. He didn't care which vegetable they served—he liked them all. But charming company or no, he had no intention of overstaying his welcome.

"May I take your coat?" Leah asked, slipping hers off and draping it over a peg. Her wide-set doe eyes peered up at him through lashes as thick and dark as the intricately curled sable hair framing her exquisite, oval face.

"Thanks." Complying with her request, he removed his hat and shrugged out of his wrap, handing them both to her. His gaze rested on her tapered fingers as she saw to the task. They matched the rest of her in grace and beauty. How was it that someone so downright captivating had no flock of stammering, drooling young bucks stampeding to her door? It didn't take a genius to recognize a treasure when he saw one. Why, if he were inclined to tying himself down at the moment, this little gal would be worth pursuing. But he'd shelved thoughts of marriage when he and Matt took up residence in the Wisconsin bush. At least until their business was well established, a life that rough was definitely not one for a gently bred young woman. He'd better keep himself well in check.

Her melodious voice cut across his musings. "Sounds like they're already at the table. Come on, I'll introduce you." Leading the way, she took him through the hall to the dining room. "We'll be needing another place, everyone," she said as they entered the cheery room with its bounty of delectable food all but covering the entire tabletop. "I've brought a guest."

"Oh. How nice." Her mother sprang up to get an extra place setting. Small and slight as her lovely daughter, she possessed many of the same features as well. And something about her manner reminded Blake of his own late mother. He immediately warmed to the homey family atmosphere as he glanced around at the tasteful furnishings with their definite feminine touches.

"This is Blake Malone," Leah supplied, then gestured to each person in turn. "My brother, Willis, his fiancée, Martha Sands, and my mother."

"Pastor Burgess already introduced him to Marty and me after church," Willis said, standing with outstretched hand. "Good to see you again."

"Same here," Blake answered, shaking the proffered hand. He then nodded to Leah's mother. "Very pleased to meet you, Mrs. Somerville. I hope you don't mind the intrusion. Your daughter was kind enough to take pity on a weary traveler."

"Malone. Why, you must be Hiram's grandson," she said graciously, moving Leah's plate to make room for another beside it. "It's our pleasure. Do sit down. I'm afraid you'll have to say your own grace. We had no idea when Leah would return from service."

"That was a lovely solo, Mr. Malone," Marty said airily. "We aren't often blessed with special music at our little church.

Willis smirked. "Mostly 'cause there's so many tin ears in the congregation."

Blake caught the ever so subtle sisterly glower as he seated Leah, then took the chair next to her. "Nevertheless, I thank you for the compliment." He grinned at Martha across the expanse of the crisp tablecloth as she handed him the platter of sliced beef.

"Do you often sing solos at your church?" she asked.

"I'm afraid I don't get out regularly to services just yet. This time of the year we're snowed in more than not, and we're out a bit from the town of Eau Claire."

"Oh, what a shame," Mrs. Somerville said, holding the bowl of mashed potatoes out to him. "My husband and I were fortunate enough to sit under the fine teaching of your late grandfather for the last few years. We were truly sorry to hear of his sudden passing. It left such a hole at church."

"Thank you, ma'am."

"We rarely missed an opportunity to worship, in fact," she continued, "until Graham suffered a stroke some weeks ago. With him confined to bed, I haven't wanted to leave him alone for any length of time."

"I do understand."

"But Mr. Malone will be attending our church while he's here," Leah said, helping herself to glazed carrots before passing them. "Pastor Burgess asked him to do another special number next week. And I'll be accompanying him."

"And I'd rather you all call me Blake," he assured them with a grin. "Mr. Malone makes me feel as old as my grandpa."

A chuckle made the rounds.

"How long do you expect to remain in the area, Blake?" Martha asked, her green eyes alight.

"I'm not exactly sure," he replied. "I have to dispose of my grandfather's holdings before I can return to Wisconsin. Could take a week or two. Maybe a month or so."

"A month! If you were here next month, we'd be thrilled to have you sing at our wedding, wouldn't we, sweetheart?" She turned her delighted gaze to her fiancé.

"We shouldn't impose on the man," Willis mumbled, shoveling in a healthy chunk of meat.

"Tell you what, miss," Blake said evenly. "In appreciation for the kind hospitality extended to me today, I'd be honored to provide a solo for your happy event."

Martha's fair features radiated her joy. "Marvelous! Perfectly marvelous!"

Thinking of all the extra practices her friend's suggestion would entail, Leah swallowed a bit too quickly and almost choked. She grabbed her glass of water and took several sips, just managing to stave off a fit of coughs. It was one thing to entertain someone as magnetizing as Blake Malone for a day or a week. But she was only human. It would take a woman of superior resistance to be near him for an extended period without succumbing to those charms of his. After all, he was hardly making a secret of his intention to leave Pennsylvania the first chance he got, and then where would she be? One heartbreak had been more than enough for her.

"Don't you think so, Miss Somerville?" she heard him ask.

"I'm sorry, I'm afraid my thoughts were elsewhere." Noticing she'd suddenly become the center of attention, she squelched a rising blush and set her glass down.

"I was commenting on the mild weather," he said. "And how unusual it seems for this time of year. I left a lot of snow behind in Wisconsin, and I remember quite a few March blizzards as a kid growing up around here."

"Oh. There did seem to be a hint of spring in the air the other day. And some of the trees look about to bud."

"Well, I, for one, won't miss winter this time," her mother supplied. "I think warmer weather will benefit your father more than anything. Perhaps we can fix up a chair out on the porch where he can soak up some fresh air and sunshine while he reads the newspaper."

"Ha!" Willis cut in. "Bad news isn't what he needs right now. It appears John Brown's hanging for treason and conspiracy to incite insurrection only added fuel to the fire in South Carolina. They may secede yet."

"You could be right," Blake said. "Too bad Lincoln was defeated in the Senate race. We could have used his moderate views to help hold the country together."

"In any event," Mother challenged in her take-charge tone, "a man likes to keep abreast of what's happening in the world, good or bad. It's of little benefit to be shut off from everything." She stood. "Now, who would care for some apple cobbler? Leah, help clear the table, dear."

When at last their guest took his leave, Leah felt as if he'd been a friend of her family forever. He seemed knowledgeable on just about every subject brought up, and his fresh, well-thought out perspectives seemed far more settled than her younger brother's rash opinions. In fact, by the time Blake finished making his points, Willis ended up viewing the man in almost hero-like awe.

"Quite the enjoyable afternoon," Marty gushed as she and Leah washed the dishes. "What a pity he isn't the marrying kind. He'd be perfect for you."

"You're not serious!" Leah exclaimed, tucking her chin down. "He lives in the backwoods. Can you envision me in some faraway outpost of civilization?"

"Oh, I don't know." Rinsing the soap from one of the serving bowls, the honey blonde turned it upside down on a towel to drain. "Who would care what was outside, if a gal had somebody like him coming home to her every night?"

Leah had to giggle. "He is a sight, isn't he?" With a silent sigh, she leaned against the sideboard, the towel dangling from her fingers. "Ah, but there's no sense daydreaming about impossibilities now, is there?"

"Who's to say things are impossible? What if he decided to stay? There is the small matter of his grandfather's place, isn't there? Just sitting empty, and all."

"Still. . ."

"And he did spend an inordinate amount of time stealing glances at you, you know."

This time Leah did blush. She'd noticed a few of those instances. Only with the greatest effort had she managed to pretend she hadn't.

"Well?" Martha prompted, her smile knowing and slightly suggestive.

"What are you saying?"

"Somebody's going to snag that man eventually, right?"

Leah tipped her head in thought. "You know I've never been that sort, Marty."

"What sort, for pity's sake?" her friend scoffed. "All you have to be is yourself, silly. And let God take care of the rest. What's the worst that could happen?"

The worst, Leah knew, would be to grow to love someone she could never have. Someone who would pick up and leave in a few weeks and never come back. She met Marty's sparkly eyes and smiled.

Blake filled his lungs and turned onto the road heading toward the lake. That's what he'd been missing in the thirteen years since his parents died—a sense of family. It had been too long since he'd experienced the warmth, caring, bantering, and easy chatter of a group of relatives around a table. Even when he and Matt had lived with Gramps, it had been only the three of them with just talk of crops and weather and God. But being at the Somervilles' these past couple hours stirred yearnings inside him he thought he'd safely banked away for some indefinite time in the future, if ever.

With very little effort he could recall the swish of feminine skirts, the soft musical quality of the women's voices—particularly Leah's. His every sense tuned to her words even when there was more than one person speaking. Did she have the slightest inkling how those pleasant tones of hers caressed a man's ear? How her most minute movement drew one's eye? A fellow could get used to having someone with her gracious, thoughtful qualities around.

Whoa! Jolted by his unwonted mental ramblings, Blake expelled a silent whistle. Had he been shut up in the woods so long he was easy prey for the first bat of an eyelash? Better remember the primary reason he'd come to Pennsylvania and see to business as quickly as possible so he could get out of here. There were plenty of good reasons he'd chosen a solitary existence at this time in his life, and most of them had practicality and hardship emblazoned across them. It would be a few more years before he could provide a decent home for a wife and perhaps a family. What was the point of entertaining delusions that his present situation could be different?

Then, entirely unbidden, an enticing vision floated across his consciousness. Leah, with her shiny dark curls and chocolate brown eyes, soft curves accented by ruffles and lace, a smile that made a heart yearn to gaze upon it permanently. *What if—*

"Forget it, idiot," he said flatly. The horse's ears flicked to the side, then turned forward again. "Just what you need, huh, boy? A fool who talks to himself." But even as he smiled grimly to himself, things didn't seem so amusing after all.

Right where he was, he lowered his eyes. *I didn't know I was so weak, Lord. I thought I had everything figured out regarding life and my future. It didn't bother me when Matt*

decided to get married. Julie already knew what she'd be get-
ting into. But some other woman. . .Leah Somerville, for
example. She'd be in over her head. Way over. It's stupid for
me to be thinking such things. I guess I'm just asking for Your
help. Get me through the solos the pastor asked for—and even
that wedding, if I'm stuck here that long. But beyond that,
Father, just help me to be strong. To remember I'll be out of
this place for good the minute Gramps's place sells. Then help
me to go away. . .alone. Even I know that's best.

After that, maybe I can afford a few harmless daydreams.
No, better not chance it. She's from this kind of setting and
deserves a far better life than I could ever offer—as if she'd even
be open to the suggestion! We've only barely met. I'm acting like
a wet-nosed schoolboy who's just fallen for the new teacher—
and she's sure to have a string of other more suitable fellows
dangling at her fingertips. Surely they can't all be blind.

He paused, unable to express the emotions warring
inside. And he made no further attempts to do so.

Chapter 4

"Should we go over it again?" Leah asked, purposely not glancing in Blake's direction.

"Good idea. Strange, I never muddle words like that. I'd better get a book and follow along this time." Exiting the platform, he plucked a hymnal from the front row and retook his place, turning to the proper number.

Leah had rarely fumbled on the keys either. *And there was no reason for her fingers to tremble merely because Blake Malone was near*, she lectured herself. She'd just have to pay closer attention to the written notes. She played the introduction, reveling once more in the sound of that glorious baritone when he joined in:

"Jesus, lover of my soul, let me to thy bosom fly,
While the nearer waters roll, while the tempest
still is high...."

Had ever lovelier thoughts been set on paper? She stole a glance at his classic profile as he continued through the verse. Or did they merely sound that way because of the quality of his voice? Regardless, the congregation was in for a treat this morning.

"Sounds splendid," Pastor Burgess remarked, giving the sanctuary his customary check to make sure the hymn books were spread around evenly.

Blake nodded, but didn't miss a beat:

"Other refuge have I none; hangs my helpless soul
    on Thee;
Leave, ah! leave me not alone, still support and
    comfort be—"

"Me," he amended, shaking his head.

Stifling a giggle, Leah drew her lips inward and kept playing, inadvertently hitting a sharp rather than a flat in the last line. She made a quick correction and went on to the third verse. Maybe they shouldn't have allowed an entire week to go by without practicing.

Her thoughts drifted back over the last few days, to the activities she'd concocted to keep too busy to dwell on Hiram Malone's aesthetic grandson. But whether she was helping Marty with the beading on her gown, doing mundane chores like laundry, or trying to find time to work on her painting, thoughts of him waltzed through her mind like a constant refrain that would not go away. A melody alternately wild with adventure, then gentle as a mountain stream. A song of nature, of outdoors.

Her preoccupation with the man made no sense whatsoever. Granted, he was dashing and gallant and pleasant to be with, and he had the voice of an angel. But her brave intentions to snag him with feminine wiles had died a swift death. He was not in the market for a wife.

And she certainly was not interested in going off to some scantily settled part of Wisconsin, either. How had he put it? Out a bit from the nearest settlement. What sort of life would that be?

Better to inquire about a position next time she went into town.

"Uh. . .that was the last verse," Blake said, his face puzzled as he turned to look at her.

"Sorry. I. . .sorry." Thoroughly embarrassed, Leah swallowed and composed her features.

The minister strode over to them. "I was going to ask you two to prepare a song for next week, but I see we're out of time. Might I impose on you to stay after the service again?"

"Sure thing," Blake said, answering for them both.

All Leah could think of was that she'd be spending another sustained period in close company with this visitor. Which, of course, would necessitate another invitation to Sunday dinner if he happened to drive her home. Oh, well, she reasoned. There were far worse ways for one to spend a Sabbath. That was the problem. If there was one thing she didn't need it was to get used to being around Blake so often. It would make his departure all that much harder to endure.

Glancing toward the sanctuary, she noticed church members beginning to trickle in. She put the hymnal she'd be using aside and took out her more involved arrangements of preludes to worship. And told herself to settle down.

Somehow she got through Blake's special without hitting a wrong note, and he sang the words perfectly. But it was with vast relief she took her place beside her younger sister, anticipating the rousing sermon to follow. Surely that would prevent her mind from straying. To her dismay, however, Pastor Burgess gave one of his quieter devotionals based on the Lord's Prayer. Leah could only wince with chagrin at the trespasses her wayward mind so easily committed.

The meeting ended much too soon. Compressing her lips together, she tiptoed to the organ during the minister's closing prayer, then played softly while the congregation drifted outside.

"So," her sister said, slender brows elevated as she joined Leah at the organ. "Will tells me you've been helping to keep our guest soloist entertained during his stay in the area."

"Come on, Nan," Leah answered defensively, trying to remove the eloquent expression from her sister's oval face. "I played a few hymns for him while he sang. Then he came to dinner. That's all. But the least I could do was invite him to eat with us. The man did drive me all the way home, and Mother always makes so much."

"Do tell. And will there be a repeat today?"

"Honestly! What is the difference, pest? The pastor requested some solos while Blake's around, and I happen to be the organist here, you know."

"So, it's Blake, is it? That didn't take long." Nancy studied her nails as if trying to contain her smile.

Leah merely rolled her eyes heavenward.

"Ready, hon?" Tim asked, stepping to Nancy's side. "I brought the buggy to the end of the walk."

She nodded. "Well, keep us posted," she tossed over her shoulder as she matched her pace with her tall husband's long-legged strides.

"Don't be a stranger, sis-in-law," Nan's auburn-haired mate called back with a toothy grin on their way to the door. "Come visit us sometime."

"I will. Soon." They did make a rather sweet couple, Leah decided, watching after them. Tim was easily a head taller than Nan. She'd hoped Nancy would have made her an aunt by now, but so far her petite frame revealed no evidence her sister was in the family way.

⟡

"And Mother's almost finished Prissy's dress for the wedding," Martha said, passing the platter of fried chicken across the table to Leah when she and Blake arrived after practice. "She's written out dozens of invitations, and Pa's intent on seeing we have enough smoked ham for the guests."

"It's amazing how quickly a special event can be orchestrated," Leah remarked almost to herself. She speared a succulent breast portion, then passed the meat on to Blake.

He nodded his thanks.

"Well," her mother cut in, "I'm sure Priscilla's thrilled to be a bridesmaid in her big sister's wedding. She'll look very grown up in the lovely gown. And what a pretty touch it will be, with Leah attired identically at the organ."

"Yes. I'm getting a little nervous," Marty confessed. "I hope everything will go smoothly. Have you chosen a song, yet, Blake?"

"I'd be happy to do a favorite, if you have one."

"Hm. I never thought of that. I'll try to choose one this afternoon so you and Leah can start working on it." Martha frowned in concentration.

"This young lady hardly needs practice," he said smoothly, bestowing a warm smile on Leah. "She knows every hymn in the book and plays them flawlessly."

Leah felt her face heating up under his admiring gaze.

"Sis always did like pounding on the player piano when the rest of us were out seeing to chores," Willis said teasingly. "That or dabbling in her paints. Anything to keep her hands soft."

"Why, I never—" Leah sputtered, while Marty scowled at her brash fiancé.

"He's only joshing you, dear," Mother said placatingly. "We all know how hard you work around here—particularly since your father took ill. Why, you've had hardly any chance to socialize. The only place you ever go is to church, and then you come directly home."

"Sure, sure," Will admitted, helping himself to another drumstick. "But she'll have plenty of time for herself and for socializing once she leaves."

"You're going somewhere?" Blake asked, tipping his blond head in curiosity.

Leah swallowed the mouthful of food she'd been chewing. "Well, naturally I won't be staying here after the wedding."

"What?" Her mother's face turned as white as the lace shawl she wore over her gown. "Why, that's preposterous, daughter. I never heard of such a thing!"

"Oh, Mother," Leah crooned.

"Well, you have a nice room right here. Upstairs," she went on, not to be deterred. "Just because there's going to be a wedding, that doesn't mean everything else has to change. There's no reason at all why things can't continue on as they always have. You know how tongues would wag if you should go off on your own, a young unattached woman. It simply isn't done. And we can certainly still use your help."

"Please," Leah said pointedly, "if you don't mind, I'd really rather not discuss this right now." She sent Marty a silent plea. "Does your mother need any help with the baking for the reception?"

Her friend shook her head. "She's already arranged for three of my aunts to lend a hand. But thank you for offering." The slender bride-to-be glanced up as the mantel clock bonged twice. "Oh. I'm afraid Mom wants me home early for a fitting. I hope you don't mind, Leah, if I don't stay to help with dishes."

"Not in the least. I can manage."

"I'll fill in for you, Martha," Blake offered as she and Will got up to leave.

Leah shot him a surprised look. "That's not necessary, really."

He merely grinned. "I've no previous commitment to run to. I don't mind helping. Not at all."

"My, how very thoughtful," her mother said graciously, despite her worried frown. Obviously she was still shocked by Leah's announcement. She rose and carried some of the used dishes to the sink. "I'll leave you two to deal with the rest, then, while I take a tray to my husband. And Leah, see if your young man would care for some sliced peaches with cream."

"Thank you," she murmured, praying Blake hadn't picked up on the slight slip of her mother's tongue. He was not *her* young man. Nan must have been filling that graying head with absurd notions.

"Do you prefer I wash or dry?" Blake asked when the table had been cleared after dessert. "I'm quite capable of either, I assure you."

No doubt, Leah concluded, *seeing as how you live alone.* But she held her peace. "I'll wash, thank you. You can set things on the sideboard." With him towering above her, she handed him a linen towel, tied a long apron over her cranberry gown, then plunged her hands into the soapy dishpan. Anything to keep from losing herself in the bewitching twinkle in those blue eyes.

"Do you mind if I ask you a personal question?" he asked casually, shifting his weight onto one foot. "For instance, what plans have you made for after your brother's wedding?"

If it had been anyone else, she'd have balked at what she considered prying. But Blake's manner exuded sincerity and real interest. And other than the way her silly pulse would go all aflutter whenever he was this close, she saw little harm in confiding in him. The fact was, she really wished she had someone to give her advice. She rinsed the plate she'd been scrubbing, then inverted it on the draining towel for him.

"Actually, the last thing I ever imagined I'd have to face was leaving Laurelwood," she answered in all candor while she worked. "The thought never once entered my mind. I love this place and its memories of a lifetime. I'd hoped it would always be my home." She emitted a resigned sigh. "But, of course, that will soon change, after all. I can't see a reason to stay. I'd only be in the way of newlyweds who deserve their privacy."

"Perhaps, but where will you go?"

"I've already inquired after some positions in town. With living quarters provided."

"But you'd be away from your family," he said, stacking the plate he was drying atop others.

"There are worse things, aren't there? I doubt you dwell with your married brother."

A wry grin spread across his lips. "You've got me there. But I'm—"

"A man," she finished. "Right?"

"Something like that. I admit it sounds presumptuous, coming from you."

"I'll be fine, Blake. Truly. There's no reason at all for anyone to be concerned. I'll get by." At her nod of emphasis, a curl tumbled free from the cluster atop her head, right into her eye. Soapy up to her elbows, she resorted to trying to blow it out of her way.

Blake reached over and plucked it off her forehead, then appeared at a loss as to what to do next. He finally tucked it behind her ear, then shrugged rather awkwardly, the tips of his own ears reddening.

Leah had to giggle. "Thanks." But the tiny spot where his knuckles had brushed her skin still tingled from his touch. She averted his gaze and fixed her attention on the dirty dishes.

<hr />

Blake had never felt anything so silky, so soft. His eyes focused on that wayward curl, just one of dozens of shiny ringlets crowning Leah's head. She was so very lovely. So talented. Her confidence in her ability to handle unexpected situations utterly fascinated him. In fact, there was nothing he did not like about her. . .and that scared him to death.

He'd known her such a short time, and yet so often she breezed across his mind like a soft wind singing through the trees. It was one thing to pack his belongings and head for Wisconsin, knowing she'd be safe and looked after. But away from her family, the home she loved?

A woman needed to be protected. Cared for. Loved.

He filled his lungs. Knowing just how easy it would be for a man to grow to love someone like Leah Somerville, he shored up his own defenses. . .because so far, he hadn't met any man good enough for her.

Chapter 5

During the slow drive home, Blake's mind refused to relinquish thoughts of Leah. He stabled the horse and strode toward the three-story structure overlooking the lake. No wonder her mother had been in such a dither over her daughter's decision, he mused, mounting the steps to the porch and verandah that stretched across the entire front of the building. Laurelwood couldn't possibly be the same without Leah's willing hands. . .hands more prone to hard work than anything else since her father had his spell. And if she didn't even socialize outside of church, that would account for the obvious lack of suitors. The eligible men around here must be too dumb to see she was worth waiting for. As far as he was concerned, her smile alone could light up a room.

He let out a troubled breath. Willis, for all his rambunctious ways, had what it took to keep things running smoothly—or would have, in time, with a practical wife like Martha to settle him down.

But Martha wasn't Leah.

"Oh, Mr. Malone," the wiry desk clerk said as Blake

entered the Lake House. "There's a message for you."

"Thanks." With a thin smile, Blake took the missive to his upstairs room. There, in the rather simple surroundings, he slit open the envelope and removed the embossed stationery, moving to the window for light as he read:

> *Dear Mr. Malone:*
>
> *Please come by my office at your earliest convenience to discuss offers made regarding your grandfather's estate.*
>
> *With best regards, I remain,*
> *Hayden Lane, attorney*

With mixed emotions, Blake refolded the document and tucked it back into the envelope. Offers. Maybe one of them would pan out. Difficult as it was to conjure up a mental picture of strangers taking over Gramps's property, there wasn't much point in hanging onto it himself. It would just deteriorate from neglect when he left it behind to return to the mill.

For a fleeting moment, Blake contemplated what it would be like to sell the Wisconsin enterprise to his younger brother and stay here. But Blake couldn't see himself being just a farmer—or laboring for somebody else to build up that person's business. Besides, Matt probably wouldn't stay in Eau Claire to compete alone against the big lumber companies, not with the latest gold strikes in Colorado and Nevada enticing so many adventurous men to head farther west and try their luck.

Blake shook his head. What had gotten into him?

Best he see to selling Gramps's property and get out of here so life could get back to normal.

But normal, he strongly suspected, would seem incredibly empty now. Empty and bland. Next thing to dead.

Leah and Marty stepped away to admire their handiwork in the newly decorated bridal chamber.

"I'm glad my grandmother chose the Wedding Ring pattern for the quilt she made for my hope chest," Martha mused. "I love the soft, pretty colors."

Leah nodded. "It does look lovely. Especially on the new bedstead Willis bought. The whole room looks different."

"I feel rather badly that your mom insisted on vacating the master bedroom," the slender blonde said quietly. "It really wasn't necessary."

Leah giggled. "As if my brother's room is fit for human habitation! Now, that would be stretching things a mite."

"You know what I mean."

Sobering, Leah gave her friend's shoulder an affirmative pat. "But perhaps Mother's right, and it really will make her life easier, caring for Daddy downstairs. She truly feels he's gaining strength and that he'll soon be able to go out on the porch for short periods. And it certainly will eliminate her having to go up and down the steps several dozen times a day."

"I'm just glad he'll be able to be at our wedding, since we'll be having the ceremony here. I hope it won't be too awfully crowded. At least we'll spare him the noise and confusion of the reception."

"Mm," Leah agreed. "Too bad it isn't summer, though. We could have it outside in the yard, instead of in the church basement.

"Well, there's one advantage we haven't mentioned. He'll get to hear Blake sing up close, rather than from a few rooms away."

Leah worked hard not to reveal that even the mention of the man's name set her heart racing. "Well, as Daddy always said, 'Things have a way of working out, somehow, when the time is just right.' God's been very good to us all. Now, let's put up those gorgeous curtains your mother made. . . ."

Later, when Marty had gone home and the rest of the family were in their beds for the night, Leah's weary sigh broke the quietness. Crossing the room, she took the painting of Laurelwood out from behind the wardrobe, where she'd propped it out of harm's way to dry completely. She held it at arm's length for a critical assessment. Knowing the house was in its glory when surrounded by variegated green grass and a riot of colorful flowers, she'd chosen a late spring/early summer setting for the scene, including lilacs and roses and every other flower which, in turn, graced the yard. She came close to adding some mountain laurel, even though none grew near the property, but decided against it. In any event, this was how she would always remember home—at its very prettiest.

She had yet to hear if she'd secured employment at any of the three possible places where she'd applied, and time was going too quickly. The wedding was barely a week away. But she tried to concentrate on something else her father had always said, how the Lord never takes something away from one of His children without replacing it with something better. Many the times he'd lectured the family on needless worry. So in her solitude, Leah read her Bible and sought the Lord's will in prayer. . .pointing out that she was approaching some dire need. Surely something would turn up. The time couldn't be any more right.

The gowns were all finished, the food preparation well in hand, and Marty was going to help decorate the living room for the ceremony. All that remained was the rehearsal, to make sure everyone knew their places. Blake had come by twice to practice Wesley's "Love Divine, All Loves Excelling" and stayed for supper both times.

The fact that Leah could act more at ease around him in no way bridled the heightened consciousness she felt whenever he was present. Once, after having caught an unfathomable expression on his face when she'd inadvertently caught him staring, she'd even dreamed about the man, imagining he had a romantic interest in her, of all things. But now that final papers for his grandfather's place had been signed and the deed transferred, she knew Blake Malone's days in the area were numbered. Leah did not permit herself to think of what it would be like after that. When he went away for good. She'd survived a similar heartache, and likely would again.

Putting the painting back into its place, she undressed and slipped on her warm night shift, then crawled into bed. What would become of Blake? Of her? Why was the future always kept hidden?

Blake arrived early the night of rehearsal. He could not

stay away longer. He knew Leah had not as yet found employment, and she'd made it clear she was more determined than ever not to remain at home after the wedding. Even her parents had reached the point of acceptance. If she did find a respectable position, they would not try to keep her from taking it. Well, he had given the matter serious prayer and hopefully had come up with his own solution. And to ensure that it was of the Lord, he'd borrowed Gideon's action—of throwing out a fleece, like the story in the sixth chapter of Judges. If he actually managed to find Leah alone and she offered him a cup of tea, he would present his case. If not, well. . .he kind of hoped there wouldn't be an if not.

Bounding up the steps to the front door, he rapped, his insides feeling like a tree that had been notched and was awaiting the final chop before falling.

And there she was. Standing in the open doorway, smiling, the ecru lace on her violet gown making her eyes darker than ever. "Blake. My, you're early. Do come in."

"Good day, Leah. You look lovely, as always." He followed her inside. Into the quiet house. His eyes made a lightning swift circuit of the confines. Empty. Deserted. "Uh, where is everyone?"

"Nobody else has arrived yet. Mother, of course, is reading to Daddy. Would you care for some tea?" She turned to him expectantly, waiting for his answer.

Blake swallowed. *Father, please don't think I'm as doubtful as Gideon, but if this is really a sign from You, let her offer me some dessert that's supposed to be for later.* "Thanks. Sounds great."

"I hope you don't mind the kitchen. I was just cutting

the pie we'll be serving after rehearsal. If you're very, very good, I'll let you sneak a piece while we wait."

His heartbeat thudded against his ribs as he tagged after her again. "Believe me, I will be good." Of its own volition, a speculative smile spread across his face. He only hoped he could convince her of his scheme. If he could get the words out without muddling them up and sounding like an idiot.

"Here you are," she said, bringing two steaming cups to the work table after gesturing for him to take a chair. "I wasn't going to sit down, as there's so much I still have to do. But everyone needs to rest for a few moments once in awhile, no matter what's waiting." She then got slices of apple pie for each of them and sat opposite him.

"I was surprised to see you here already," she repeated after grace. "But the others will arrive shortly, I'm sure."

He sampled a forkful of the pastry. "Actually, I was hoping to catch you alone. I've something to discuss with you."

"Oh?" She sipped her tea, then set down her cup and started on her pie.

He nodded. "Heard anything about a position yet?"

"No, I'm afraid not. But I'm still hoping. Something could turn up anytime."

"What if it doesn't?"

She tipped her head back and forth in thought. "I guess I'll suddenly find it imperative to visit Nan for a few weeks. She lives in town. If something opens up, I'd be right there to snatch it."

"Is that what you want? Not knowing what lies ahead? Having to settle for the first thing that comes along?" he asked quietly.

Leah stopped chewing. "No. But sometimes we let a few too many choices get by us. Then we have to take what we can. Nothing's forever."

"Some things are." He sliced another chunk of pie and ate it.

Staring at him with a perplexed frown, she did not respond.

"So I've come to lay another possibility at your feet. One that wouldn't be temporary. I only ask that you let me spell it out, without interrupting."

"As you wish," she said, her demeanor questioning.

"I'd like you to come back to Wisconsin with me. As my wife."

Her mouth fell open on a tiny cough. "I beg your pardon?"

"Hey, no interrupting, remember?"

"But—"

He held up a hand. "I've been thinking about this for some time, Leah. And praying night and day, asking God to provide you exactly what you need, according to His will. And it came to me. I'm it."

She blinked once. Slowly. Incredulously.

"What I mean is, we need each other. I didn't come back to Pennsylvania looking for a wife. It was the farthest thing from my mind. . .until I met you. Now I can't imagine going back home without you by my side. Would you please think about it?"

Again, no response.

"Leah?"

"Am I permitted to speak at last?"

He nodded. But he felt far from the calm exterior he

hoped he was portraying.

"I don't know what to say. I wasn't expecting anything like this. But I've always believed people who marry should be in love. Should be convinced they can't live apart from each other."

"Are you saying you dislike me?" he asked, uncertainty beginning to creep in.

"No. Never. I think you're a wonderful person. An incredible man."

"Do I detect a 'but' there?"

She cut him a look rife with doubt. "What did you expect, Blake? You come here out of the blue, a man I've known only a little more than a month—if that—and now you're proposing marriage. I can't even think." Rising, she brushed a hand over her face and took a few steps away, then turned. "Marriage. I mean, that really is forever." She looked straight at him. "Do you. . .love me?"

Blake could not keep from going to her. He sensed it was not the proper time to take her in his arms, so he did the next best thing and took her hands in both of his as he searched those lovely eyes of hers. "I don't know. I've never felt like this before. I know I'm very attracted to you, that I think about you constantly. I love everything about you. I believe I'm growing to love you. And I expect those feelings will continue to deepen as we get to know each other. And we're already good friends. That's better than a lot of married folks can say when they start out."

She regarded him steadily, her shock still quite visible. "This is just so sudden. I need time to think, to pray."

"Well, I can't give you a lot of that. There's only a week until the wedding. After that, I have to go. Will you at least consider my proposal? And I mean seriously. This is no spur of the moment thing for me. I've already been mulling it over and seeking the Lord's counsel."

She nibbled her bottom lip.

At least she hadn't said no. He pressed on. "I don't exactly have a lot to offer someone like you right off. As I said, I wasn't planning to marry for some time. But I promise I'll be a good and loving husband. And I'll do my utmost to make a decent life for you. I'll always take care of you."

"I'll. . .think about it."

"Good. I won't pressure you. I won't even bring it up again, unless you do."

"Thank you. I—"

The front door slammed just then, and Willis and Martha came into the kitchen, with Marty's pigtailed sister Priscilla in tow. Will looked from his sister to Blake and back again. "Are we interrupting something here, Sis? You look all flushed."

"You know, he's right," Blake admitted.

"I. . .I was cutting the warm pie. For afterward," she stammered. Then she grabbed Marty's hand. "Come on upstairs. We need to talk."

Chapter 6

W hat is it?" Marty's voice penetrated the haze of Leah's thoughts as she closed the master bedroom door after them.

"I need some advice," said Leah, turning toward her friend.

"What kind of advice? You're white as the snow angels we used to make."

"I hardly know how to start." Leah waved one hand in a helpless gesture. "Oh, never mind. I shouldn't bother you with this. I should just pray about it and make my own decision."

But the willowy blonde crossed her arms and planted her feet where she stood, pursed lips indicating her determination. "Perhaps you could get rid of some people like that, but you happen to be talking to your best friend. Of course you can bother me with whatever's troubling you."

Leah released a pent-up breath and sank to the nearest chair, while Martha crossed to the bed and sat on one edge, a leg curled under her.

It took several moments before Leah could speak, and when she did, the words were almost inaudible. "Oh,

Marty, I'm really mixed up. I don't know what to do."

"About what? Has a position opened up in town? Or more than one and you can't decide? What?"

Shaking her head, Leah kneaded her throbbing temples. "No, nothing's turned up as far as working goes. It's something else. A different offer."

"Well, spit it out, for pity's sake!" The fair-haired girl came to kneel beside her. "Surely it can't be so horrid you can't even mention it."

Leah met her friend's concerned gaze, seeing the worry creases in her otherwise smooth forehead. "It's. . . Blake. He's asked me—" How could she even say the words? In a rush, she spilled out her news, "To marry him and go back to Wisconsin with him."

Martha's jaw fell open. "You can't be serious! Why, that's wonderful!" But the initial enthusiasm faded under Leah's steady stare. "Well, isn't it?"

"I don't know," Leah moaned. "It's all so sudden I don't know what to think. I wasn't expecting something like this." Then she blushed. "Well, all right, I sort of daydreamed about it when it all seemed next to impossible. I couldn't see much harm in that. But for him to actually propose. . ."

"Well, I think it's perfect." With that declaration, Marty rose. "Blake Malone is a wonderful man, a committed Christian who certainly shows responsibility and enterprise, as well as loyalty to family. He treats you with the utmost respect—and only a blind person could miss his blatant attraction to you. I think he'll make you a marvelous husband."

"But he doesn't know if he loves me," Leah said flatly.

"Do you love him?"

"I don't know." Releasing a heartfelt sigh, she searched her friend's face. "I was positive I loved Lance Brainerd once, remember? And when he chose Sheila Patterson instead, I wanted to die. I told myself I never wanted to feel that way again. So I've shied away from putting myself in that position a second time. I've refused every man who ever made overtures, turned them away so often they finally gave up."

"And where has it gotten you?" Marty asked softly.

"Well, at least Laurelwood's been a safe place, one where I didn't have to fear getting hurt. I've been happy here."

"But you have so much to give, Leah. Why be content with a life of solitude, when the Lord's brought someone across your path who has far nobler qualities than Lance could ever hope to have?"

"Do you truly think God brought Blake here?"

"Yes," she said with conviction. "I told you early on that he was perfect for you, didn't I?"

Leah's eyes clouded with fear. "But what if he's just been putting his best foot forward and doesn't really love me? What if all we feel for each other is surface attraction, and someday. . ."

Marty placed a comforting hand on Leah's forearm. "There's nobody in this world who can be sure about the future, Leah. Love or no love. All we can do is follow the Lord's leading and be the best we can be while He takes care of the rest."

"But still. Marriage. It's a huge step. I barely know Blake Malone."

"But what you do know about him is all good, isn't it?"

A tentative smile tugged at the corners of Leah's lips. She nodded.

"Well, I would suggest you thank the Lord for His blessings and accept Blake's proposal."

"Really?"

"Really." Suddenly Martha's expression glowed like a bright burst of fireworks. "Leah! We could have a double wedding!"

"What?"

"See? It couldn't be more perfect. Everyone we know will already be coming here next weekend for a wedding, right? Well, how fortuitous is that, I ask? You have a lovely new dress, your mother can take over the piano end of things. . ."

With a jumble of thoughts making her head spin, Leah clasped her hands together, nibbling on her steepled index fingers. "What would she and Daddy say?"

Marty shrugged. "If it's of the Lord, I can't see them objecting. They both like Blake a lot and admire not only his background, but his purpose for the future. And they haven't exactly been pushing you toward any of the other single men they know."

With a small huff, Leah smiled wryly. "Actually they seemed more than a little relieved that I never chose any of them."

"Because they hoped the Lord had someone better in mind for their oldest daughter."

Leah's smile widened into a grin. "You have an answer for everything. That's something I've always admired about you."

"Mostly, I just love my dearest friend," Marty replied, "and want to see her happy."

Considering everything the girl had said, Leah felt most of her doubts vanishing like the dew of morning. Nevertheless, she still wanted to pray about it, to seek her own answer from the Lord. A decision like she was about to make was not one to be taken lightly. It would affect the rest of her life.

"Do you, Willis Arthur Somerville, take this woman, Martha Elaine Sands, to be your wedded wife?"

"I do," he said, raising his chin confidently.

"And do you, Martha, take Willis to be your wedded husband?"

"I do."

Pastor Burgess turned slightly. "And do you, Blake Nicholas Malone, take this woman, Leah Abigail Somerville, to be your wedded wife?"

"I do." He gave her a tender smile.

"Do you, Leah, take Blake to be your wedded husband?"

Her gaze still fixed on this man to whom she was committing her entire future, she gave him an answering smile. "I do."

"Then, by the power vested in me by God and the Commonwealth of Pennsylvania, I now pronounce you husbands and wives. Whom God hath joined together, let not man put asunder. You may kiss your brides."

Leah was hardly conscious of the murmured sighs and comments made by the onlookers as Blake took her shoulders and gently drew her to him. The tempered strength in his touch quelled her trembling as her husband's head lowered, his lips descending to claim hers. And as long as she lived, she would not forget the reverence and love in his kiss. When at last he drew away, the warm glow of a dozen candles flickered in his eyes as they smiled into hers. She thought he had looked dashing before, but the obvious extra effort he'd put into looking his resplendent best for the ceremony made her heart swell with pride and a joy beyond words.

"Congratulations!" the minister said, breaking the lovely spell, and the gathering of relatives and friends surged forward to envelop the two couples in hugs and good wishes.

Out of them all, Leah remembered only her father's misty-eyed smile, his halting "God. . .bless." She knew he had much more to say but could not put the words together. She felt them all in the slight squeeze he gave her hand.

Stooping to hug the frail shoulders, she blinked back the moisture gathering on her lashes and kissed his cheek. "I love you, Daddy," she whispered, unable to trust her voice. Then she straightened and turned to her mother's loving arms, reveling in the soft crush of rose satin and crinolines as the two women hugged.

"It's been quite a day," the older woman managed, dabbing at her eyes with a lace-edged handkerchief. "Gaining one daughter, while losing another. But I pray you'll all be happy."

"I'll do my best, Mother Somerville," Blake promised when she embraced him, "to be a good husband to your daughter."

Mother smiled, her azure eyes awash in tears. "If I had the slightest doubt of that, I wouldn't have allowed this wedding to take place. Now, go catch up with the others. There's some delicious smoked ham and wedding cake waiting for you at the church. We'll save the good-byes for later."

That evening, her belongings stowed in the back of Blake's buggy, along with the newly painted portrait of Laurelwood she'd wrapped in heavy paper for protection, Leah somehow managed to contain most of her tears. Parting embraces and whispered endearments were over, and a prayer of blessing had been uttered to usher them on their way. She turned for one last wave to the family she'd be leaving behind while she went off to begin a whole new life. There was no way of knowing if she'd ever see her father again on this earth, but she squelched that sad thought as best she could. Then Blake's calloused hand squeezed hers empathetically, and the buggy pulled away.

As her home slipped from sight, the floodgates let loose. Helpless against them, Leah could only bow her head and let the tears fall.

Beside her, Blake said nothing, but he put his arm around her and let her lean against his strong form as he headed toward the road to the lake, where they would spend this first night of married life before departing for Wisconsin on the morrow.

As the sobs gradually subsided, Leah drew a cleansing breath to help assuage her nervousness. She ventured a glance through her damp lashes up at her husband, and he smiled a lingering smile, holding her gaze. Then his eyes closed, and he brushed her lips with his.

There hadn't been time for a conventional courtship, and likely they had much to learn about each other. . .so different would this life be from the safe, predictable world she had envisioned for herself. But as the peach and mauve glow from the setting sun filtered through the lacy crowns of the winter-bare trees and glistened over irregular patches of melting snow, a wondrous peace flowed through Leah. She felt God's joy. The future was in His hands. Surely everything would work out right.

Chapter 7

W isconsin is so much like Pennsylvania," Leah exclaimed. "I'm amazed."

Loving the sound of his wife's voice, Blake drew her nearer on the wagon seat beside him. "I left a lot of browns and grays and drab whites behind when I went to dispose of Gramps's estate. I'm glad spring has made its appearance."

He surveyed the familiar rolling, tree-covered hills and peaceful valleys as they passed through, gratified that the meadows were lush with water and that the landscape sported an abundance of multi-colored spring flowers. The hills looked as if a traveling painter had taken a great brush and lightly coated them in soft greens, and he hoped Leah, as an artist, would view them that way. He wanted her to be happy here.

As his faithful work horse, Butch, drew the supply wagon over the hilly, winding road between La Crosse and his lumber camp a little north of Eau Claire, Blake inhaled the scents of the warming trees on the wind, the pines, resins, and balsams softening on the southern slopes. The lumber camps along the way were bustling, and he could hardly wait to get back to his own enterprise. He'd wired Matthew of his expected date of arrival, but never told him he'd gotten married, preferring to keep it a surprise. But now a niggle of apprehension crept up Blake's spine. He hadn't actually prepared Leah, either.

He watched as she made yet another attempt to brush some of the travel smudges from her russet traveling ensemble. But she flashed him a stalwart smile, and his heart crimped. He breathed a prayer of thanks to the Lord for bringing her into his life. With each passing day as they shared their love and grew to know the various facets of each other's past, he pledged inwardly that he would never cause her to rue the day they'd wed. "This trip must seem endless to you."

She pursed her lips. "I don't think I care to set eyes on another train for a very long time," she said, stifling a yawn as she laced her fingers through his. "But I did enjoy seeing Chicago and spending a night in La Crosse. That was an adventure."

A companionable silence passed. "Do you think your brother and his wife will like me?" she finally asked, the slight waver in her voice revealing her nervousness.

"How could they help it?" He hugged her against his side and kissed her cheek. "Your husband is positively wild about you. And he does have some influence on the underlings."

Her light giggle erased some of the tiredness from her features. "How much farther did you say it was until we reach your place?"

"Only a couple more days. We'll probably have to sleep in the wagon the next two nights. I hope you don't mind. You can rest on that pallet we fixed up whenever you get tired of watching the scenery. I promise to wake you when we're almost home."

"Home. Now that does sound pleasant. If you're positive you don't mind, I think I will close my eyes for a bit. I probably won't sleep, though. I'm far too excited." She climbed over the seat back and stretched out. In less than a mile, she was sound asleep.

Blake smiled to himself as a red-winged blackbird swooped in front of them, cavorting about in the fragrant spring morning. Somewhere off to the side a partridge drummed, and Blake was almost certain he'd glimpsed a robin. His thoughts drifted to other springs and summers, some of the pleasant times he and Matt had shared despite the often back-breaking labor and long hours they put in to build up their business.

He hoped most fervently that Leah would find beauty in the raw landscape, would see beyond the present to the good life he envisioned for the two of them.

Roused from an afternoon nap when the wheels jounced over a particularly rough section of the road, Leah rubbed sleep from her eyes and sat up. "I must have dozed off." She braced herself against the bumps as she stood and climbed onto the seat beside Blake, her heart swelling with pride and love under the warmth of his smile. "Is it much farther to your place?"

"No, just over that rise, actually." He raised his gloved hand and pointed ahead, where the trace meandered through the thick woods surrounding them.

Leah peered in the direction indicated, and her pulse

rate increased. She knew she must look a sight, but the best she could do was tuck stray hairs inside her bonnet and smooth some of the wrinkles from her skirt, hoping to make a good impression on the couple who would be part of her new family. Glancing at her husband, she sensed a certain uneasiness in him, and she hoped his brother had kept everything running smoothly.

At last the wagon emerged into a broad clearing, occupied by a small camp.

A very small camp. And primitive. No one was about. She detected a glimmer of water through the trees, however, and concluded it was the Chippewa River Blake had mentioned. In the distance, she could hear the sound of axes and the occasional shout.

Leah's spirits sagged. Besides a collection of sheds which she surmised must house wagons, horses and assorted equipment, she counted a mere handful of more substantial buildings. One, likely the bunkhouse, was significantly larger than the others, but they were all plainly constructed and dwarfed by the huge trees that ringed the open area. She searched beyond them for a house, but her view was limited by the thick forest.

"It's kind of dead right now," Blake told her, "but in a few weeks there'll be so much activity it'll make your head spin. You'll see." He halted the wagon in front of a tiny cabin made of logs and turned to her with a tentative, rather embarrassed smile. "Well, this is it."

"What?"

"Home. Our place. This is where we live. It. . .isn't much, yet."

Speechless at his understatement, she could only stare

as he hopped down and held out his arms for her. It was no better than some hunter's crude shanty.

"From your expression, I can see it isn't exactly what you were expecting," he said apologetically, "but it's only temporary. It'll do until I have time to build something better."

Leah told herself she must be dreaming, having a nightmare. But as she got up and leaned into Blake's strong hands to be set on the hard ground, it felt all too real.

He scooped her into his arms and shoved the door of the tiny structure open with his boot, carrying her over the threshold.

Into the hovel.

Leah swallowed.

A single, unadorned window emitted a sickly shaft of outside light into the drab walls chinked with moss and mud, low sidewalls, and a steep gabled roof. On one end, a sort of bunk made of pine boughs with blankets spread over them indicated the sleeping chamber. A stone fireplace occupied one wall, and in front of it, several pairs of woolen underwear and socks had been draped to dry over a rough hewn pole suspended from the ceiling. That would account for the peculiar odor, Leah reasoned caustically, then spied a heavy work jacket hanging on a rack of antlers beside the door. Wordlessly, Blake set her down on the plank floor.

She couldn't bring herself to speak.

"I'll. . .get our things and bring in the supplies," he stammered and within moments carried in their trunks, valises, and the crates of goods they'd bought in La Crosse. "While you unpack, I'd better check in with Matt, spring the news of our marriage. We'll eat at the mess hall tonight." And with that, he was gone.

Leah turned a slow circle in the dismal surroundings, noting the thrown-together table and two chairs, the open hearth where she would be doing the cooking. She had left her beautiful farm for this? She sank down on her trunk, buried her face in her hands, and wept.

She didn't know how much time passed. But the hot tears gradually subsided, overcome by the realization that she had come here of her own volition and now must make the best of the situation, make this rustic shack a fit place to live. There was no other choice. She gave fleeting thought to wishing she could tear Marty's hair out for convincing her to come here, then quickly dismissed the less than charitable idea. For better or worse, she was married to Blake Malone. For life. And the fact that he treated her with the utmost tenderness and consideration during their trip here had caused her feelings for him to grow deeper by the day.

But in her heart, she had expected he'd bring her to something a trifle better than this.

A half-filled bucket of water sat near the hearth. Carrying it to the door, Leah spilled off the layer of dust which had accumulated on the surface, then poured some into a basin to repair her face. She felt somewhat better after washing up. Straightening her shoulders, she removed the hatpin from her bonnet and puzzled as to where she could put it and the other articles of clothing she'd brought. Well, unpacking her wardrobe could wait for some other time. Perhaps Blake would put up some pegs or nails for her use. Anything but more antlers!

She set the stylish hat on the bunk and assessed her surroundings with a practical eye. Pathetic, perhaps, but it was all they had. There must be some way to make it more livable. Starting with airing the place out. She snatched the stiff underwear and socks from the pole and folded them. Then she opened the door wide and swept the small confines with the rough pine broom she'd seen in the corner. The ratty blankets she tore up for use in dusting and scrubbing.

It seemed a shame to waste her pretty new linens and embroidered pillowcases on that makeshift pallet, but she'd only brought the few niceties she'd saved in her hope chest. She'd make some new ones later. The Log Cabin quilt her mother made brought a wry smile as she shook it open and spread it over the crisp sheets just tucked in place. Little had either of them known how appropriate the pattern would be. And the smooth linen tablecloth did wonders to hide the imperfections of the little table. Last, she unwrapped the painting of Laurelwood, somehow staving off the tears that sprang to her eyes at the very sight of the lovely old homestead she'd likely never see again. There wasn't a nail where she could hang it, but the narrow mantel above the fireplace would suffice. Propping it there, she stepped back to appraise her work.

Blake chose that moment to return. She heard his manly strides crossing the compound from wherever he'd been. Was it was her imagination that they seemed to lose a measure of confidence as he approached the open door? He peered inside cautiously before entering. "Safe to come in?"

Still standing there, arms crossed, Leah slanted a scathing look up at his hangdog expression.

"I. . .hope you'll forgive me," he began, mercilessly

crushing the brim of the hat he held. "I should have warned you, I know. I did try once or twice, I swear. But I couldn't."

"Well, that's a rather moot point now, isn't it?" she asked evenly, already more or less resigned to her fate. It was a long, long way back to Pennsylvania.

Blake came the rest of the way inside, and his sky blue eyes rounded as he looked around, a softly crackling fire and the warm glow of the kerosene lamp casting a soft golden hue over everything. "Man alive! You've done wonders with the place already. It looks nice. Real nice."

She gave a nod of mute concession.

"And you must be starved by now. Julie's got supper ready over at the mess hall. She's anxious to meet you."

Until he mentioned food, Leah hadn't realize what an appetite she'd worked up. Her stomach contracted painfully. "I'll just freshen up a bit."

"No need, really," Blake said. "You look fine. Julie isn't one to fuss over things like appearance—and it'll be just them and us anyway."

Leah's shoulders sagged. She plucked her shawl from the back of the nearby chair and tossed it about herself as the two of them walked to the building adjacent to the bunkhouse. Rectangular in shape, it was also slightly elevated to fit the roll of the land, and they mounted the two steps to the door.

The extended open room glowed from a profusion of lanterns positioned evenly throughout, and Leah noted its tidiness as she perused the three long tables with benches, plus what obviously was the cook shanty at the far end. The whole place smelled enticingly of hearty food.

A smiling young blonde woman approached, clad in men's attire, with a large apron covering most of her. A protruding tummy indicated she was in the family way. "You must be Leah," she said, her voice airy and decidedly feminine. "I'm Julie. I couldn't believe it when Blake stuck his head in here and told me he'd brought a bride home with him! Please sit down and make yourself at home. Supper will be on the table in a jiffy. I'm so glad to have another female around here to talk to! And do excuse my clothes. I've sort of grown beyond dress seams, and Matt's shirts are so much roomier right now."

"Pleased to meet you," Leah replied, taking an instant liking to the unpretentious girl as Blake smiled and gestured toward where several places had been set for the meal.

Moments later, the door opened to admit a wiry young man with Blake's fair coloring. He lacked several inches of his brother's height but was equally handsome in his own way, with a grin as broad as his muscular shoulders and eyes a similar blue. He had a little tyke by the hand. The two stared at her all the way across the room as they came to the table.

"Matt," Blake said, "I'd like you to meet my wife, Leah. Leah, this is my kid brother, Matt, and his son, Timmy."

Matt grinned and reached to shake her hand. "Well, well. A pleasure to meet the gal crazy enough to take on my big brother. Remind me to ask you how you managed that, by the way."

Timmy sidled closer to his dad but offered a shy smile.

"Have a good trip?" Matt asked Leah, but his gaze included them both.

"Not bad," Blake answered. "Leah's probably worn out, though. Especially with unpacking and settling in. She already has the place fixed up nicer than it's ever been."

"Anything would improve that cabin of yours," Julie chided, bringing a platter of tasty venison steaks to the table. "If you'd have given us fair warning, I would've spruced it up a bit for Leah." Shaking her head, she then went for the roasted potatoes and a bowl of green beans and set them near the plate of sliced bread. She took the place beside her son, giving him a hug.

Blake offered grace, and they all dug in.

"So you didn't have any problems while I was gone?" Blake asked, slathering butter on the hunk of bread he'd taken.

"Nothin' we couldn't handle," Matt told him. "Almost didn't make that last shingle order for Piersons, but finished up right under the wire. Frank and Mel came by to see if we're hiring yet. I told them to check back in a week, which'll be up any day."

"Hire 'em," Blake said. "And anybody else who happens by. I need to get ahead on a few things."

His brother nodded.

Leah felt Julie's stare, and glanced up to meet the girl's friendly smile. "How old is. . .Timmy, isn't it?" she asked, looking at the little towhead.

"He is in those terrible twos," moaned the young mother. "Into everything, impossible to keep in one place for long. Sometimes I must resort to tying a rope around his middle and attaching it to the clothesline outside, just so I know where he is when I'm busy. He doesn't seem to mind, though he'd rather be out 'helping' his daddy."

It was hard to imagine such an innocent looking child finding ways to get into trouble, but then Leah had not been around children very often. She chewed a bite of steak slowly, weariness of the long day catching up to her. Her thoughts drifted homeward, and she wondered how Will and Marty were getting along, if her father was still showing improvement, how Mom was coping. Just this short time she'd been gone, and it seemed like ages.

Somehow she couldn't picture herself writing a glowing letter to her family about her new life in Wisconsin. Not just yet, anyway. Did mail even make it this far? And how far away from the lumber camp was this aforementioned town called Eau Claire? Would she be shut off from civilization forever?

"Would anyone like dessert?" Julie asked, interrupting Leah's ponderings as she brought over a layer cake iced with chocolate.

"Sounds great," Blake said with enthusiasm. "And after that, I'll take my little bride home. I think this day's been long enough for her."

"I should help Julie with the dishes," Leah said.

"No," the girl answered smoothly. "It'll only take me a few minutes to clean up. Breakfast is at 5:30. . .unless you sleep in. In which case, I'll fix yours whenever you get up."

As tired as she was, Leah wasn't about to put up much of a fight. Perhaps tomorrow she'd be more help. With that tiny cabin of Blake's to look after, obviously it was going to take something like aiding her new sister-in-law to occupy all the time she'd undoubtedly find on her hands. What on earth had she gotten herself into?

Chapter 8

By the time Blake finished giving Leah a tour of his lumber operation, her head was spinning with unfamiliar terms like sawyer, chipper, cant hook, froe, peavy, and skidding tongs. He and Matt demonstrated how trees were notched and then cut with a crosscut saw to fall in precise positions. She watched them lop off the slender tops and side branches, then put the Malone mark on the log with an engraved hammer. After that it would be measured by a scaler and labeled for the sawyer to cut into lengths between ten and eighteen feet, then skidded to the logging road to be hauled by horse-drawn wagons to the river. There, huge rafts of logs would be floated down to the sawmills in Eau Claire. "It's ever so fascinating," Leah told him honestly.

He grinned and hugged her hard, planting a kiss on her nose. "Just wanted you to see what we do all day," he said lightly.

She admired the way Blake looked in his blue and white striped hickory work shirts, the stagged pants that were cut off at the knee and ran into the heavy woolen stockings worn inside the leather spiked boots. Somehow it added to the dashing picture she had in her mind of the man from faraway who had stolen her heart. This man who, she soon learned, left the warmth of their bed at dawn every morning and did not return until a little past dark.

The next few weeks found her cultivating her new-found friendship with Julie Malone, who at Leah's age of twenty-two, lived for the sole purpose of making Matthew and their son happy. That, and keeping the newly hired workers at the mill fed. With the days slowly lengthening, the crew was putting in incredibly long hours.

"So you had no idea you'd wind up married to a lumberjack either?" Leah asked incredulously. She sipped the tea Julie had poured for her while they chatted, mending their husbands' worn work clothes. Timmy lay on the wood floor nearby, playing with a carved logging wagon, complete with horses.

The girl flicked a lock of wheat-blonde hair over her shoulder and giggled. "I was supposed to become a school-teacher, since I'd been raised all proper, with the correct qualifications and abilities. But the summer I graduated, I came here to visit my Aunt Jen and Uncle Zach, who was one of the top sawyers in the area. When he signed on with Blake, Aunt Jen took it upon herself to become the best camp cook who ever lived—or so all the men declared. Anyway, I started helping out. That's how I met Matthew. One look from those gorgeous blue eyes, and I was a goner."

"I know exactly how you felt," Leah confessed.

Julie smiled and continued. "Auntie Jen was thrilled that I wanted to stay permanently. Especially after my uncle died in an accident on a log raft. She and I had grand times, up until she went out by herself picking berries for pies and got bit by a snake. Nobody went looking for her until it was too late. So. . .that left me, more's the pity. I sure miss her." A sigh as sad as her smile brought a pause. "My parents weren't exactly enthralled with my choice, but they've since grown to adore Matt."

Leah had given no thought to snakes and only a little to the faraway howls she attributed to dogs. In all likelihood they were wolves. She shivered. "But don't you ever. . .miss civilization?" she had to ask.

"At times. But usually if there's a stormy spell and the ground's too mucky for work, we all hop into the boat and head downriver to town. Sure as not, we're out of one supply or another. We eat at one of the restaurants, sometimes even take in a traveling show. Then when we come home, I'm all set to get back to my routine."

Leah wondered how long it would be before she could feel the same way. With each passing day, she missed Laurelwood more. The fact that Blake was the tender and loving husband he'd promised made her life bearable. . . when he was around. But that was getting to be far too seldom for her liking. Except for half a day each Sunday, he was always out working. And lately she'd noticed an odd queasiness, especially in the morning, as if she'd eaten something that hadn't agreed with her. Sometimes she didn't bother to come to breakfast at all, telling Julie afterward that she wasn't hungry.

As Julie glanced over at the clock on the sideboard, Leah realized the two of them needed to finish fixing supper for the famished men. They'd be ravenous, as always, certain to devour every scrap set before them. Gulping the remainder of their drinks, they sprang up and tended to the beans and bacon Julie had simmered overnight in a bean hole outside. The beans bubbled over the hearth fire as several trays of biscuits cooled on the sideboard.

Leah lifted the lid of the kettle to stir the beans, and the sight of the greasy bacon on top made her stomach lurch. She swallowed and stepped away, clutching her middle.

"Something wrong?" Julie asked, puzzled. She peered into the pot and gave the mixture a few stirs.

"I'm just not feeling all that well these days. The change of water, no doubt."

A peculiar smile tipped up the expectant mother's lips at the corners. "How long has this been going on?"

Leah shrugged. "Oh, I don't know. Since a little after Blake and I arrived."

"And what about your cycle?"

"It's—" As Leah calculated the weeks in her mind, she slowly arrived at the conclusion Julie's satisfied expression revealed. "You mean, I'm. . ."

Her fair-haired friend nodded.

The certainty overwhelmed Leah, and an incredible feeling of warmth spread through her. At last, something wonderful to write Mother and Marty! "I–I guess I'll have to tell Blake tonight when we're alone. Do you think he'll be glad?"

Julie gave an off-handed shrug. "No reason for him not to be. Except maybe how crowded that teeny little cabin's gonna be pretty soon. You'll have to get him to build you something bigger, like Matt did for me. Of course, they're pretty busy right now."

"Yes. But surely he'll give the matter some thought, at least, knowing how desperately we'll be needing more room."

But when Blake trudged in that evening, shoulders sagging, eyelids drooping, even his voice husky from exhaustion, she merely dished up some of the beans she'd brought home for him and put off telling her news.

And that went on for days.

Fortunately, Julie had been sworn to secrecy. Leah ceased helping with meals now that she wasn't feeling up to snuff. But the more time she spent on her own, gazing at her painting of Laurelwood as she battled through morning sickness and other queasy periods, the more she longed for her home and family back in Pennsylvania. Back there the sweet babe would be coddled and doted upon by his grandparents and relatives. What sort of life would he know here, brought up in the dangers of back-woods Wisconsin? She was fairly certain of one thing: If the hours Blake was putting in gave any indication of what they could expect in the future, their child would see precious little of the father of the house.

And what if something went wrong with her or the baby? How long would it take for help to arrive from Eau Claire? Maybe this hadn't been such a prudent choice, after all. That possibility made her feel weepy, and she hated feeling weepy.

One afternoon over tea, Julie patted Leah's hand, drawing her back from a million miles away. "I found some extra flannel in a trunk at home. Do you think you could put it to use? I still have most of Timmy's outgrown things, and have already made our new baby plenty of new ones."

Leah brightened. "Truly? That would be wonderful. Thank you so much. I never once thought ahead to bring any yard goods with me. Our marriage happened so fast."

"I just thought maybe it would help you fill a few hours," the girl added gently.

"I certainly have plenty of those to fill." The bitterness in her tone surprised even Leah. But a quick glance at Julie gave no indication that she'd picked up on it. "You know," Leah said without thinking, "your voice is about the only human one I ever hear, most of the time. Blake comes home dragging his feet, gulps his food practically whole, and falls into bed. Then at first light, he's out the door. Even Sundays, when the rest of the crew is off, Blake and Matt still put in quite a few hours of work. How do you stand it?"

Julie smiled and answered in a casual tone. "It's not always like this, I promise. But summer's when they have to get as much accomplished as possible. Once the weather turns cold, the days grow too short for them to do so much. Some of their time is spent at the shingle mill. They're underfoot a lot then. You'll see."

"I suppose there's hope," Leah answered wistfully.

So during the lonely summer days, Leah began sewing tiny garments. And as each new article was completed, she would take it over to show her friend. She often thought back on the conversation she'd had with Julie that day. In particular, the idle comment about rarely hearing another human voice. And the truth of it really started to grate on Leah.

Inwardly, she began to seethe. "I've been much too nice to someone who treats me this way," she declared in the oppressive silence of the cabin. "When he comes home tonight, I'll be polite, but nothing more. See how he likes that! He hasn't even given me a chance to tell him he's going to be a father yet, for pity's sake." Pressing her lips together, she imagined her repentant husband fawning all over her, begging her to forgive him for his thoughtlessness, promising to quit work earlier and spend time with her.

Hours later, she heard his familiar step approaching. Hiking her chin, she dished his stew while he washed up outside.

"Hi, sweetheart," he said wearily, as he came in. He gave her a peck on the cheek.

She said nothing.

"Supper smells good."

She plunked the bowl unceremoniously on the table.

With a thin smile, he pulled out a chair and sat. He buttered some bread and began eating.

Leah took the other chair and moved it nearer the firelight, then took her sewing out of the basket nearby.

"You're pretty quiet," he finally remarked.

She merely shrugged. "I can't think of anything to say." *Especially since you prefer being with those silly trees to being with me,* she wanted to add, but she bit her tongue.

"Was there something you wanted to tell me yesterday? Seems I remember you mentioning a matter I should know about. I must've dozed off before you got to it."

Leah tried for extreme nonchalance as she kept stitching. "Oh, it was nothing, really. Just about the baby." She flicked a glance at him, mostly to gauge the effect, if any, the flat statement made on him.

"What baby?" His eyes opened to a surprising width, considering the dark circles under them.

"Ours." She returned her attention to her project.

His chair scraped over the floor and toppled in his haste to get up. "You–you mean we're gonna. . .that I'm. . . you're— Why didn't you say so!" Jubilant, he grabbed her and all but crushed her against his solid frame as he swung her in a circle. "Oh, Leah, my love. This is just wonderful. It's great news. Great news."

Her own heart softening under the display of the old tenderness she'd been missing, Leah had to smile. Her decision to remain aloof from Blake fell by the wayside as he rocked her in his embrace. "You mean, you're truly happy about it?"

"Happy! I have never been happier in my life. Just think. A son, to help in the business."

"Or a daughter," she reminded him, tipping her head back so she could see his face.

"Naw, it'll be a son. A man can tell these things." He gave an assertive nod.

"I promise to do my best to see that you're not disappointed," she said with a disbelieving smile.

"You've never disappointed me, wife." He tweaked her nose. "But I might be a little put off right now if you tell me there's no dessert."

Her own joy dimmed a little, and Leah had to force a smile. He never once mentioned the fact they'd be needing more space pretty soon. . .that there wasn't room in here for a cradle or a rocking chair.

Men. All they cared about were their stomachs.

Chapter 9

Five endless months of this persistent nausea. Would she ever feel normal again? Battling yet another wave of queasiness, Leah lugged the bucket of mop water outside.

"Why don't you let me do that for you, love?" Blake asked, hurrying over to her.

But she'd purposely saved the chore until he was around. She had a point to make. "I'm used to doing things for myself," she said coolly, not even glancing his way. She didn't need to look at him. His whole bearing showed how her tone stung him. *Good. Let him know I can get by on my own. He's taught me well enough.*

The caustic thoughts railed against her conscience. But Leah didn't care. She was weary of being alone hour after hour, day after day, not having anyone to talk to except on Sunday mornings. She was tired of being nothing but a cook, a washerwoman, tired of clothes that were too tight. She detested this rustic cabin and hated having her pretty linens snag on the rough wood. She couldn't even pray anymore. . .and she alternated between hating that most of all and pretending she didn't care a whit.

Life was nothing like she'd hoped or dreamed in her naive past. She was fed up. She wanted to go home.

Home to Laurelwood. And somehow, she'd find a way to do it.

Returning inside, Leah brushed past her bewildered husband, avoiding the arms that reached out to her—even though he'd put in the longest day yet and looked utterly spent. Turning away, she shimmied out of her work dress and climbed into bed without a word. And there she lay stiff as a board, facing the wall.

But she would not cry. She was sick of tears.

"Are you sure pregnancy's supposed to be like this?" Blake asked Matt as the two of them fastened logs together to float them downriver. "Man, it's almost like she can't stand the sight of me anymore."

His brother grinned and brushed wood splinters from his work gloves. "What, you don't remember the moaning I did when Julie was carryin' Tim?" He shook his head. "Least little thing would set her off. She'd be fine one minute, sobbin' the next—liked to drove me crazy, walkin' on eggshells all those months. At least she's havin' it easier with this one, praise be. And now with her mom here to help out with her time bein' so close, it's less worry for me. Once Leah's got that little bundle in her arms to hold and love, she'll revert back to her normal self. You'll see."

Somewhat encouraged, Blake still couldn't relinquish all his doubts. He prayed for Leah constantly, pleaded that God would give him patience, help him to see beyond this tough spot to happier times ahead. He knew he'd been neglecting her for far too long. This afternoon he'd quit early and take her for a little drive.

ᐤ

Leah heard the wagon pull up. Curious, she peeked out the window and glimpsed her husband striding toward the door. *In the middle of the afternoon?* she thought waspishly. *All these weeks and months I've been aching for him to come home and spend time with me, and he finally decides to do it?* She gave a little huff and feigned intense interest in the infant sacque she'd just finished embroidering.

The door opened, admitting her cheerful blond giant, an equally cheery smile on his handsome face, dimples and all. "It's a nice day out. Thought we'd take a drive. The leaves are beginning to turn, and the woods are getting pretty."

Leah steeled herself against the ridiculous pounding of her heart. "Thank you, but I'd rather not."

"Don't be silly," he said evenly. "You've been cooped up in here nigh onto forever. The fresh air will do you good."

"I'm really quite busy just now," she fudged, poking her needle into an already completed flower.

He stood there for a few seconds, as if expecting her to change her mind.

Leah was not about to give in. It was too late for him to dote on her now. Too late for him to be charming. If she waited long enough, he'd give up and go back to work. That's what he preferred anyway. He'd more than proved that since dragging her here.

But Blake didn't give up. And he didn't go away. Completely ignoring her stubborn display, he plucked her cloak from the antler rack and crossed the room. In one smooth movement, he swirled it about her shoulders, then scooped her up into his arms. "You need to get out more, sweetheart. Trust me."

Mortified as he carried her out the door and set her onto the wagon seat, Leah clenched her teeth. So he was bigger than she was. That didn't make him boss. She'd said she didn't want to go, and he was making her go anyway. *Well, fine. Try your hardest, Blake Malone. I'll just sit like a post until you bring me back.*

He flicked the reins over Butch's rump and turned the wagon in a wide circle, heading down one of his logging traces, in a slightly southerly direction. The nonsensical tune he whistled made her all the madder.

Her arms folded across her chest, Leah didn't let on that she noticed the kiss of autumn on the forest. The crew had cleared a huge patch of trees since he'd first escorted her around his holdings, evidence of a lot of hard work. And she couldn't help but see the golds and reds of fall beginning to gild the edges of the leaves on the perimeter. No doubt Wisconsin would be every bit as breathtakingly beautiful as Pennsylvania in autumn's full glory.

Neither of them spoke as the horse plodded over a carpet of pine needles, dredging up the tangy scent of pine sap. Leah wondered how long he'd keep her out. There wasn't anyplace to go to in this direction, not with such thick forest all around them.

Shortly, quite unexpectedly, the wagon emerged from the cover of trees into a wide clearing. One occupied by a building well under construction.

Blake pulled up on the reins, halting Butch.

Leah's heart leaped with recognition. Her throat

clogged. "Laurelwood!" she choked out. "All this time, and–and you've been building me Laurelwood!" Burying her face in her hands, she burst into tears.

Blake slid a comforting arm around her, drawing her close. "I had it in mind to surprise you when it was closer to being finished," he said huskily, caressing her as she wept. "But the Lord finally got it through my thick skull that I had my priorities all mixed up. I should have been nurturing our marriage. I hope you can forgive me for being such a cad, for neglecting you so shamefully. I do love you, Leah."

"But I've been a wretch and a shrew," she managed between sobs. "A horrid wife. I don't deserve you. I am the one who needs to ask forgiveness. From you and from the Lord. I am so very sorry."

He cupped her face in his work-hardened hand. "Both of us are a little new at this marriage business, my love. I just hope all the secrets I had to keep haven't caused permanent damage. I had my crew working double time on this at the end of every work day. And you might as well know, Julie was in on it—otherwise she'd have been all over Matt for deserting her, too."

Listening to the voice which had drawn her heart from the very beginning, Leah gradually regained her composure. This demonstration of love humbled her beyond words. She didn't know if she'd ever be able to forgive herself for acting like a spoiled child rather than a grownup married woman. She should have trusted him.

"We'll do our utmost to finish it before winter sets in," Blake told her. "I thought you'd want our son—or daughter—to be born here. Start our own traditions." He smiled into her eyes. "I hope you approve."

Thinking back on how she'd once questioned the depth of his feelings for her, Leah very nearly started crying again. But she hung on to her control with every ounce of strength she possessed. "I. . .don't know how to thank you for this, dearest Blake. I'll never doubt you again. Ever. And I'll be the wife I promised you on our wedding day. I'll make this house every bit as special as Laurelwood ever was. Because you'll be here, and where you are, my heart will always be."

"And I'll be the husband you've been needing all this time. . .with no more surprises."

Losing herself in his love-filled eyes, Leah raised her lips to his. And she realized at last that it was true, what people said. . . .

Home is where the heart is.

SALLY LAITY

Sally spent the first twenty years of her life in Dallas, Pennsylvania, and calls herself a small-town girl at heart. She and her husband Don have lived in New York, Pennsylvania, Illinois, Alberta (Canada), and now reside in Bakersfield, CA. They are active in a large Baptist church, where Don teaches Sunday school and Sally sings in the choir. They have four children and twelve grandchildren.

Sally always loved to write, and after her children were grown, she took college writing courses and attended Christian writing conferences. She has written both historical and contemporary romances and considers it a joy to know that the Lord can touch other hearts through her stories.

Having successfully written several novels, including a co-authored series for Tyndale, three Barbour novellas, and six Heartsong Presents titles, one of this author's favorite things these days is counseling new authors via the Internet.

New Beginnings

by DiAnn Mills

Dedication

*This novella is dedicated to Beau and Allison
as they step out in their own new beginnings.*

Charlene,
    Blessings &
joy in this time of
good will & peace
towards men.
                        Love
                        Di Ann
                    12-17-99

Chapter 1

Wisconsin, 1899

Betsy Anne Wingert had always believed her wedding day would be filled with happiness, laughter, and the excited anticipation of dreams coming true. Instead she felt trapped and miserable.

But what good did remorse do now? In less than half an hour, standing before the mahogany and brick fireplace in the Malone parlor, she'd pledge her life and devotion to Nicholas Parker Malone. She'd carry the title of his wife until the day she died.

Betsy's eyes flooded with bitter tears. How could she have agreed to this? They'd grown up together, like brother and sister. Everyone expected them to marry—pointed to it when they played house as children. But to Betsy, it had been a game. She should have been honest, voiced her true feelings—and certainly never agreed to be his wife.

A lie.

A sin.

Now she'd pay for it the rest of her life.

Studing her reflection in the full-length mirror of the

Malone's guest bedroom, Betsy bit back another well of sorrow. *Dry your eyes!* she ordered. *No one must know, least of all Nicholas.* Peering at herself, she decided giving herself to her husband would be something she could endure. Nicholas's embraces were ardent, but gentle.

She shook her head in an effort to dispel the shame racing through her veins. He loved her so much—she'd seen it in his clear blue eyes.

Dear, sweet Nicholas with hair the color of corn silk and such handsome features. His lively spirit attracted young and old, male and female. She'd long since recognized his caring, devotion. . .pure adoration as God intended for a man to cherish his wife.

Help me, Lord, she prayed. *If this is what You want for me, a marriage bereft of love, then help me to bear it. I want to love Nicholas, truly I do.*

The door creaked open, and Eloise Wingert slipped inside the bedroom. Betsy turned to greet her, feigning happiness for the sake of her beloved mother. Despite her resolve, at the sight of the dark-haired woman, Betsy's eyes moistened.

"Oh, my precious darling," her mother murmured, gathering Betsy into her arms. "I shouldn't have left you alone. This is such a special, joyous time for you." She slowly brought her to arm's length and gazed into Betsy's face. "A bride's joyful tears are drops of gold in the eyes of God."

"Thank you, Mother," she replied, wishing she could have remained forever in the security of that embrace.

She cupped Betsy's chin and smiled adoringly. "You are so beautiful, my little girl all grown up." Her mother hastily whisked away any traces of emotion and smiled. "Let me stand back and take a look at you. I want to see the whole gown."

Obediently, Betsy turned around, catching a glimpse of herself in the mirror. Her mother had sewn the wedding dress from a picture she'd seen in *The Ladies' Standard* and purchased the ivory silk brocade from New York—the very latest in fashion. Little three-leaf clovers embellished the fabric, making it appear to shimmer in the light. The tight-fitting bodice closed in front with many mother-of-pearl buttons, and layers of ecru lace trimmed the collar and sleeves.

She whirled around to see the full view of the back. An ivory sash tied at the waist, and tiny pleats gathered at the bustle, leading to a flowing train.

"Mother, I love my dress. Thank you for making it for me," Betsy said, and she meant it. Her mother had always given so much of herself to her family, completely, unselfishly. "I want to be just like you," she whispered.

Her mother shook her head. "I have so many faults, but I do strive to be what God intended. I guess if I have any last bit of advice, it is exactly that. Let the Lord have His way with you. Follow His leading, no matter if you don't understand why."

She nodded and attempted a faint smile. From the worried frown etched across her mother's forehead, Betsy realized she knew something troubled her. Disconcerted, she avoided her mother's gaze and toyed with the pearl buttons on her bodice.

"You don't really want to marry, do you?" she asked ever so softly.

Betsy's silence echoed around her.

"This must be why you've been so quiet the last few weeks. Darling, you don't have to go through with the wedding."

"I must, Mother. I gave my word."

"It's not too late." Her gray eyes narrowed.

"Yes, it is. I won't hurt him." Betsy sighed and swallowed the lump in her throat. "Nicholas is a good man, and he loves me."

"But what of your happiness?"

She picked up her ivory skirts and bravely faced her mother's loving concern. "Mother, downstairs he's waiting for me, just like he always has since we were children. How could I ever disappoint Nicholas and his family by not marrying him?"

"There's no talking you out of this?" Her mother pressed her lips together in an obvious effort to hold back tears.

She shook her head. "I only wish we weren't leaving in the morning."

"I feel the same way, Betsy, but I've heard him talk. Farming has always been a great love for Nicholas, not like his father and grandfather who loved the lumber mill. I, too, detest the thought of you moving to Ohio."

She touched her ivory gloved hand to her mother's mouth. "No more of this," she whispered. "It will all work out." Turning away to the window, she spoke the words of her heart. "I simply wish his Grandfather Parker hadn't left him that land in Ohio. He never asked me if I wanted to be a farmer's wife."

Betsy viewed the many carriages and wagons parked

up and down both sides of the road. So many treasured family and friends had gathered at the Malone home for the wedding. The last remains of March snow had melted, and in its place shoots of green burst forth from the rich earth. Earlier the sky had threatened rain, but now beams of sunlight flickered through the treetops. It raised her spirits, giving her hope. Perhaps God had blessed this day after all.

Nicholas deserved a beautiful wedding. She may even see him and feel something more than the childhood friendship they'd always shared. Maybe living on a farm wouldn't be so bad. . .watching things grow and seeing new life in plants and animals.

Deep inside, though, she doubted it.

"I really understand how you feel, but Nicholas thought you'd be thrilled with his surprise," her mother said gently.

"I acted like it was wonderful," Betsy pointed out, chewing on her lip. "And I vow he will never perceive the difference."

"I know you believe this is for the best, but pretending will not make you happy. He'll eventually learn the truth—about it all." Betsy's mother walked over to the window and stood beside her. "If I can't change your mind about today, then I'll simply pray that working together on a farm will be a blessing to your marriage." She touched her cheek. "You need time alone with Nicholas, without your family or his."

A light knock at the door relieved Betsy from her mother's penetrating questions. "Betsy, Eloise, it's time," Benjamin Wingert's booming voice announced.

"All right, Father," Betsy replied, hugging her mother once more. "Come on in. I'm ready."

Her father spanned the width and height of the doorway. Dressed in a dark brown suit, he stood incredibly handsome. His thick silver hair and muscular shoulders made him look so healthy and alive. Betsy took a deep breath. Oh, how she'd miss her father's robust voice and gentle ways. For a moment he merely stared as though stunned.

"Father, is everything all right?" she asked, unaccustomed to viewing him speechless.

He strode across the room and lightly took her hand into both of his. "I've thought about this day since you were born," he said, his voice heavy with emotion. "And you are lovelier than I could ever have imagined."

Betsy felt her eyes grow liquid again. "Oh, thank you. Mother did a splendid job with my gown."

"Nonsense with the gown. I'm pleased with the young woman wearing it. You remind me so much of your mother." He glanced at his wife endearingly. "It's as though time has drifted back to our wedding day." Expelling a deep breath, he turned his attention back to his daughter. "Nicholas is a fine man, and I'm pleased to call him son. May God bless you both richly."

"Can we pray?" Betsy asked timidly.

His mustache twitched upward in an approving smile. "Yes, of course." The three grasped hands, and Betsy willed her shaking to cease. Slowly he began. "Heavenly Father, we praise You for the gift of love. Thank You for allowing Eloise and me to raise such a fine young woman. She's Yours, Lord, just as she's always been. Today I give her to

Nicholas as his wife. Bless their union and be with them as they leave us tomorrow. All these things we ask in Your precious and holy name. Amen." He lifted watery eyes and pressed his lips together for a slight smile.

"Oh, Father," she breathed as he drew her close to him. He held her for several long moments until the sound of the piano downstairs pulled them apart.

Her mother tugged and straightened Betsy's gown until it was arranged to perfection. Meeting her gaze, Betsy saw compassion and concern.

"Hurry now, Mama," she whispered. "You'll want to see me descending the stairs."

The beginning chords of another hymn urged them to part. The wedding of Betsy Anne Wingert and Nicholas Parker Malone would take place as planned.

Standing in his father's library amid the floor-to-ceiling books, Nicholas watched the throng of people mingle through the parlor and hallway. Some took seats in over-stuffed and straight-backed chairs, and others stood talking in subtle whispers. Instantly they hushed as the pianist struck the chords of "Come Thou Fount of Every Blessing."

Betsy is my blessing, he thought, feeling nervous and impatient. *And I must tell her that every day of our married life.* He loved her with everything in him. She had her father's blue-green eyes, a pert little nose, and a wide smile that caused her whole face to glow. Nicholas grinned to himself, recalling how he used to tease her about her large mouth. She'd cry and tell her mother, and then he'd be forced to apologize. Odd, how one skinny little girl could grow up to be so lovely. Her musical laughter and sweet voice stayed with him constantly—always had, since they were children. Yes, he would love her forever.

Both families had wanted this marriage, and he happily accepted their wishes, although he would have pursued her with or without their blessings. Suddenly he remembered the two of them as children playing in the apple orchard.

"Now, Nicholas, when we're married, we must have juicy, red apples like these. Don't you agree?" she'd asked with a nod of her walnut-colored curls.

"Of course. And if our house doesn't have an apple tree, then I'll plant one," he replied.

"Oh, would you, Nicholas? Just for me?"

"Anything you want."

"May I have a home near my mother?"

"Yes, I promise."

The reminiscing about childhood days left an empty feeling in the pit of his stomach. *I'm taking her away from her family,* he reflected. *I broke my promise.* But they were not children anymore. He was twenty, and Betsy nearly eighteen. He remembered again her reaction to his surprise of inheriting the farm. She hadn't become upset, but she hadn't been overly excited either. Surely she'd have expressed her disappointment.

Nonsense. I'm worrying about something needlessly. Today, Betsy and I will be married, and tomorrow we'll leave for our new home in Ohio. And with God's help, I'll be the best husband and farmer this country has ever seen.

He felt a tap on his shoulder. "Son, everyone is seated for the ceremony. It's time."

Roused from his musings, Nicholas stared into the blue eyes of his father, Phillip Malone. He took a deep breath. "I'm ready."

"Do you have the ring?" he asked with a teasing grin.

"Yes, sir."

His father placed an arm around his shoulders. "I'm very proud of you—your selection of a wife, your decision to farm, and the godly man you've become."

"Thank you. Sometimes I worry that I'm not doing the right thing, but I feel God's calling to Ohio and my inheritance. You know I'm going to miss you and Mother."

"And we are already wishing you were still here in Wisconsin."

They both hesitated. His father initiated a handshake, but his arm slid up to Nicholas's shoulder and neck, ending in a vigorous hug. Finally the elder Malone broke away. "We best take our place. Betsy surely doesn't want a wedding without a groom."

The two walked side by side from the library into the parlor. At the sight of the small crowd, a siege of nervousness erupted inside Nicholas. He wanted and needed to see Betsy. She and she alone would put to rest the unsettling in his soul. Anxiously, he waited her.

Then he saw his bride.

More ethereal than he'd ever imagined, Betsy appeared to fairly float down the circular staircase, clinging to her father's arm. Radient in ivory silk and lace, wearing a fragile smile, she trembled.

Nicholas's mind stepped back to a time when he'd thrown a rock into an elm tree only to have a nest with three tiny, blue robin eggs topple to the ground. She'd screamed at him, hit him with her little fists, then fell into his arms sobbing. He'd felt so wretched and then protective.

And he'd protect his angel now.

The Reverend Dale Schmidt lifted his head and silently commanded everyone's attention. "Dearly beloved: Forasmuch as marriage is a holy estate, ordained of God, and to be held in honor by all, it becometh those who enter therein to weigh, with reverent minds, what the Word of God teacheth concerning it.

"The Lord God said, 'It is not good that the man should be alone; I will make him an help meet for him.'

"Our Lord Jesus Christ said, 'Have ye not read, that He which made them at the beginning made them male and female, and said, For this cause shall a man leave his father and mother, and shall cleave to his wife: and they twain shall be one flesh? Wherefore, they are no more twain, but one flesh. What therefore God hath joined together, let not man put asunder.'"

Nicholas stole a look at his bride. Tears dampened her cheeks. That was his Betsy, so easily moved to sentiment. He loved her kind heart and gentle ways. For a moment he thought he'd explode with the joy filling his soul.

The pastor continued. "Into this holy estate this man and this woman come now to be united. If anyone, therefore, can show just cause why they may not be lawfully joined together, let him now speak, or else forever hold his peace."

Nicholas felt her quiver, and he fought an immense urge to hold her until she calmed.

"Wilt thou have this woman to thy wedded wife, to

live together after God's ordinance in the holy estate of matrimony? Wilt thou love her, comfort her, honor and keep her in sickness and in health, and, forsaking all others, keep thee only unto her, so long as ye both shall live?"

"I will," Nicholas said, hearing his voice sound loud and clear.

"Wilt thou have this man to thy wedded husband, to live together after God's ordinance in the holy estate of matrimony? Wilt thou love him, comfort him, honor and keep him in sickness and in health, and, forsaking all others, keep thee only unto him, so long as ye both shall live?"

Betsy hesitated. Silence followed. Nicholas turned to her and smiled. She seemed so frightened. Poor girl, he knew how crowds of people left her speechless.

"I will," she whispered, with a shaky smile.

The ceremony soon ended. "I now pronounce you man and wife. You may kiss your bride," the pastor instructed.

Nicholas gazed deeply into the blue-green eyes of his wife. A twinge of alarm rang through his mind and shattered his senses. He didn't see love in her eyes. He saw fear. . .and distrust.

Long after the Malone home hushed and Betsy heard the even breathing of her husband beside her, she reflected over the afternoon. Feeling certain her secret lay secure, she pondered over the uneasiness settling in the core of her being. Guilt robbed her of sleep, and she desperately needed rest for the journey ahead.

The guests had been most kind, bidding congratulations and encouragement for their future. Some prayed God's blessing on their marriage, and Betsy wondered if she would be struck dead for thanking them. As she'd expressed gratitude to each one for sharing in her and Nicholas's special day, she felt her mother watch and silently comfort her. What would she ever do without her constant presence? She hated thinking about it.

When the last guest had departed, Betsy found herself standing in front of the fireplace where she'd taken her vows. Glancing up into a painting of the very same house, she felt an odd sense of peace. At the time she wondered if it was the replica or God Himself letting her know of His presence.

"You like the picture of Laurelwood?" Deborah Malone had asked softly.

"Yes. I've never seen a painting reflect such serenity. Why is it called Laurelwood when that's not what you call your home?" she asked curiously.

The woman laughed softly. "Oh, it's not this house. The painting is of Leah Malone's girlhood home in Pennsylvania—Nicholas's grandmother."

Betsy glanced at her, quite perplexed.

"Ask Nicholas to tell you about it," she suggested. "That will give you two something else to talk about on your way to Ohio," she sighed dreamily. "It's such a romantic story."

Betsy smiled genuinely. She did love Deborah Malone. Regretfully, she wouldn't get to know her better. "I'll be sure to ask him about it. And, thank you again for this lovely wedding. . . ."

Nicholas stirred in his sleep, and she felt his gaze upon her. "Betsy, are you all right?"

"Yes, I'm fine."

"But you're not sleeping." He sounded concerned, so much like him.

"Oh, Nicholas, I was only thinking of today."

"Of course," he murmured, wrapping his arm around her. "I should have known."

I'll be a good wife, she vowed silently to God. *Just watch me make him happy.*

Chapter 2

A slow drizzle dampened Betsy's new determination to make the most of her marriage and chilled her to the bone. It began near dawn when she first heard Nicholas rousing, no doubt anxious for the journey to Ohio. Like the many times she'd seen him excited about adventures and new ideas, he suddenly began talking and sharing his dreams about the farm—their future—as though she lay fully awake and felt the same enthusiasm.

Don't pretend, she scolded herself through the fogginess of faint reality. *Wake up and share his dreams. Tell him all the things he should hear from his wife.*

"And we'll be there in plenty of time before plowing and planting," he said, leaning over to her and gracing her cheek with a kiss.

Betsy opened her eyes and forced a smile.

"Good morning, Mrs. Malone," he whispered. She saw the glowing light of love in his clear blue eyes.

"Good morning." She smiled at his tenderness. "Is it time?"

"Yes, I believe so. Do you mind getting up so early?

Well, I mean once we are living on our farm, every day will be like this." His face flushed with confident expectation.

She dared not spoil their first day by revealing her disappointment. The idea of leaving her family and friends left her numb and. . .unforgiving. "Is it raining?" she asked, lifting her head from the pillow.

Nicholas stroked her thick hair and drew her close to his chest. "We can wait a few more minutes. It's not even daylight yet, and Mother would never hear of us leaving before sunrise."

"Thank you, Nicholas," she murmured, slowly drifting off to sleep.

"I love you," he whispered.

And she smiled in response.

It seemed she'd barely gotten to sleep again when he awakened her. Odd, she'd been dreaming that he'd changed his mind and decided to stay in Wisconsin and work with his father at the lumber mill. Such a delightful thought, but nevertheless only a dream.

With heavy eyes, Betsy rose and prepared herself. Last night Nicholas had packed their belongings into a wagon so their departure would be much easier. Some of their wedding gifts she hadn't even seen, but since she secretly felt unworthy of them, it didn't matter. They'd be unpacked and put to use in Ohio.

Still, the rain lingered, and she felt the nagging chill. A cozy day by the fire seemed much more to her liking. At least it wasn't snow.

Then Betsy remembered an envelope her mother had given her the previous evening. She hadn't opened it last night but laid it on the cherry dresser of Nicholas's bedroom. Picking it up, she eased it open:

> *To my darling daughter,*
>
> *As you step out in this new life with Nicholas, I want to share this verse to speed you on your way. My heart aches with the fact you're leaving, but I know it's God will for your life. My love and prayers go with you.*
>
> *"Now unto him that is able to do exceeding abundantly above all that we ask or think, according to the power that worketh in us, Unto him be glory in the church by Christ Jesus throughout all ages, world without end. Amen." Ephesians 3:20–21.*
>
> *With all my love,*
Mother

Betsy blinked back the tears threatening to spill. Mother knew the right verses to give her the strength and courage to face the days ahead. She tucked it into her Bible and carried it downstairs to meet Nicholas.

After a hearty breakfast with Deborah and Phillip Malone, they stepped out into a pink tinted sky to bid farewell. Already she missed her parents, but she'd said good-bye to them after the wedding. Betsy had shed enough tears yesterday to last a long time, but again they threatened to surface when she viewed a pair of fine mares in a dapple color hitched to the heavily laden wagon.

"We have something else for you," Phillip said, with a glint in his blue eyes.

"Father, we have no more room," Nicholas insisted.

The older man ignored his protests. "Excuse me while I get it. We'll find room."

Betsy turned to Deborah, whose eyes contained the familiar merriment she'd often found in Nicholas's gaze. Moments later, Phillip returned with a large, rectangular-shaped object draped in an old quilt.

"What is this?" Betsy asked, without an inkling of what he carried.

"Laurelwood," Deborah whispered. "It will always be a reminder of home and those who love you."

Nicholas objected, shaking his blond head. "But we haven't room."

"It's not for you as much as Betsy," his mother stated firmly. "She needs to see something familiar when her family is so far away."

"Oh, thank you," Betsy breathed, thinking of the many wonderful hours she'd spent with her parents at the Malone home. "Please, Nicholas. Can't we find a spot for the painting?"

He sighed deeply, then a warm smile spread over his face. "To see you this happy, I'd almost leave a sack of seed corn." Then he laughed. "Well, almost."

Betsy clapped her hands. Elation made her want to dance and shout. "I'm so thrilled. When I'm lonesome, I'll just gaze into it and envision Mother and Father sitting on the front porch with you. It will be so grand."

Phillip ran his fingers through his blond and silver hair, then scanned the length of the wagon until he saw where he could slip the painting between a trunk and two boxes. He wrapped it tightly with an additional quilt before he and Nicholas anchored it in place.

"And I know a perfect place for it in our new home," Nicholas said, reaching around Betsy's waist.

"That's right," Deborah replied. "You've seen the house, but she hasn't. For a moment I'd forgotten the two months you were gone last fall tending to the property."

"And you'll see it, too," Nicholas said. "Father tells me you plan to visit us next spring."

"With the Wingerts," she added.

Betsy beamed. Now, she really had something to look forward to. A year seemed endless, but things could change. Her heart could soften and she could become the wife Nicholas deserved. She stole a look at him. He tried so hard, just like he'd always done.

"Then I'll plant half the tillable soil in wheat and the other half in corn. And we'll have plenty of good spring water. Why the place is overfilling with them, and a creek flows through the middle. It makes for great picnics and good pasture for the cows." Nicholas rattled on as the horses ambled down the road.

"What cows?" Betsy interrupted.

He leaned over and lightly kissed her cheek. "Oh, I bought three good Holsteins last fall. Willy Barrett, a neighbor, is feeding them for me."

"Milk cows?" she asked hesitantly, wondering if he'd already told her this.

"Yes," he replied, a dimple in his cheek deepening. "Didn't I tell you?"

She cringed. "Maybe, I'm sorry but I don't remember."

"You, Mrs. Malone, were too busy planning our wedding. Some days you were so distracted, that I worried you might have another fella." He laughed.

Betsy felt the all too familiar churning in the pit of her stomach. "Oh, you silly man. Just when would I have seen someone else?"

"Don't know. Don't matter now, anyhow, 'cause you're mine."

"That's right," she said with a nod, pulling her woolen coat closer around her shoulders. When the clouds covered the sun, a biting chill remained. "There's never been anyone else." And those words were true. "Can I name the cows?"

"Of course."

She thought for a moment, biting her lip.

Nicholas laughed. "Don't work too hard at it. They're only cows."

She joined in his mirth. "Guess I need to see them first, but you can tell me all about the neighbors."

"The Barretts live about three miles from us on a farm with about the same amount of acreage—eighty in case you forgot. Willy and Ella are their names, and she's very nice. And they have seven or eight kids. I think she'll be a good friend to you."

"I hope so," she whispered as he squeezed her hand. She couldn't imagine filling her days with nothing but chores while he worked the fields.

Betsy listened to Nicholas talk about the farm. He'd told her so many times about the house and barn that she had the layout permanently engraved in her mind. They'd have a kitchen parlor, bedroom, and back porch with a root cellar for storing vegetables in the winter. She knew they would never run out of things to talk about because

Nicholas always had a topic floating about in his head. Not like her, where too often melancholia set in and left her all too willing to shut herself away from the world. Mother said that wasn't good and to ask God's help in overcoming it. Once she did, but her moods didn't seem so terrible to her.

"And there's a church right down the road from us," Nicholas continued.

"What's it called?"

"Loss Creek Church, just like the name of the road we'll live on. I attended there last fall, good people, good minister. He preached the word unashamedly."

She nodded, making sure she remembered everything he'd just told her. "How far is the nearest town? I know you told me before, but I'm asking again."

"Seven miles, and it's called Crestline, a railroad town. Seems like a growing community to me. Bucyrus is about fourteen miles away, and it's bigger, right on the banks of the Sandusky River."

Betsy sighed. *Heavenly Father, I want to feel the same expectations as Nicholas. I hate pretending every moment of the day. If it all could be real. Perhaps someday it will. I want so to find myself loving him and the life he's chosen for us. Lord, only you can do miracles, and I desperately need one.*

The first night Betsy and Nicholas slept at a cousin's home about twenty miles east of Eau Claire. Sore and aching all over from jostling in the wagon, she welcomed a hot bath and a comfortable bed. For the most part, the two would be spending their evenings in hotels and boardinghouses, but he'd prepared her for the times when they might need to sleep under the stars. She hoped the snow and ice had finished, but with the unpredictability of weather in March, it was hard to tell.

The two planned to cover nearly four hundred and twenty-four miles before reaching their destination—approximately three weeks of travel, barring any severe weather changes. By the time they reached Ohio and finally turned onto Loss Creek Road, Betsy believed every muscle in her body ached, yet she sensed an eagerness to see her new home.

Nicholas pulled the wagon to a halt.

"Why are we stopping?" she asked puzzled, especially since he'd been in such a hurry to reach the farm before dark.

"For you to close your eyes," he grinned, his blond hair picking up highlights from the late afternoon sun.

Obediently, she shut them tightly and hooked her arm into his as the horses meandered ahead.

"We just passed the Barretts'," he informed her. "But don't open your eyes. There's plenty of time for you to see their farm later."

"Nicholas, this is taking forever," she claimed, wanting desperately to view the countryside.

"Patience," he soothed. "I can see our house now."

"Can't I see, too?"

"No, this is my surprise. When I first saw the house, I could see you planting flowers and me working the land."

With nothing to see but blackness, her other senses became more acute. She heard the calling of a bobwhite and detected the scent of dark, rich soil. "Now?" she asked. "I can't wait much longer."

"Just a moment more. I may need a kiss first before I

can give my consent," he teased.

"You can have two."

He laughed, and Betsy did love to hear him laugh. "Whoa," he shouted to the horses.

She felt his nearness and smiled. Sometimes Nicholas made life so much fun. He kissed her tenderly. "One," he whispered. His arms gathered her close and this time he lingered on her lips, making her feel warm. . .and loved. "All right, you paid the price. Open your eyes and welcome to the Malone farm."

Immediately her gaze flew to a small white frame home resting on a hill, nestled between two large maple trees. Peering closer, she saw it looked in much better condition than she'd ever envisioned.

Her hand flew to her mouth. "Nicholas, it looks very nice—not at all what I expected." She grimaced. "I mean, I didn't know what our home would look like."

He chuckled, seemingly delighted in her response. "Well, I did repair the roof and add the porch when I arrived last fall."

"That's why you were gone two months. Please, I want down from this wagon," she said, clasping her hands. "I want to see the inside, and, oh, is that a lilac bush I see?"

He jumped to the ground and turned to grasp her waist, lifting her gently down to the soft, green earth. "I understand the blooms are purple, the kind you like."

"I can almost smell them now—well, in a couple of months for sure."

He laughed and took her hand. "I can see you can't wait a minute more. Let's go inside." Once they climbed the hill and then the porch steps, he hesitated. "Now,

Betsy, I need to build us some furniture. There's not much inside, 'cept a table, two chairs, a cookstove, and I built you a cupboard for your dishes. We have a bed and dresser in the wagon—"

"Nonsense, Nicholas. It will be fine. I'm simply glad to finally be here." She gazed up at him shyly, and he touched her nose with a kiss.

He opened the door and ushered her inside. Although small and very old, it looked in excellent condition. In the dim light, she saw he must have done a considerable amount of work during his previous visit. A red brick fireplace took in the entire wall of a rectangular parlor. As she gazed above a cherry mantel, he whispered, "For the painting."

Betsy nodded and saw the kitchen looked sufficiently roomy. "The cupboard is beautiful," she breathed, touching its oaken sides. He'd carved a scroll-like leaf pattern across the very top. "This took time," she said, gingerly fingering the engraving. "You're definitely a gifted carpenter. We'll be the envy of all the neighbors."

He slipped his arm around her waist. "I have so many plans, Betsy. Someday I'll build you a big, beautiful house full of fine things. But for now, we have to settle for being poor farmers."

She felt her emotions rise and fall. She'd never gone without in her life, yet this was where her new husband had brought her. Forcing an encouraging smile, she elected to search about the small home. After all, Nicholas deserved a devoted, loving wife, not what he'd gotten. "You're a fine man. I'm very fortunate to have you," Betsy said sincerely. Things could be much worse.

Hand in hand they walked into the bedroom. It looked bare and plain, but of course when their things were unloaded she'd make it quite homey. Mother had given her yard goods to sew curtains, and she'd packed a number of colorful quilts, along with a rug to keep their feet warm in winter.

Feeling both relief to be at the farm and gratitude for Nicholas's preparing the home, she faced him and lifted his other hand from his side. "I do want to be a good wife to you."

"All I ever want is your love," he replied. "Without that, I have nothing."

Chapter 3

The following morning before breakfast, Betsy and Nicholas walked out over their farm. He pointed out the many bubbling springs and skipped stones across a shady creek. In a shallow part, they crossed over on moss-covered rocks with Nicholas steadying her balance.

"This will be a perfect picnic spot," she said, glancing about her. "I can bring you lunch when you're working near here in the fields. It will be delightful."

"Delightful? I imagine I'll be plenty sweaty and smelly."

She feigned annoyance but burst into laughter. "Then you can wash up and dangle your feet in the water."

Hand in hand they strode on toward the fields where he planned to grow corn. "Over there's the cows." He gestured. "Want to see them so you can give them a proper name?" He grinned, and she poked his ribs.

"All right," she replied a few moments later when they reached the grazing animals. "See the one that keeps tossing her head?"

"Yes, she's practicing for the flies this summer."

She rolled her eyes. "Maybe so, but she's Bossy. I think the smaller one should be Prudence, and the medium one that keeps backing away from me, ah, well, Miss Skittish."

Nicholas roared, his blue eyes dancing. "Miss Skittish?"

She nodded and tried unsuccessfully to pat the cow. "She deserves special treatment until she feels comfortable."

He grimaced. "If she doesn't kick me when I try to milk her."

On they walked, and he pointed out moist areas in the woods where sponge mushrooms would most likely come up in April or early May after a good rain. The smell of fresh earth teased her nostrils, and the colorful signs of spring were a welcome sight.

"This is beautiful," she murmured.

He replied with a long, lingering kiss. Breaking away, Betsy swore she could eat a loaf of bread by herself so they ventured back to the house for breakfast. Nicholas dug through the wagon for the coffeepot while Betsy mixed up flour, lard, baking powder, and salt for biscuits. A bit of smoked ham and a jar of apple butter made for a tasty meal. While she cleaned up the kitchen, he hung the painting.

"Come see, Betsy," he called when the hammering ceased.

He had it centered above the mantle. "It's perfect," she complimented, drying her hands on her apron. "Some day you must tell me the story about the painting."

"I will," he said, "but not now. Too much to do."

Slowly the wagon shed its heavy load, or rather it shifted to the kitchen floor until Betsy could go through their belongings. He put together the black iron bed and she made it up with new sheets, embroidered pillowcases from her hope chest, and a quilt her mother had pieced from scraps of Betsy's childhood dresses.

That evening Willy and Ella Barrett stopped in for a visit, bringing a jar of rhubarb preserves and a loaf of freshly baked bread. They'd left their eight children at home, and Betsy saw they were expecting another.

Willy, a rather squarely built fellow, spoke softly and looked very strong. He had small, dark eyes that seemed to disappear into his round face when he laughed—and he did that a lot.

Ella, a tiny woman, had the most flaming red hair Betsy had ever seen. A patch of tan freckles dotted her nose, and sky blue eyes twinkled mischievously. She hardly looked like the mother of so many children.

Betsy put on coffee for them all before they moved outside to the porch steps, since they had only two chairs. She felt a bit uncomfortable about the seating arrangement, but the Barretts didn't seem to mind.

"What can I do for you?" Ella asked. "I know you must be tired from riding all this way."

"I am," Betsy admitted, "mostly sore, but it's exciting to finally be here. We unloaded everything today, and both of us worked inside and out, putting things in order."

"I do want to help in some way," Ella said, with a tilt of her head.

"You can be my friend," she replied gently. "Nothing else would make me happier." Nicholas reached for her hand and squeezed it lightly. She'd pleased him, but her reasons for friendship were selfish.

"Your husband and I plan to help each other off and on," Willy announced. "Sharing in some of the hard work makes it easier."

"Especially for one like me who needs to learn more about farming." Nicholas chuckled. "Starting tomorrow I milk my own cows."

Betsy felt a warm sensation growing inside her at the knowledge of finding such good friends near her new home. She excused herself to pour the fresh coffee, and Ella followed. "I can really get this. You most likely have your share of serving others," Betsy said.

Ella picked up two cups and held them out. "This is my ninth baby, and I feel fine. If I allowed myself to slow down, I'd get lazy." She glanced around and saw the yard goods piled in the corner of the kitchen. "Curtains?"

"Yes, hopefully I can get started on them after Sunday."

"We could get them done in one afternoon," Ella offered. "My two older girls are good seamstresses." In the lamplight, her hair looked like spun fire.

Betsy bit her lip in anticipation. "Are you sure you'd want to spend the time sewing my curtains?"

"Of course. We could come Monday right after lunch, and by suppertime we'll be finished."

"That would be wonderful."

Long after the Barretts left, Nicholas talked about the farms, their plans, and all the other things he desired until Betsy began nodding off to sleep. She didn't want to hear anymore about his dreams. For that's all they were—his dreams.

The next morning, Nicholas woke before dawn and milked the cows while Betsy sleepily made breakfast after he brought the milk to the house. He left right after sunrise and returned at noon, starved, yet eager to continue.

Betsy warmed him ham and bread along with some of Ella's apple butter.

"I sure could have used a dipper of water about mid-morning," he said, slightly irritated.

She looked up startled. "I'm sorry. I did not know to bring you any." Silence followed. "I will remember tomorrow."

"So what did you do all morning?" he finally asked.

"Washed dishes and the other things we unpacked from the wagon," she replied, staring into his slightly reddened face. "I also cleaned and dried our clothes and put away the supplies we purchased in Bucyrus."

Again quiet prevailed.

"I'm sorry I was short with you," he finally said. "I just expected more things to be done."

"What else would you have me do?" Her voice rose, unfairness showering over her like the dirty laundry water from the morning.

Concern etched across his brow. "Not you, Betsy, me. I wanted more accomplished this morning. I must work faster if I'm to be a good farmer."

Wringing her hands in her lap, she wanted to speak fitting words that a good wife would use to encourage her husband. "You're simply learning, Nicholas. It will get faster."

He combed his fingers through his blond hair. "Yes, you're right." For the first time, he smiled and reached up to stroke her cheek with his thumb. "I love you."

"I know you do," she replied, wishing she could return the same affectionate words.

A few moments later he left for the fields, leaving

Betsy waving good-bye from the porch.

"I'll bring you a jar of cool spring water during mid-afternoon," she called from the front porch.

He turned and eyed her curiously, almost suspiciously. "I love you," he called.

She blew him a kiss.

On Sunday morning Nicholas proudly drove the wagon for their first visit to Loss Creek Church. It was a smaller church than the one in Eau Claire, but the people welcomed them, most of whom remembered him from the previous fall. Many church members introduced themselves to Betsy, and he watched her graciously return their greetings.

The Barretts attended, and for the first time she met all eight children. They looked like an army of red hair and sky blue eyes. Betsy looked a bit overwhelmed at the brood and rightfully so. That many children meant a lot of mouths to feed.

Nicholas enjoyed Pastor Johnson's sermon on the first three Beatitudes and looked forward to hearing him in weeks to come. Observing his wife, he felt proud of the way she responded to the church folk. People took to Betsy easily. Her sweet and sometimes shy disposition seemed to bring out the best in them. Of course, he didn't think she realized her own capabilities and talents. He'd seen her teach a children's Bible study class, silently commanding even the rowdiest little boy's attention. Other times he watched her heart melt at the sight of an injured bird or animal, nursing it back to health.

And Betsy always told the truth, which accounted for

why her lack of affection plagued him. He knew she feigned sleep at night to discourage him. It hurt and alarmed him. Yesterday morning while plowing, he tried to remember the last time she'd said "I love you." It must have been her fifteenth birthday.

They were seated in her mother's gazebo amidst bushes of red roses, and he'd brought her ribbons for her hair along with special words from his heart.

"These are lovely," she said, carefully removing them from the box. "And you remembered lavender is my favorite color."

Nicholas stammered and looked down at his freshly shined boots. He felt extremely awkward, not at all like the man of eighteen that he professed to be. "I. . .I thought they'd look pretty with your dark hair. . .and I want to tell you something." He met her wide smile and perfectly straight white teeth.

"Tell me what?" she asked innocently.

He picked up her hand as though she were made of the most delicate porcelain. Wetting his lips and staring into her beloved face, he suddenly forgot everything he'd planned to say. His face warmed and his hands dampened. "Betsy," he slowly began. "I. . .I want you to know that you are the most beautiful girl in all the world. . .and I love you."

Tears formed in her blue-green eyes, causing them to look even more green. She tilted her head slightly and the smile never left her. "And I love you, too," she whispered.

Standing in the midst of his partially plowed field, Nicholas took a ragged breath. Guess he'd simply took it for granted she'd meant those words to last a lifetime.

Nevertheless, he needed to hear them soon or he'd explode.

On Monday morning, Nicholas left for the fields, taking with him a jar to fill with cool, sparkling spring water whenever he needed it. He appreciated the spring air, still crisp before the heat of summer set in. At noontime Betsy brought their lunch, and beside the rippling creek, they ate fried chicken and green beans from the night before and biscuits from breakfast. He simply didn't have much to say, especially with the worrisome thoughts rolling around in his head about Betsy.

"You've gotten a lot done this morning," she commented, handing him a generous portion of chicken. "When do you think the plowing will be done?"

"Probably the end of next week."

Setting aside her plate, she eyed him curiously. "Is something wrong?"

He shook his head, feeling lonelier than he could remember. "Should there be?"

Betsy stiffened, then smoothed the skirt of her green-flowered dress. She plucked a blade of grass and studied it. "I don't really know. Did I not pack enough food for your lunch? Is it that Ella and her girls are coming this afternoon?"

For a moment he pushed the nagging thought from his head. Gazing out over the creek bank, so placid—unaffected by human emotions and turmoil—Nicholas wondered if he'd been wrong.

She grasped his hand resting across his lap. "Is all this too much work?" she asked softly. "Do you want me to help you in the fields or take over milking the cows?"

His agitation dissipated at the sound of her voice. He couldn't resist stroking a loose strand of walnut-colored hair that she'd elected to wear down about her shoulders. His precious Betsy, so much a child and yet his wife. Of course nothing was amiss. She only needed time to adjust to the farm, Ohio. . .and to him.

"I'm sorry," he said. "You already do more than enough to help me. I didn't expect the plowing to take this long, even though Willy told me otherwise."

"You've been terribly tired."

He smiled sadly. "And a bear. I'll toughen up to this real soon. It's not like working at the lumber mill. I worked hard there, but I saw the fruits of my labor faster."

"You'll be just fine," she soothed, avoiding his eyes. "And I'll cook you a wonderful dinner tonight. Is there something special you'd like to have?"

He shook his head and hesitated. "I love you, Betsy Malone."

"I know," she whispered. "God and you, what more could I ask?"

Betsy hurried back to the house, realizing the time neared of Ella's arrival. The expectation of spending the afternoon with her new friend made her feel a bit giddy.

Without warning, a slow, mounting fear seized her as though threatening to choke the life out of her resolve. Nicholas knew. She couldn't hide it from him much longer. He almost asked her about it today.

Oh, God, what is wrong with me? I want to tell him I love him, but not unless I mean it. Help me be the woman You desire of me. She remembered the verses from Ephesians that her mother had given and repeated them in her mind. *Now unto him that is able to do exceeding abundantly above all that we ask or think, according to the power that worketh in us, Unto him be glory in the church by Christ Jesus throughout all ages, world without end. Amen.*

It will happen, she told herself firmly. *I simply need faith.*

Inside her home, Betsy glanced up at the painting of Laurelwood. Her eyes took it in at least a dozen times a day. Nicholas still hadn't shared the story behind it. She needed to ask, to know if the love behind his grandparents and parents came from a deep secret hidden within the home.

Her guests soon arrived. Ella and her two daughters, Belle and Verna, quickly set to task helping Betsy cut out and stitch curtains for the kitchen, parlor, and bedroom windows. A third daughter, Marie, stayed behind to tend to the younger children. After much deliberation, Betsy decided to embroider lilac and yellow flowers on the ones in the bedroom to match the pillowcases she'd done before the wedding. The afternoon sped by, much faster than any of them had anticipated.

"Mercy, look at the time," Ella said with a start.

Betsy glanced up at the clock sitting on the parlor mantle. "Oh, my, it is getting late. Our men will be wanting dinner before we know it."

"And we're not quite finished," Ella continued.

"Mama, we can hurry home and cook," Belle offered, a pretty young girl with a flawless complexion and the same shade of red hair as her mother.

"Yes, Mama, you can stay and finish with Mrs. Malone," Verna added, complete with freckles and strawberry-blonde hair.

Ella appeared to ponder the matter. "All right. I think that would be a fine idea."

Betsy checked on her own roast and potatoes simmering on the stove and returned to help her friend. The curtains looked beautiful, and she could do the embroidering in the evenings while Nicholas read from his Bible.

"You and Nicholas look so happy," Ella commented, after her daughters had left.

"He is a very good man," she said. A nudging at her mind prompted her to seek answers from her new friend. "Tell me, when did you first realize that you loved Willy?"

Ella laughed lightly. "Well, we married when I was barely sixteen years old, scarcely old enough for a girl to know what love really is or means."

Betsy nodded and smiled. "So you just always knew?"

"Oh, no. When I first met Willy, he impressed me with his calm ways and good nature. I felt a tremendous amount of respect for him—the way he worked hard and loved the Lord. When he did ask my father for my hand, I felt really confused. I didn't love him, but I sensed God leading me to take the step."

"Without reservation?" Betsy felt her heart pound against her chest.

Ella leaned into her. "I had never been so scared in my entire life." She sat back and a faint smile played upon her upturned lips. "But God is faithful. I prayed that I would be the wife God desired of me, and it happened!"

"When? How long did you have to wait?"

Ella sewed a few more stitches before replying, then she rested the fabric in her lap. "During the eighth month of my first baby, it all happened. Goodness, I felt like I carried a bushel basket of potatoes inside me."

Both women laughed, and Betsy attempted to relax.

"Well, one summer evening I saw Willy heading up from the fields. He always went straight to the well to wash up a bit, so I stood at the kitchen window and watched him. Suddenly, a strange feeling came over me. It seemed like I was looking at him for the first time. He stood erect, the muscles bulging from his tanned neck, grinning to himself. Later, he told me that he secretly hoped our first baby would be a girl. Anyway, a feeling of love spilled out over me like the water gushing out of the bucket rising from the well."

A faraway look settled in her blue eyes. "Poor Willy. I ran outside and threw my arms around his neck, laughing and crying at the same time. He didn't know what to think. I must have told him a hundred times I loved him." She glanced over at Betsy. "And everyday I love him more. We've had some rough times, but God molds us through adversity."

"Thank you," Betsy managed. "It's a beautiful story." Unfortunately she hadn't felt like that around Nicholas since they were much younger.

With the curtains completed, Ella gathered up her sewing basket, and the two hugged good-bye.

"This has been such a perfect afternoon," Betsy said. "I praise God for you, Ella."

Her friend smiled. "He put us together for a reason. I'll pray for you and Nicholas—that God will bless you richly with His unfailing love."

For a moment, Betsy feared even Ella knew her darkest secret.

Chapter 4

Several long, lonely weeks slipped by, turning into months. One morning Betsy woke up, missing home more than ever—and everything about it. A lump formed in her throat, and tears leaked out each time she contemplated her dire circumstances. She felt miserable, alone, and afraid that the rest of her life would be no better than this. Praying didn't seem to help—neither did reading her Bible. The blackness persisted for three days until she no longer felt like talking to Nicholas in the early mornings or evenings. All she wanted was her mother and home, not the lonely existence of Nicholas's farm.

A few nights later, she attempted to mend his socks, although depression threatened to suffocate her.

"It's been three days, Betsy. What can I do to help you out of this?" Nicholas asked, closing his Bible.

She shook her head, fighting the melancholy and not wanting him to see her misery. In one breath, she felt ashamed of her gloom, and in the next she wanted desperately to blame him.

"Nothing? You're unhappy about something." He spoke kindly, making her feel like a child. "Is it me?" His blond hair fell across his forehead, and when he brushed it away she saw the concern in his eyes.

Betsy blinked away the tears, giving her attention to darning his socks. "I'll be all right. It's nothing, really."

"You can't keep things from me, Betsy. You've never been able to." He pulled his chair closer to hers. She almost reached out and touched him, wanting him to draw her close for a few minutes so she could close her eyes and wish the awfulness away. Except she didn't want to pretend any longer. God hadn't answered her prayers. She was forever stuck on this forsaken piece of land—away from home and family with a man she didn't love. What bothered her the most was the haunting realization that she would soon come to despise him for everything. If she hadn't already.

"I'm lonely," she finally said. "I miss home."

"What about Ella?"

Betsy swallowed hard. "Ella is a wonderful friend, but I'm still having a difficult time."

He nodded thoughtfully. "Willy offered me a puppy a few days ago. I could get it for you."

She wanted to scream at him, tell him that nothing would help short of going home, but she knew Nicholas's heart. "A puppy sounds nice," she said forcing a smile.

"All right," he said standing. "I'll go get it now. The mother only had one, so there's not several to choose from."

"You don't need to go now," she protested, sensing the lateness of the hour. "Wait until tomorrow."

He bent down to her. "No, I want you happy, and I'll do anything to make sure of it." He stepped out into the night with a look of weariness upon his handsome features.

Betsy stared after the door, deep in thought, feeling utter guilt for her behavior and feelings. How long before Nicholas decided to quit? He'd always done everything within his power to make her happy. Her recollections of his selfless giving and generosity pulled at her heartstrings. He deserved more than a child-bride brooding over pangs of homesickness. She wanted a marriage where both the husband and wife gave to the other, like she'd seen in her parents' relationship. But then she continued in her selfishness, brought down by black moods. When would it change? Why hadn't God answered her prayers?

In less than an hour, Nicholas carried in a yellowish brown, yapping puppy. Betsy laughed at the sight of him. "He needs to grow into his feet and ears," she giggled, taking him from Nicholas's arms. "What shall we call him?"

"You name him. He's your dog," he replied, scratching beneath the puppy's chin.

"Well, he kind of reminds me of Father's old yellow dog, Jasper. Do you remember him when we were children?"

"Sure do. He had the longest tongue of any dog I'd ever seen."

Betsy held him close. "Maybe I could call him Jasper. What do you think?" She glanced up into Nicholas's face and saw the fatigue creasing his brow and etching tiny lines under his eyes. "Oh, Nicholas. You do need to go to bed. You look so tired."

"First, let's get the puppy situated for the night."

"No, I will fix him a spot by the stove. You go on to bed." She smiled and shooed him on. "Go on now. I'll be there in a little bit."

Betsy waited until she heard his even breathing before snatching up the puppy. With one hand on the lantern, she headed to the barn. She remembered a wooden crate that would make a perfect bed for Jasper. It also gave her time to think.

She simply needed more things to keep her occupied. A garden needed planting—Nicholas had already worked the spot and purchased additional seeds to go with the tiny plants flourishing under his care. She loved flowers, and the lilac bush would be blooming in May, but she'd like more. Ella had plenty of peonies to share, and Mother had given her seeds for petunias and geraniums. A moment later, Betsy remembered one of Ella's daughters, Verna, wanted to learn embroidery. She could teach her. But most of all, she wanted to do more for Nicholas. And starting in the morning, she'd begin anew.

The following morning when he stirred before dawn, Betsy lay still until he left. Every morning she stayed in bed until the very last minute before rising to prepare his breakfast, but not today.

Flinging back the covers, she hurried into the kitchen and added wood to the cookstove. Striking a match against the cast iron side, she lit some dry kindling. The flame rose and danced, slightly igniting the wood around it. A short while later, the nutty aroma of fresh coffee filled the kitchen.

While the coffee brewed, Betsy dressed and allowed her hair to cascade down her back. Nicholas liked it that way. She fed and petted Jasper, then poured her husband a steaming mug of coffee. Humming a tune, she opened the door to a still-darkened morning and cast her eyes in the direction of a flickering lantern where she knew Nicholas did his chores.

Stepping into the barn, she saw Nicholas bent beneath Bossy and heard the *swish swish* sound of his milking.

"Good morning," she called softly.

Startled, he glanced up. "Why Betsy, what are you doing out here?"

She knelt at his side and handed him the coffee. He smiled and it warmed her heart. "I thought you might enjoy this before breakfast."

"Thank you, sweetheart," he managed, taking the mug and abandoning his work. "You look beautiful. I thought you were an angel."

"No," she said softly. "Just your wife, but thank you for the compliment."

He reached for her hand, paused, then spoke. "You would tell me if you regretted marrying me, wouldn't you?"

She stifled a gasp. "You are my best friend, the one I've always told my dreams and secrets. You taught me how to fish and whistle, even when Mother said it was unladylike. Nicholas, you know me better than I know myself. How could I be discontent with such a wonderful man?"

He squeezed her hand gently but said nothing.

Longing to free herself of the awkwardness, she kissed his nose, then rose from the barn floor. "Now, Mr. Malone, you finish your chores so you can enjoy a long breakfast with your wife."

Outside, she lifted her head and inhaled deeply. She could do this, and she did care about Nicholas—in a brotherly way. He'd been her companion forever. Hopefully her answer had set his mind at ease, but a strange chill tormented her. He'd always understood her actions and words, and even saw through any lies or deception. Had he already guessed the truth? *Oh, Lord, help me. I'm so scared.*

She lived in anticipation that one day she might look outside her window and feel the tingly sensation of love just as Ella had. She had to believe it. No more melancholy or regrets, she'd simply concentrate on making Nicholas happy.

Out in the barn, Nicholas wanted to kick over the bucket of milk, punch the cow, and then for good measure set fire to the barn. What he'd feared for so long had just hit him in the bottom of his stomach. Pounding his fist into his hand, he fought the hurt and devastation whirling like a twister inside him.

Betsy didn't love him. He couldn't deny it any longer. They were simply childhood playmates who had grown up together and married out of convenience and a desire to please their parents—at least that's how she must surely view their wedded state.

Burning tears filled his eyes and he roughly brushed them away. Ever since he could remember, he'd loved Betsy with a fervor so strong that he failed to understand the depth of it. He'd done everything within his power and leaned on God's strength to make her life peaceful and happy. What he'd seen in her eyes and neglected to hear from her lips had stabbed him and wrenched out his heart.

Wondering if he should confront her or continue to

ignore her lack of caring, Nicholas sought a place to kneel on the fresh hay. *Oh, heavenly Father, Creator of the universe, giver of love, I confess I am a sinful man, and I humbly ask You for guidance. Betsy is not a cruel woman. You know her heart, Lord. She wants to do all the right things, and I find no fault with her as my wife. She tries so hard. Look at how she just now brought me coffee. But I love her, and I know she doesn't feel the same. What am I supposed to do? Keep hoping and praying things will change. . .or send her back to Wisconsin?*

The idea of living without Betsy had not occurred to him before, and he paled at the thought of living without her. *Lord, I couldn't send her away! I'd rather she never love me than to be separated.*

Aren't I sufficient? came that still small voice.

Yes, Lord, You are my portion and my strength.

Don't you want her to be happy? Is love selfish?

You know I want the best for Betsy, but to live without her? The words of Psalm 34:8 raced across his mind: *Oh, taste and see that the Lord is good; blessed is the man that trusteth in him.*

Nicholas blinked away the moisture filling his eyes. He'd obey. His wife had not been given to him as a pet, like he'd given her the puppy. She must choose to stay, or he must send her back to the family she loved. Struggling to regain his composure, he finished milking and made his way to the house for breakfast.

The wounds of rejection still churned inside him, fresh and bleeding. His whole life had been centered around God and Betsy. Now he'd seen the truth about his wife, and God wanted him to set her free.

Why had she consented to marry him if she felt nothing? Anger quelled the hurt, and he clenched his fists. Their marriage, their relationship meant nothing but a game to her. He felt like such a fool. How could she live a lie?

How long could he continue the masquerade?

He trudged up the hill and climbed the back porch steps, but surprisingly enough, the aroma of bacon and eggs greeted his nostrils. Betsy never cooked breakfast this early, and certainly nothing more than bread and jam from the night before. Startled, he entered the kitchen and eyed the table overflowing with butter, honey, biscuits, and oatmeal in addition to what had already tantalized his taste buds.

"Are you pleased?" Betsy asked, setting a skillet of bacon and eggs onto the table. Her face flushed from the heat of the stove, and she smiled sweetly.

Frustration settled upon him at the sight of the food. Was this supposed to soothe his hurt feelings? Jasper scampered beneath his feet, causing him to nearly trip and aggravating him even more. He could already see the dog was a mistake. She scooped up the puppy and placed him in a box near the cookstove.

"Nicholas?" she questioned, wringing her hands. "Is there something wrong?"

Avoiding her gaze, he clamped his jaw and brushed past her to refill his coffee. Nicholas didn't need her breakfast—or guilt sacrifice. "I'm not hungry," he grumbled. "I've got work to do."

"But. . .but you should eat."

He snatched up a strip of bacon and two biscuits on

his way out. "This is enough," he muttered, slamming the door.

Strange, he ought to feel better not giving into her trickery—her "playing house" game, but instead a sick feeling swirled around in his stomach. He lifted his chin and looked up into the early morning sky breaking into shades of pink and orange. *Lord, she deserves to be shunned for what she's done.*

He walked into the barn and lifted the halter from the peg near the horses' stall. Usually he experienced a sense of joy in preparing to till the earth, but not today. A part of him wanted to turn and apologize for his rudeness, but the biggest part wanted to punish her for breaking his heart. He wanted her to feel the same gut-piercing pain.

Chapter 5

Bewildered, Betsy glared at the door. Her hand flew to her mouth as she shrunk into a chair. He knew the truth! What she'd dreaded for so long had happened. Any other time, he'd have been happy to see the spread of food so early in the morning. Instead he acted angry and couldn't wait to leave the house. How could she blame him? The realization had no doubt devastated him.

Liquid emotion spilled down her cheeks as she looked helplessly about her. Shame needled at her. Nicholas had seen through her attempt at portraying the perfect wife. Her gaze swept over the table. Steam rose and disappeared from the oatmeal and eggs, just like his dreams of their marriage.

Jasper yelped, seizing her attention. Through misty eyes, she held him to her bosom, clinging to the puppy as though the warm body could coax things right in her world. The longer she held him, the more tears welled up in her eyes. What a mess she'd made of her and Nicholas's life. She'd hurt the gentlest of all men.

Inhaling deeply, she searched for the words to pray.

She still wanted to love him, but it might be too late. Betsy had a terrible thought that even if she ran after him shouting words of endearment, he wouldn't believe her. *God, I don't know how to fix this. I know You can. Help me, I beg of You.*

The morning dragged. She ironed and then checked on the tiny sprouting tomatoes and other vegetables growing in a corner of the kitchen. Sensing a warm spring day, she carried them outside to the rear of the house. Soon they'd mature enough to transplant outdoors. Yesterday the prospect sounded exciting, but not today.

Watching Jasper play sparked an occasional smile. The puppy barked at a family of sparrows and pulled at a stubborn weed.

She longed to see Ella and her family. The sight of her friend's smiling face and sparkling eyes always lifted her spirits. Ella's time fast approached, and in these last days before the new baby, she stayed close to home.

Betsy considered walking the three miles to the Barrett farm after delivering Nicholas's noon meal. Mother always said visiting with other folks helped a person forget their own problems. She also remembered her mother saying all anybody ever needed was the Lord. She spoke words of wisdom, even when Betsy didn't want to hear them. Remembering the verses from Ephesians tucked away in her Bible, Betsy called the Scripture to mind. *Now unto him that is able to do exceeding abundantly above all that we ask or think, according to the power that worketh in us, Unto him be glory in the church by Christ Jesus throughout all ages, world without end. Amen.*

As the morning wore on, she tried to focus on her

relationship with God and not on the problems in her marriage. Each time she felt a fresh sprinkling of tears or shame creep across her mind, she prayed for answers. Begrudgingly she admitted she couldn't fix anything in her life; only God could do those things. In short, Betsy Malone needed a touch from the Father.

When the sun peaked high in the sky, she toted Nicholas's lunch in a wooden pail toward a far field. She'd covered it with a red checkered cloth and packed plenty of food, knowing he'd be hungry. Hopefully he had calmed down a bit. Maybe today, she'd see him and feel that peculiar twinge of love that Ella spoke about.

Jasper trailed after her, running and scampering about, exploring his new world. He chased a butterfly and scared up a rabbit. His antics made her laugh, and for a brief moment she forgot the earlier unpleasantness.

In the distance Betsy spied Nicholas driving the horse and plow toward her and she waved. She remembered tomorrow he wanted to plant the last of the corn. He lifted his head, but instantly cast his gaze back to the ground. Nibbling at her lip and wearing a shaky smile, she sauntered his way.

"I'll be at the creek bank when you're ready," she managed.

"All right," he muttered and continued down to the end of the row.

Without glancing behind her, Betsy headed in the direction of their familiar picnic spot. Setting down the lunch pail, she walked to the water's edge and listened to it gurgle over and around the rocks. It sounded so peaceful, not at all like the turmoil raging inside her. Nicholas's shadow fell across the water, and with a deep breath she turned to face him.

"You don't have to stay and eat with me," he said impassively.

Her heart pounded against her chest. "I'd like to, if you don't mind."

"I'm not in a good mood."

"I can see that. . .I'm sorry."

He lifted a brow and frowned. "Sorry about what?"

She swallowed hard. "For upsetting you."

"Who said you did?"

She stared into his clear blue eyes, dark and forbidding. "I don't want to play games, Nicholas."

"And who are you to accuse me of such nonsense?" he shouted, his voice echoing about them.

She trembled, not recognizing the stranger before her. "I want us to work this out and go on with our lives," she said.

"Why don't you tell me what we need to work out?"

"Our differences—the things separating us," she replied. "Can we sit down and talk about it?"

He chuckled sardonically. "And what exactly is our problem?"

Betsy knew she neared tears. This was her fault, and now she'd damaged their marriage, possibly beyond repair. "I'm not a good wife," she whispered.

"And why is that?" he demanded.

Lifting watery eyes to meet his gaze, she silently pleaded for understanding. Angry eyes met hers.

"Betsy, answer me."

She felt so ashamed. "I don't love you as I should."

"Oh?" he questioned harshly. "When did you come to this conclusion?"

Silence.

"When?"

"While planning our wedding day."

Nicholas still stood on the hill of the creek, glaring down at her like a furious giant. "Did you think I'd never find out? Am I stupid?"

She shook her head and wrung her hands. "I didn't want to hurt you."

He pointed to his heart. "And what do you call this?

"I'm sorry," she mumbled. "I've been praying. . . ."

"Praying? For what, that I'd never find out?"

Regret squeezed from her eyes. "No, Nicholas, for God. . . ."

"I've heard enough," he interrupted. "I think you should go on back to the house while I decide what's best."

She wanted to argue and tell him that they needed to talk right then—pray about the problem together, but instead she acquiesced to his request. Sensing his wrath would not dissipate in a moment's time, she nodded and climbed the hill, brushing past him on the path home.

Too shaken to cry, Betsy concentrated on Nicholas's final statement. She spun on her heels and saw his back. Obviously he was too provoked to watch her leave. With reluctant steps, she plodded on toward the house. Jasper yapped at her heels, causing her to remember when as a child, she'd trailed after Nicholas, begging to tag along no matter what he had planned to do.

Those days were gone. She could no longer invite the frivolous antics of a child or the impetuous temperament of a young girl. She must commit to the responsibilities of a wife, if she still had that role.

Betsy dreaded the afternoon, realizing it would be dark before Nicholas returned from the fields. She had to find something to occupy the empty hours. Perhaps visiting Ella would help, but she didn't dare confess her failing marriage. No one need know her misery.

Chewing on her lip, she glanced up into a cloudless sky. *Oh, Lord, I've made such a mess of things. Help me. I don't know what to do.*

Once he finished with his noon meal, Nicholas stuffed the checkered cloth into the wooden pail. He leaned back on the soft grass and clasped his hands behind his neck. The food sat heavily on his stomach just like the weight on his mind. He really should get back to work, but he had no desire to do so. The farm, his life, held no meaning without Betsy. He never should have brought her to Ohio. At least in Wisconsin she had her family to give her some sort of meaning to her loveless marriage. She would have been happy and content there.

His heart ached with the acknowledgment. *Betsy didn't love him.* Before he'd suspected it; now he'd heard it from her own lips. A tear trickled down his cheek. He shouldn't have been so harsh. Perhaps talking about it might bring about an end to it all—and get it over with.

For the next hour, Nicholas closed his eyes and fought the memories of Betsy plaguing his mind, from the time she was a little girl of six and he a boy of nine. He'd watched her grow into a woman. His Betsy. His love. His wife.

If he really loved her, he would send her back to Wisconsin.

Finally rising to his feet, he shuffled back to the fields, feeling too miserable to pray.

Midafternoon, Betsy decided she'd visit Ella after all. Anything had to be better than watching for Nicholas or crying. She washed her face, hoping her swollen eyes and blotchy skin didn't give away her anguish.

Leaving Jasper at home, she treaded down the road toward the Barrett farm. Just the sight of the farmhouse lifted her spirits. One of the younger boys spied her and raced her way.

"Hallo, Miz Malone. How do you like the puppy?" Boyd asked, a red-haired, freckle-faced boy with a toothless grin.

"Just fine. He wanted his mama pretty bad last night, but he'll be fine."

The boy frowned. "Papa said he'd do fine."

"Oh, he will. It takes time for him to get adjusted to his new home." *Just like me,* she thought sadly.

He nodded, apparently satisfied with her reply. "What did you name him?"

"Jasper."

He paused a moment. "That's a good name."

By now they were nearing the house. "How's your mama feeling?"

"All right, as far as I know. She's been doing all kinds of things today—washing, baking pies, and planting the garden."

Betsy smiled and ruffled his hair. "Guess she'll keep

me busy while we visit."

She found Ella taking down clothes with little Audrey hanging onto her skirt. Betsy immediately began helping her. "Don't you think you should be resting?" she asked.

"Not when I don't feel like it," Ella replied with a smile. "This baby isn't ready to come, and I'm not slowing down a bit until I have to." She glanced at Betsy and frowned. "What's the matter?"

"Why, nothing."

"Nonsense. Your eyes are red and you're pale." Still staring, she waited for Betsy to reply.

Swallowing another onslaught of emotion, she shook her head in denial.

"You and Nicholas have a spat?"

Betsy reluctantly nodded, losing the battle against tears. "I didn't really come here to burden you with my troubles."

Ella smiled and placed a hand on her rounded stomach. "That's not what the Bible says. We're supposed to share in each other's problems. Now, I might not be able to help, but I sure can listen. Let's a take a little walk and tell me what happened."

In the next several minutes, Betsy explained it all, even confessing her lack of affection for Nicholas. "I've prayed, but nothing's changed."

"And he found this out today?"

Betsy fought the tears. "Well, I think he suspected it before."

"And what are you willing to do about it?"

Ella's question stunned her. "I don't understand. I mean. . .I intend to keep the promises I made to God when we married."

"What about honesty between you and Nicholas?"

"You mean talking about it, instead of covering it up?" Ella nodded. "Remember the truth sets you free."

Betsy sighed. "I tried today, but he's pretty angry."

"Most likely more hurt than anything. A man has an awful lot of pride and Nicholas's has been crushed. But he seems to be a sensible, God-fearing man. Give him a little time to sort things out."

"I hope you're right." She hesitated and looked beyond Ella to the older girls taking down the remainder of the laundry and the younger ones playing. "I wonder if a child would make things right," she said wistfully.

Ella studied her and tilted her head. "Babies are a miracle—they don't cause them. Only God does that."

Betsy sighed deeply, feeling her eyes moisten. She blinked back the tears, not wanting her friend to see any more weeping.

"Are you expecting?" Ella asked softly, compassion lacing her words.

Betsy could only nod. "It's been over two months, but I don't want to tell him when he's already upset."

"How do you feel about a baby?"

"I don't know for sure," she honestly replied. "I'm a little frightened, and I don't know what Nicholas will say about it."

Ella's hand slipped into hers. "I think this is a matter for the Lord. Let's take a moment and ask Him to direct you and your husband." When Betsy silently agreed, Ella began. "Oh heavenly Father, You know all things and You know us better than we know ourselves. Betsy and

Nicholas need a touch from You to restore their marriage and have their relationship glorify You. Oh, Father, You are love, and You bestow it lavishly upon us. Help them to find joy in You and in each other. Thank You for the gift of this precious child, and give Betsy wisdom in telling Nicholas about the baby. In Jesus' name, Amen."

"Thank you," Betsy whispered, reaching to give her friend a hug.

"You're welcome." Ella smiled. "How about a cup of coffee and a piece of sugar cake? Belle just made it this afternoon and it smells delicious."

The two wrapped their arms around each other's waists and strolled across the yard past the children and on to the house.

For the first time, Betsy felt a little better, but how would she ever tell Nicholas about the baby?

He might decide he didn't want either of them.

Chapter 6

Nicholas finished the milking and glanced around the barn for more chores. He'd purposely dawdled, finding all sorts of things to do rather than head to the house. With a heavy sigh, he shut and latched the barn door. Leaning his back against it, he prayed for strength and control. He watched the smoke curl up the chimney of the house and disappear into the shadowed sky—a sight that usually warmed his spirit. And normally the lantern glowing from the kitchen looked cozy and inviting, but not tonight. Distrust and heartbreaking conclusions lay behind those doors.

He still radiated anger—hot, intense, and dangerously quiet. Peering up at the starless sky, he remembered his earlier resolve. He had a job to do, and he'd best tell Betsy his decision tonight.

The closer he walked to the door, the harder it was to put one foot in front of the other. He wanted her to think he didn't care about her rejection, but he feared his heavy heart would shatter into irreparable pieces.

Smelling his favorite meal of chicken and dumplings furthered his resentment. He didn't want special food or a neat, clean house. What he craved rested in what Betsy couldn't give. His large hand turned the knob on the door, and he stepped inside, avoiding the one he loved more than anyone else on earth.

Refusing to meet her gaze, he headed directly to the water-filled basin and washed up. All the while, her puppy played at his heels.

"I have your supper ready," Betsy said barely above a whisper, reaching down to gather up Jasper. "I'm sorry he worries you so." She placed him in a box near the stove before setting the pot of chicken and dumplings on the table.

She sat across from him with her hands clasped firmly in her lap. He ladled the steamy food into his plate and immediately scooped up a mouthful, burning his tongue.

"Nicholas, aren't you going to ask the blessing?"

He felt a twinge of guilt. "No," he replied.

Lowering her head, she closed her eyes for a few moments. For the first time, he stole a look at her. Her face pale and splotchy, he saw she'd been crying for quite a while. When she opened her eyes, he saw they were red and swollen. Hastily he looked away and forked another dumpling and bite of chicken. Betsy wouldn't get any sympathy from him.

She didn't eat, but he ignored her empty plate.

"Nicholas, can we talk?" she finally asked.

Finished with the hearty meal, he pushed back his plate. "I believe so."

Betsy sighed. "Can we pray first?"

He hadn't talked to God since that morning in the barn. Why start now? "That's not necessary," he grumbled, finding the courage to stare into her face.

She drew in a deep breath. "May I?"

Leaning back on the chair, he thought she didn't look very well at all. Good. She deserved a miserable day. "Go ahead, if it makes you feel any better."

Her lips quivered as she lowered her head and folded her hands. "Dear Lord, I've hurt my husband badly today."

"Betsy, please," he interrupted.

She continued praying. "But I want to work this out. It can't be done, unless You touch our hearts with love and understanding. Give us wisdom and patience in dealing with the problems between us. In Jesus' name, Amen."

He rubbed his whiskered jaw. "Before you say anything, I'd like for you to hear me out."

"All right," she replied, her hands still primly folded.

"I've thought all day about us and how you don't have feelings for me." He hesitated, fearing if she broke into sobs he'd be tempted to take her into his arms. Lifting his coffee cup to his lips, he maintained his stand. "Because of all this, I'm riding into Crestline first thing in the morning and purchasing a ticket for you—back to Wisconsin."

Her face blanched and the dreaded tears rolled swiftly down her cheeks. "I don't think that would solve anything," she said, dabbing her eyes with her apron.

"Yes, it does," he replied with a determined shake of his head. "You don't love me, so there's no reason for you to live here as my wife. You just go on home and carry on your life as though we were never married."

"No, please, Nicholas!" she protested. "We made a promise to God. . ."

"You lied!" He pounded the table with his fist.

Startled, she rose from her chair and hurried to the door. "Where are you going?" he demanded.

"Outside," she managed. "I'm. . .I'm sick."

Nicholas paced the floor until she returned. He said nothing while she bathed her face but stood and watched her try to calm down. Knowing Betsy, she'd be upset for hours, and he didn't want to see or hear it.

"Are you in control of yourself now?" he demanded.

Her eyes looked incredibly green, and their haunting gaze bore into his—accusing, hurtful. "Yes," she whispered.

"Now, I don't want to hear you sniffling about." Never had he been so harsh with her, but he couldn't stop himself. If he stopped for one minute, he'd be apologizing for his cruelty.

"I'll be quiet."

"And put that dog in the barn. I don't want him yapping all night again."

"I will."

With her reply, he stepped outside to get a breath of fresh air. Seating himself on the porch step, he took a ragged breath. There, he'd done it. He'd been mean and hateful so she'd think he no longer cared for her. After purchasing the train ticket tomorrow, she'd be on her way home. Guess he'd been pretty stupid right from the start.

A little girl's voice echoed in his mind. She was nine years old, and she'd just flung her arms around his neck when he consented to let her tag along to the fishing hole. "Oh, Nicholas, I'll always love you. You're better than a big brother 'cause you make me so happy."

I'm a fool, he told himself, *time to grow up and act like a man.*

Setting the teakettle on to boil water for dishes, Betsy felt her emotions vacillate from raw and bleeding to numb. She'd never imagined Nicholas would send her away—back to Wisconsin. As badly as she missed her old home, she detested the thought of returning there without him. Her parents, his parents. . .they'd be utterly disappointed. Now, even more shame settled upon her.

Lord, this isn't what I prayed for, she lamented. Her hand instantly covered her mouth to swallow the sobs threatening to escape. *I wanted You to show me how to love him, not drive me away from him! This can't be happening. Oh, Lord, please work this out.*

She cleared the table, waiting for the kettle to sing, waiting for Nicholas to come back inside, and waiting for God to answer her prayers. Only the water began to boil.

Much later she lifted Jasper into her arms for the trek to the barn. Nicholas had still not come inside, and she fretted over his state of mind. Only when his pony died one cold winter had she seen such fathomless despair. Passing through the parlor, shadows from her lantern lit up faint features of the painting above the fireplace. He'd never explained it to her. How, in nearly three months of marriage, had they not talked of his parents' home? Would he now? She doubted it, but perhaps it might help to discuss something other than their own private grief and disappointment.

The door creaked open, and she saw the outline of her husband standing in the grassy area between the house and barn. "Jasper, please be quiet," she whispered to the puppy. She had no reason to believe her husband would honor her request, but she had to try.

Upon the door opening, he walked in the opposite direction. "Nicholas," she called lightly.

Stopping, but not turning toward her, he replied simply, "Yes."

"Would you tell me the story of the painting?" She held her breath and nervously stroked the puppy, waiting for his answer.

"My mother can tell you when you get home."

"I'd hoped you'd tell me about it." Silence met her, as heavy as the blanket of black around them. "Please."

"It doesn't matter anymore," he claimed, jamming his hands inside his overall pockets.

"All right," she replied, resigned to the devastation of him sending her away. "I'm taking Jasper to the barn. If you change your mind, I'll be right back."

In the short time it took to settle in the puppy, Nicholas had already disappeared inside the house and gone to bed. He neither spoke nor moved when she joined him on the other side.

After a silent breakfast the following morning, Nicholas saddled up the dappled mare and rode off.

What do I do now? Betsy asked God, glancing up into the heavens. Looking about her she marveled at the beauty of life unfolding around her. Birds were pouring out their praises, and plants craned and arched their necks to get closer to the Creator. *How did Mother handle distress?*

Sitting on the front porch rocker, she deliberated those times at the Wingert household when the world cast them into ill fortune. *Mother and Father prayed,* she remembered.

Father read his Bible, and Mother busied herself and sang.
Retrieving her Bible, she elected to do the same.

Betsy prayed, then read through the book of Ephesians, her mother's favorite epistle. She dwelled a moment on chapter four, verse twenty-six and felt totally
self-righteous about Nicholas's treatment of her. *Be ye
angry, and sin not; let not the sun go down upon your wrath.*
Then she read in chapter six how Nicholas had loved her
exactly as God instructed, and she experienced true chas-
tisement. Odd, Mother had told her those things, but she
never knew they were a commandment of God. *Oh, Father,
forgive me,* she prayed. *If given another chance, I'll put You
first in my marriage and follow Your ways with Nicholas. I'll
learn to love him.* . . . Whether or not her husband changed
his mind, she meant to live every day for the Lord.

Nicholas lingered outside the train station for over thirty
minutes before he gained enough daring to step inside.
Purchasing Betsy's ticket didn't sit well with him at all.
But how could he continue living with a woman who
admittedly shared no love for him, at least not the kind a
wife should feel for her husband?

Things could change, he told himself. *She could grow to
care for me. Ours wouldn't be the first marriage that started
out this way.* Except he never thought about those circumstances for himself. Clenching his jaw, he stepped
into the train station and bought the ticket.

Moments later, he walked back into the sunlight.
"Hey, Nicholas," a familiar voice called.

Recognizing Willy, he waved and watched his neighbor cross the street to meet him. "Guess we're letting a

good morning of work go by," his neighbor said with a lopsided grin.

"Suppose so," Nicholas replied, extending his hand to greet him.

Willy grasped it firmly. "Is something wrong? You look rather haggard."

He lifted his dusty hat and combed his fingers through his hair. "Oh, nothing to concern you about, just a few personal matters."

"I see," Willy said, his dark eyes studying Nicholas. "What brings you to town?"

"Oh, I needed to get something for Betsy," he replied with a sigh.

"At the train station?"

Nicholas sighed. "Yeah. . .I purchased a ticket back to Wisconsin for her."

Willy raised a brow and eyed him curiously. "Awfully soon to go sending her for a visit, isn't it? I mean with summer coming—the garden and the like. I'd think you'd wait till fall. Course it's none of my business."

He felt a tremendous need to tell Willy everything. This godly man, his neighbor and friend, might give him insight into his miserable problem. "I don't know what to do about Betsy," he finally blurted out.

"Would you like to get a cup of coffee and talk?"

Nicholas hesitated, then nodded. "Might as well. Don't feel much like ridin' home."

A couple hours later, he rode his horse beside Willy's wagon en route to their farms. The horses ambled on with Nicholas deep in thought. So far, his friend had only lent an ear—sometimes asking a question, but mostly listening.

"I hope I've done the right thing," Nicholas said, giving a heavy sigh.

"And you've already gotten the ticket?"

"Yeah, it's in my hip pocket."

"Nicholas, have you prayed about this?"

He shifted uneasily in the saddle. "Not since she confessed yesterday morning."

"Supposin' God wanted her to tell you the truth. Have you considered that for the first time since you were married, Betsy was honest? She could have lied, and you'd never have known the difference. What I'm saying is God brought you two together, and He wants you to stay together."

"Maybe so," Nicholas said. "But why would God have me choose a woman who didn't love me?"

Willy shook his head, then spoke softly. "We don't know God's plans and what He has in mind for us. What do you say we stop right here and pray?"

"Aw, you go right ahead. I'm not interested. Doesn't matter anyhow."

Willy pulled in the reins on his pair of horses and lowered his head. "Lord, we've got a big problem here with Nicholas and Betsy's marriage. He's hurting 'cause he loves her and wants her to feel the same. If he's not supposed to send her back to Wisconsin, would You kindly make it real clear to him? Thank You, Lord, for all Your many blessings. In Jesus' name, Amen."

Nicholas felt close to tears, and it embarrassed him. Hastily blinking them back, he chose to stare down the road. "Thanks," he mumbled. "I should be praying, but the words won't come."

"The Lord understands our hearts, and I'll be talking more to Him about you as the day goes on."

Nicholas nodded. "Appreciate it." Up ahead he could see the outline of his house and barn. Any other time, the sight would fill him with pride and anticipation of his dreams for him and Betsy. Now the thought of the days and weeks ahead without her grieved him. But he'd get used to it. Wouldn't he?

Chapter 7

Betsy watched the sun directly overhead and noted her growling stomach. She hadn't intended to be gone for so long, but the urge to walk and pray kept her away from home much longer than she expected. Most likely Nicholas would want his noon meal, and she wasn't there to prepare it. She'd left him a note explaining her desire to go for a walk.

She smiled and patted her stomach. Strange—but such a blessing, how spending a few hours with the Lord could fill her with such peace. . .and excitement for the new life growing inside her. She felt certain the problems between her and Nicholas would work out. Wonderfully contended, she hummed the hymn "Blessed Assurance."

I must not forget this glorious time with the Lord, she told herself. *I may need to remind myself of it later.* Shaking her head as though to dispel any unpleasant thoughts, she lifted her gaze to the cottony sky and sang. "This is my story, this is my song, praising my Savior all the day long."

Jasper barked, and she laughed. Surely a lovely morning like this meant Nicholas had changed his mind and wouldn't send her away.

By the time Betsy returned to the house, Nicholas had been there and gone. No doubt he'd hurried on to the fields, and she'd missed him on her way back. Glancing about the kitchen, she saw the remains of a ham sandwich, cold fried potatoes, and crumbs from a piece of chocolate cake. Her note had been moved, but he hadn't added anything to it. A big part of her wished he'd written something.

Rolling up the sleeves to her dress, she pulled out flour, salt, and yeast to make bread. Nicholas loved hot, fresh rolls, and she planned to churn butter as soon as the bread started to rise. While on her walk, she'd picked some fresh dandelion greens to add to the night's supper of pork chops and creamed corn. She prayed for a softening of his heart and the courage to tell him about the baby.

That evening when she heard the cow bells signaling time for the milking, she poured a dipper of cold water into a jar and walked it out to Nicholas. Nervous and trembling, she left Jasper inside the house so the puppy wouldn't get underfoot.

His back to her, he leaned into Prudence's side, and she heard the familiar *ping ping* hit the pail. "Good evening," she greeted, hoping her voice sounded more confident than she truly felt. "Thought you might enjoy a cool drink of water."

"Thank you. Just set it on that bail of hay," he said, without so much as a nod her way.

Setting it where he directed, Betsy drew a deep breath. "Mind if I stay? Supper is nearly done."

He sighed. "I'm not much company."

"Yes, you are. Even if you aren't in the mood to talk, I'd rather be here than alone in the house." And she sincerely meant it.

He stopped milking but still didn't give her any eye contact. "Don't say things you don't mean, Betsy," he muttered.

"I said exactly how I felt," she said. "And I'd like to talk after we eat. I have some things to say."

"All right," he replied, resuming milking the cow.

"Will you tell me about the painting tonight?" she hesitantly asked.

He paused for several long moments. "Guess it wouldn't hurt."

Betsy sat there beside him in silence until he completed the milking. Their dinner was finished except for putting it on the table, and she could do that while he washed up. All the while, her mind whirled, wondering how she'd tell him about the baby—and if it would make a difference in his wanting to send her back to Wisconsin.

At supper they ate without conversation until she elected to tell him about her walk, making certain she revealed all the fascinating little areas about the farm. She'd discovered marsh marigolds blooming above one of the springs and purple violets near the woods. While picking dandelion greens, she'd noted some large yellow blooms but discovered they were newly hatched baby chickens. Since they didn't own any chickens, she wondered where the hen belonged. Although Nicholas failed to respond, her chatter filled the quiet, empty moments.

Standing, Nicholas pulled something from his rear

pocket and laid it on the table beside her. Instantly she recognized the train ticket. "I bought this today, just as I said I would. It's for the day after tomorrow, so you'll have time to pack your things."

She held her breath in horror. *Help me, Lord. Give me the right words to change his mind.* "Isn't it rather soon?" she asked, fighting the trepidation wreaking havoc through her body.

"No, considering the circumstances." He grasped his coffee cup and took a large gulp before continuing. "I want you to be happy, Betsy, and you aren't with me."

She wet her lips. "I don't want to go home. I belong here."

He lifted his chin and tightened his jaw. "It's settled. You can tell your folks, my folks, anything you like."

"That's not the point," she gently argued. "I made a commitment to be your wife—"

"And I'm releasing you of it."

Understanding their words weren't going anywhere, she prayed for a different topic and then struck upon an idea. "Would you tell me about the painting now?"

His ragged breath gave away his sentiments. "I suppose you will bother me until I do." He scooted his chair across the kitchen floor, scraping it along the way. "Let's go into the parlor and get this over with." He snatched up the lantern and carried it into the room.

Obediently she followed and carried her chair, but he chose to stand beside the fireplace. "Laurelwood is not a painting of my parents' home," he began. "It's of my grandmother's childhood home in Pennsylvania." He pointed to an apple tree. "You can see the landscaping is different from the one in Wisconsin. My grandparents moved there from Pennsylvania right after they married.

"Grandpa owned a lumber mill and worked so many long hours that my grandmother thought he didn't care about her. One day, she became so angry about him being gone so much that he promptly ushered her into a carriage and drove her to the home he'd just completed. It was identical to the one she'd left behind, and it was the real reason he'd spent time away from her." He shifted uncomfortably. "My father and I were born there, married there too."

"What a beautiful story," Betsy whispered. "So your grandparents had problems starting out in their marriage, too?"

He flashed her an angry scowl. "It's not the same."

"But still," she insisted. "They stayed together and worked it out."

"I'm not my grandfather, and you aren't my grandmother."

His words stung, but she knew he felt betrayed—and rightfully so. "I want to stay with you, Nicholas. I believe God will bless our marriage."

"I've given up on God," he fairly shouted, then his voice quieted. "I'm sorry to raise my voice. It's settled. Day after tomorrow you will board the train in Crestline and head back to Wisconsin." He walked toward the door.

"Wait," she urged. "Can we talk a little more? I have something important to tell you."

His shoulders slumped, and she felt like the most detestable creature God ever created. Without turning, he replied. "Tell me now. I have things to do."

Taking a deep breath and wetting her lips, she began. "I have wronged you terribly, Nicholas, and hurt you so deeply. Even now you can't look at me. It's my fault, and there is nothing I can do but beg your forgiveness. If you really want me to leave here after I finish, then I will go and not argue. But please understand this, I don't want to live anywhere except with you." She sighed and willed her queasy stomach to stop churning.

"I'm not sure what love is. You and I have been together since we were children. No one else has ever mattered or meant anything to me, but you. You were my big brother, my hero, my teacher, and my husband. I may not know or comprehend exactly how I'm supposed to react as your wife, but we do have another reason to stay together."

He slowly turned to face her, frustration clearly written across his handsome features. "What's that?"

Someone pounded hard on the door, startling both of them. "Mr. Malone, Mrs. Malone, please open the door."

Nicholas flung it open wide to see Ed Barrett, Willy and Ella's eldest son, standing before them. He'd been running, and his efforts to talk were futile between his pants for air.

"Slow down, boy," Nicholas urged, grasping him gently by the shoulders. "What's wrong? Somebody hurt?"

Ed took a few deep breaths. "It's Mama," he finally said. "She's having the baby early. Pa went to get Mrs. Lanefield, the midwife, and sent me after you, Mrs. Malone. Can you come and help?"

"Of course," she replied and glanced hastily at Nicholas. "Would you come, too?"

He nodded. "Yes, I can keep the other children busy."

"I'm going back home," Ed announced, seemingly in more control.

"Wait, I'll get the buckboard," Nicholas said.

"No, I can run faster than it would take you to hitch it up." With those words, the boy took off in the shadows of night.

Betsy rose and touched Nicholas's arm. "Please, just saddle up the mare. We can ride together, and it'll be faster."

For the first time, he met her gaze. She saw the pained look in his blue eyes, the torment she'd caused. Instantly he looked the other way. "All right then, let's go."

The Barrett home looked quiet and peaceful when they arrived, but the moment Nicholas tied the mare to a post, Ed rushed to meet them.

"Thanks for coming," he breathed. "Papa's not back yet. Belle and Verna are with Mama, and Marie is tending to the others."

Betsy gave him a reassuring smile. She felt frightened and knew nothing about birthing a baby, unless Ella could talk her through it. Glancing up at Nicholas, she saw a worried frown pass over his face. "I'm going to her," she whispered, and he reached out and touched her hand.

"You'll be fine." For the first time since her early morning confession in the barn, he nodded encouragingly and revealed a glimpse of the Nicholas she knew. . .and loved.

She shook with the realization, except this wasn't the time or the place to tell him. "Pray for Ella," she said, passing through the door.

Verna directed Betsy to her mother's side where Belle dabbed the perspiration from Ella's forehead. At the sight of Betsy, the girl smiled weakly.

Betsy returned the gesture, but her gaze quickly rested upon her friend's face, pale and drawn. "I'll take over now," she whispered to Belle. "I'm sure your papa and Mrs. Lanefield will be here soon. Everything is going to be just fine."

The young girl kissed her mother's forehead, whisked away an errant tear, and disappeared. As soon as the door closed, Betsy took Ella's hand as she attempted to speak through a shallow breath. "This baby is coming fast, and it's much too soon."

Wetting her lips, Betsy vowed to stay calm and not reveal her fright. "Tell me what to do," she managed.

"Get the girls to boil water and fetch my sewing basket—oh," she moaned. "The pains are getting closer." Holding her breath, she squeezed Betsy's hand until the labor subsided. "I'm glad you're with me."

"Does that mean the midwife might not arrive before the baby? I've never helped give birth before." Betsy felt herself shaking.

Ella smiled feebly. "I'll do all the work. You just follow my instructions. Giving birth is an opportunity to see one of God's special miracles." She squeezed Betsy's hand, perspiration beading on her forehead. When the contraction was over, Ella closed her eyes. "Are you ready for my ninth child?" she asked. Gripping Betsy's hand again, a faint groan escaped her lips. "Pray for my baby," she whispered.

"I will, I am," Betsy replied, wiping her damp brow.

"The girls. . ."

She nodded and turned to the door. "Belle, I need one of you girls to bring me your sewing basket—now!"

Within ten minutes, a tiny voice hailed his coming into the world.

"He's small," Ella whispered, crying, cradling the baby boy in her arms. "Dear God, he's much too small."

Chapter 8

"He's beautiful," Betsy soothed. Her ears perked at the sound of voices. "Willy and Mrs. Lanefield are here."

Ella glanced up through watery blue eyes. "Dear God, I'm afraid our little boy won't live. Betsy, get Willy for me, please."

A plump, matronly lady stole into the room with the most angelic smile that Betsy had ever seen. "Why, Ella, you've gone and had this baby without me."

"But he's too little," she cried. "Please, I've got to see Willy."

"Sure, honey." And she motioned to Betsy. "Let me look him over, Ella, clean him up. Goodness, he's got a good set of lungs."

Betsy found Willy and the children outside on the front porch, some talking, others silent in the lantern light, but they'd all heard the baby's cries and brimmed with excitement. Her gaze immediately went to Nicholas and silently pleaded for help. Smiling, she moved to Willy seated on the porch swing and kneeled in front of him. "Ella wants to see you," she whispered.

He fairly beamed. "The baby?"

"It's a boy," Betsy replied, then lowered her voice. "Willy, he's very small, and she's frightened. Please go to her, she needs you."

Immediately he stood, and his eyes clouded over. A worried frown replaced the laugh lines. "He was early," he reiterated.

"But Mrs. Lanefield says his lungs are good, and he certainly looks fine to me." She felt Nicholas's strong arms around her shoulders.

"You go on in," he urged. "Me and Betsy will have this group praying."

Willy nodded and stepped inside. Nicholas summoned the children's attention. "We need to pray for your mama and your new baby brother."

"Praise God," Ed said, with his father's same lopsided grin. "Now we've got another brother to help even the odds."

"That's wonderful," Nicholas continued and chuckled despite the grim circumstances. "But the baby is very small. We need to ask God to make him strong and healthy."

Instantly quietness fell, reminding Betsy of the dreadful stillness she'd experienced in the house when she realized Nicholas wanted to send her away. She didn't want the children to feel helpless; they needed the peace of God.

"Let's gather in a circle and hold hands," she suggested.

In moments, Nicholas stood with Betsy across from him and children on both sides. "I'm going to start praying," he said. "When I've finished, each one of you will have an opportunity to say something. Let's bow our heads and go to the Lord in prayer. Heavenly Father, we come to You right now thanking You for the gift of this new baby. We're real concerned, Lord, 'cause he came early and he's very little. We pray You'll place Your healing hand on him, making him strong and healthy. His mama is upset and she needs to hear from You that everything will be fine. Give her peace and courage in this time of trouble." He paused and waited for one of the children to begin.

"Help me to be a good big brother and help Papa more," Ed said.

"And Lord, I would really like to help Mama with this baby like I did with little Audrey," Belle added.

"And if you'll make this baby healthy, I won't ever grumble again about taking care of the younger ones," Marie vowed.

"I won't be pestering the others so much," Herbert promised.

A sob escaped from Verna. "I won't try to get out of helping with my chores."

Betsy took a deep breath. "Lord, you know the desires of my heart. I haven't served You as well as I should, but I want to be a better neighbor and not just lean on Ella. Please help the baby grow strong in health and in You." She paused. "And help me be the kind of wife that Nicholas deserves." She wanted to raise her eyes to see if he responded, but in the dark, she wouldn't be able to see him.

"I'll share my mud pies with the new baby," Laura said softly.

Audrey and Boyd uttered a "please, Jesus" before

Nicholas spoke a hearty "Amen." They raised their heads to find Willy observing them from the doorway.

"Mrs. Lanefield says he's strong and healthy," he called with a smile. "That was the sweetest prayer this side of heaven." With a deep sigh he walked toward them. "And it makes me proud of my family and my neighbors." Glancing about, he hugged his children. "Want to know what we've named him?"

"Yes," the children shouted.

"John," he stated. "Like the youngest of our Lord's disciples."

"Fine name," Nicholas complimented.

"Thanks, that's how we feel."

Shortly thereafter Mrs. Lanefield called from the doorway. "Here he is. Got him clean and wrapped up nice. Would you children like to take a peek?" She handed the tiny bundle to Willy, and the others took turns ooing and ahhing. Finally, he handed baby John to Nicholas. "Here, you two can have him for just a minute while we check on Ella. She said Betsy did a wonderful job during the birthing. I thank you, Betsy. We both are grateful for what you and Nicholas have done here tonight." Willy and his children filed into the house like an army on a mission, and Betsy laughed softly.

Nicholas sat in the porch swing and held the baby a bit awkwardly.

Betsy took a deep breath. "Isn't he beautiful?" she whispered, sitting down beside him.

"Yeah, a new little one sure is a blessing."

"Ella called them miracles."

"That, too." He hesitated, then looked into her face.

"I've been thinking tonight, Betsy, about the painting and us. Well, as you said, my grandparents had it hard in the beginning—starting out in a strange place—but they ended up with a wonderful marriage. I know I already have the train ticket, but. . .but if you'd rather stay a little longer. . .well, I'd appreciate it. I don't really think God wants us apart."

Her eyes swelled with the liquid emotion filling her soul. "Oh, thank you, Nicholas. I don't want to leave you."

He cleared his throat. "I didn't treat you very good these last few days. I've asked God to forgive me for turning my back on Him, and now I'm asking if you will forgive me for being so cruel."

"But, I hurt you—deceived you," she insisted.

"That's no excuse for a man to act as I did toward the woman he loves. I think, Betsy. . ." He looked down at the baby, before glancing back at her. In the dim light, she could see a tear slip down his face, and she gently wiped it away with her finger. "I think I'd rather have you with me, even if you don't share in the same feelings, than live without you."

She tilted her head and swallowed hard. "I realized something tonight, too. Ever since I can remember, you've always been there for me—patching up my scrapes and bruises, playing house, listening to my girlish dreams, and most importantly loving me. You've been patient and kind, even when I acted horribly." She grasped his hand holding onto the baby blanket. "That's like God. All this time, you've loved me without asking anything in return. I took you for granted, just as I have our heavenly Father. Guess I just thought you'd always be there. Then, at the thought of losing you completely, I panicked. Facing the future without you caused me to see how much I really do love you—and always have. Please forgive me, Nicholas, for being such a child and not treasuring all the wonderful things you've done for me."

"Do you mean it?" he asked quietly, staring into her face.

"Oh, yes," she replied. Feeling a bit shy, she leaned over and brushed a kiss across his lips. "Nicholas Malone, I love you." She sat back on the swing and viewed the serene portrait he painted with the sleeping baby in his arms. A sweet little twinge danced across the bottom of her stomach, and she remembered Ella's words. "Oh, Nicholas, I want to be with you forever," she murmured, "until God sees fit to part us."

"That's my kind of wife," he said and entwined his fingers around hers. "Come back here," he ordered huskily and pulled her to him. When her face nearly touched his, he kissed her tenderly, and she longingly returned his kiss.

She leaned her head on his shoulder, and the swing slowly began to sway back and forth. "You're doing a great job with baby John," she noted, feeling happier than she could ever remember.

"Thank you, but I feel strange holding this little one."

"Do you think you could get over that feeling, say in the next six or so months?"

Stunned, he searched her face, but all she could do was smile in her excitement. "Am. . .am I going to be a father?" he stuttered.

"And a fine one you'll make, too," she replied, planting

a kiss on his cheek. "Maybe for nine or ten."

"My grandparents didn't have nine or ten. They just had three. Why, I'll just have to start plans for a larger house, maybe bigger than the one in the painting."

"With God's help," she said.

"With God's help," he echoed. His lips found hers, sealing the commitment of husband and wife for a lifetime of love.

DIANN MILLS

DiAnn lives in Houston, Texas, with her husband, Dean. They have four sons. DiAnn wrote from the time she could hold a pencil, but not seriously until God made it clear that she should write for Him. After three years of serious writing, her first book *Rehoboth* was released by **Heartsong Presents** and soon followed by another. Her other publishing credits include magazine articles and short stories, devotionals, poetry, and internal writing for her church.

DiAnn is an active choir member, leads a ladies' Bible study, and is a church librarian. She also enjoys reading, research, and music.

Turbulent Times

by Andrea Boeshaar

To Gina Merritt

Thanks for your help with this story.
You're a groovy friend!

Chapter 1

Kent, Ohio, February 1969

A my Lorraine Bartley, or "Raine" as she preferred, stood gaping at her boyfriend before she let out a grunt-sounding gasp. "What? Marriage? Are you stoned, Nick?"

He shook his head. "No way. I'm totally straight."

"Well, maybe you need to get stoned."

"Raine, I don't need any grass to help me think. I know right from wrong, and we can't be together if we're not married." He shrugged, his voice softening. "My conscience has been bothering me lately. . .a lot."

She strode toward him, enjoying the very look of this man. Nicholas Parker Malone. His soft, blond hair hung in waves to his shoulders, and reddish-blond sideburns grew down his jaw line in thick rectangles. His features were ruggedly handsome, and he had a nice athletic build.

"I like your shirt," she said, eyeing up the long-sleeved, white, cotton tunic with a painted-on abstract design on its front and shoulders. Wrapping her arms around his waist, Raine stood on tiptoes to plant a quick kiss on his mouth. "Did you make it in one of your art classes?"

"Yeah." Nick paused to enjoy the kiss, then pushed her gently away. "Don't change the subject, Raine."

She sighed. "I don't want to get married. I want to be free. We're free, remember? Our generation is the one that's going to change the world. Man, let's not get caught in the same trap our parents did."

Nick sauntered to the window of the tiny apartment. "I didn't have parents," he stated caustically, "so I guess I don't know what trap you're talking about."

Raine felt like biting off her tongue. "Sorry, Nick. I didn't think."

She stopped short, knowing the subject was a painful one for him. When he was just a little boy of five years old, his parents had been killed in a train accident while they vacationed overseas. Nick, their only child, was given to his paternal grandfather and namesake, Nicholas Malone, who took over the parenting from then on. But over the years, Nick felt he'd gotten robbed, cheated out of growing up in a real home with real parents. Raine suspected that's likely why he insisted on getting married now. She'd recently found out she was pregnant, and no doubt, Nick was hoping to create a nice, cozy family.

Fine for him, except that wasn't what Raine wanted. She had a family, complete with domineering father, Geoffery Bartley, who ruled his wife and kids with an iron fist. Raine's mother, Amelia, had lost heart long ago, her spirit crushed, and consequently she allowed Raine's father to tell her how to think. . .how to feel. Raine's older sister and brother were much the same way. Puppets.

But not Raine.

"I've got to be free, Nick," she uttered once more, cringing at the thought of such a binding commitment as marriage.

"And how free do you think you really are?" he countered, spinning from the window. "Your folks pay your rent, your tuition to Kent State. You don't have to work a job to support yourself. Yeah, you're free, all right. It's just a good thing you've got those establishment 'old folks at home' who take care of you, or else you'd really be free—and living on the street!"

"That's enough, Nick," Raine said, folding her arms and glaring at him. She couldn't stand it when he got on one of his high-and-mighty trips.

When Nick turned away and didn't reply, she stomped into the kitchen and pulled a cola from out of the fridge. She suddenly regretted telling him about her pregnancy. But last week, when she'd discovered the news, she'd felt so scared and confused that she had to tell *someone,* and Nick was her best friend, not to mention the father of her child. However, things were different now. This week she felt more determined than ever to guard her freedom.

"Did you hear the news today, Nick?" Raine asked, hoping to get his mind off of her and onto another of his passions—protesting the war. "Fighting in Saigon. About a hundred people got killed."

"Yeah, I heard," he muttered.

Raine frowned. Usually talking about the war got Nick all fired up with ideas about overthrowing the government and working for world peace. *Man,* she thought, taking a long swallow of her cola, *this marriage thing is too weird.*

Nick finally turned from the window. "Raine," he

asked, "would you at least *consider* marrying me? We have been together for a couple of years. We love each other. . . ."

She could barely stand the vulnerable look in his blue-green eyes. She turned away, saying nothing.

Later, after Nick left for work, Raine had time alone to think. Sure, she had it better than most students. Her parents paid for everything so she could concentrate on studying music—and she let them pay her way. But Geoff Bartley didn't control her with his money. No way!

Nick, on the other hand, worked two jobs, one at the campus bookstore and the other as a teacher's assistant conducting Introduction to Painting, a class that ran Tuesday and Thursday afternoons. He was less radical than she was, but equally as fervent in his efforts to stop the war in Vietnam and promote social justice. But if she had to narrow it down, she'd say Nick's three passions in life were his painting, his relationship with Raine, and the SDS (Students for a Democratic Society)—but not necessarily in that order. And, yes, she loved him—more than she had ever loved anyone in her life. But could she marry him?

Marriage. The very idea caused her to groan. It definitely wasn't for radicals.

Picking up her guitar, Raine began to strum the chords to the Pete Seeger tune "Where Have All the Flowers Gone?". It was one of Nick's favorite protest songs.

Where have all the flowers gone, long time passing?
Where have all the flowers gone, long time ago?

Raine sang through the verses till she got to the fourth one.

Where have all the soldiers gone, long time passing?
Where have all the soldiers gone, long time ago?

Thinking about the killing in Vietnam, she nearly choked on the last two lines.

Gone to graveyards every one.
When will they ever learn? When will they ever learn?

With a heavy heart, Raine set down her guitar. She wished the war would end. Why wasn't the government listening? Why weren't things changing?

Steering her thoughts back to Nick and the situation at hand, she glanced around her apartment. It was neat for the most part. Her parents had given her the brown-and-black checked sleeper sofa and the matching armchair. The bathroom was to the right and the kitchen to the left. The appliances came with the apartment, and a long, built-in, wooden counter served as a table. She felt comfortable. It was home.

But what do I do when the baby comes?

She sighed, leaning against the couch. The doctor at the clinic said she was about three months along. She'd be a mother in six months. Her freedom would be gone forever.

Unless she had an abortion. . . ?

Raine considered it—again—but didn't think she could go through with such a procedure. If she did, she'd have blood on her hands. How would she ever march in another anti-war demonstration, shouting, "War is murder!" knowing she'd done the same thing as the government that had drafted the guys in Nam? Very simply, she couldn't.

Adoption. . . ?

Raine sighed. Perhaps. However, a deep gnawing inside her said that if she gave away their baby, she'd lose Nick forever. He'd never forgive her, and even if he did, he'd never forget. That was Nick. Sensitive-to-a-fault Nick.

Standing, Raine walked to one of the many paintings she'd hung on her walls. Nick's creations. All of them. Some were crudely framed, others were not. She reverently touched one of the oils. It was an abstract—a house torn into three sections. Its severed edges were tinged in red, like blood, and the windows of the place were slanted in such a way that the painting emanated pain. Nick said it represented the feeling he had—one he still recalled—upon hearing of his parents' death. He said his home had been torn asunder.

Raine shook her head sadly. Poor, sweet Nick. How could she hurt him?

She walked to the coatrack beside the door and pulled on her winter jacket. Stepping out of her apartment, she locked the door and then left the building. Outside, it was sleeting, but she didn't care. She needed air. She needed to think. She needed to talk. . .to Nick. The situation was making her crazy. She simply had to come to some sort of decision. . .tonight. Now!

Her trek to the campus took fifteen minutes in the

dark, cold, and slippery night. When she arrived at the bookstore, she found it locked up tight. Glancing at her watch, Raine realized the shop had closed long before she'd left her apartment. For all of her musing, she'd lost track of the time.

Nibbling her lower lip in contemplation, Raine wondered where Nick would go. Home? Probably. She headed that way.

Another twenty minutes and she climbed the front porch steps of the four-bedroom bungalow that Nick shared with eight other guys.

"Naw, he's not here," one of his roommates said.

"Are you sure, Pat? He got off of work forty-five minutes ago."

"Want to come in and check?" he invited.

Raine shook her head. From her vantage point, she could see the place was a dump, and Steppenwolf's "Born to Be Wild" blared from the stereo. "I suppose you're, um, studying," she said sarcastically. A person in his right mind wouldn't be able to hear himself think in such a ruckus. Then again, most of these guys were seldom in their "right minds," and Nick, the exception, probably found a quieter place to do his homework.

"Sure, I'm studying, but you won't bother me, Rainy Day," Pat replied. "Come on in." He opened his arms wide. "You can get high and feel the love while you wait for Nick-the-paint-stick to get home."

"That's okay. I'll check around campus for him."

Pat shrugged, then closed the door, and Raine walked back to the university. She looked for Nick in the Student Union, but didn't find him. She searched the library. Not there. Finally she gave up and walked back to her apartment as the freezing drizzle pelted her. When she reached her apartment building, Raine felt soaked to the bone. Her teeth were chattering from the cold.

With frozen fingers, she unlocked her apartment door. *Nick, where are you?* she wondered. She felt more than a little perturbed with him. *Where are you when I need you? You should be here for me.*

Her selfish haze gradually burned itself off, but then as she changed into dry clothes, a sudden, horrible thought took its place. What if Nick found some other chick? He wouldn't, of course, she quickly reasoned. But what if. . . ? What if Nick decided he didn't want the responsibility of a pregnant girlfriend? What if he said, "Hey, baby, you're on your own"?

Raine swallowed a lump of consternation. Most guys she knew wouldn't be talking marriage. They'd be figuring out how to. . .keep their freedom.

Freedom. Suddenly the word didn't hold quite the same appeal if she didn't have Nick to be free with her. She was like a kite, dancing on the breeze, and he was the one below, holding onto her string, guiding her, making sure she didn't crash to earth and shatter into pieces.

But what if he let her go?

She'd be lost without him.

A knock sounded on her door, and she jumped. "Who's there?"

"Nick."

Relief flooded her being. Running to the door, she flung it open. "Where have you been? I was looking for you everywhere!"

His blond hair was drenched, as were his clothes. "Pat said you'd stopped by. I got worried maybe something was wrong."

"Where were you?" she asked again, ignoring his concern for the time being.

He smiled and stepped into the apartment. "I was at the Haunted House, listening to this guy. . .man! What an intellect! He's got some right-on ideas, but mostly no one agreed with them 'cause the guy is way too passive. He's not into the coming revolution."

Raine released a slow breath. She should have known. The Haunted House. It was an old structure just a block from the Water Street bars where students roomed. A young married couple rented the upper apartment, and since they'd moved in last year, the Haunted House had become one of the more popular intellectual centers around campus.

"I left when the debate started heating up," Nick continued, "and met up with one of my students. We started rapping, and I ended up going to her dorm room to look at some of her artwork. Pretty good, too."

"Her?" Raine lifted an inquiring brow.

"Yeah." He shivered. "Hey, how 'bout making some coffee?"

Raine didn't move. She just stared at him. Young, handsome, talented. . .if she didn't want Nick Malone, another woman would.

"Nick," she said in a broken, little voice, "will you just hold me in your arms and tell me you love me?"

Confusion momentarily crossed his features, but then he shrugged. "Sure." Shedding his wet wool coat, he gathered her into his arms. "I love you, Raine," he whispered close to her ear. "You know that. I've never loved anyone else the way I love you. Never will."

She laid her head on his shoulder and closed her eyes. She'd heard them before, but tonight his words were like a beautiful melody. "Hey, Nick?"

"Hm. . . ? "

"Let's get married."

Chapter 2

Behind the wheel of his 1961 blue Volkswagen bus, Nick rattled and sputtered across the state of Ohio to where his grandfather lived near Bucyrus. What had once been fertile farmland was now a thriving subdivision, and Grandpa's single-story ranch-styled home stood in the forefront.

Nick pulled into the driveway, barely able to recall when Grandpa had sold his land, razed the original farmhouse, and bought this one. Nick was only nine years old when Grandma died—just four years after his parents' tragic accident. If Grandpa had taken his son's death hard, he'd been devastated by his wife's passing, and there hadn't been any room in the old man's heart for nurturing a little boy. It wasn't until Nick's high school years that his grandfather woke up to his namesake's activities, namely trouble, trouble, and more trouble. Consequently, their relationship had been a stormy one, and when Nick turned eighteen, he'd moved out, enrolled in Kent State, and hadn't been back since.

Until now.

Climbing out of the VW, Nick conceded that the old

man had experienced some change of heart. He'd been trying for the past three or four years to reconcile their relationship, but Nick had ignored his efforts, refusing to acknowledge the birthday and Christmas cards and all the letters in between. However, something had changed. Nick sensed it. Maybe the situation with Raine prompted it. Whatever the case might be, he knew the time had come to pay his grandfather, Nicholas Parker Malone, a visit.

He got as far as the back walkway, when the door opened and a man with a shiny bald head, hollow cheeks, and large, liquid-blue eyes greeted him.

"Nick?" he asked in a whispered croak.

"Grandpa?" He scarcely recognized him. He'd aged considerably in the past seven years.

Then his grandfather further shocked him by bursting into tears. "Nick! Oh, Nick. . ."

He watched in mild horror as the man who had seemed so devoid of emotion all his growing up years now wept uncontrollably in front of his very eyes. "Maybe this is, um, a bad time. I can come back."

"No, no, please don't go away." Hastily wiping the moisture from his eyes, the old man stepped down from the back stoop and slowly made his way over to Nick. Throwing his spindly arms around him, he added, "I have been praying you'd come home."

Confounded by the impassioned welcome, he merely patted his grandfather's shoulder, then pushed him gently away. "Well, here I am," he said guardedly.

The ninety-one-year-old man stood just a foot away and seemed to drink in his every feature. "You've got your grandmother's blue-green eyes."

Nick shrugged. "That's nice. . .I guess. But they've always been there. Nothing new."

"Of course, of course. Only this old fool never noticed before, or if I did, I never said anything. I never said a lot of things, son. Come in, will you? Please, come in."

Nick nodded and his grandfather took his arm, hanging onto it for strength and balance as they made their way into the house.

"Have you been sick, Grandpa?" Nick asked, noting the phenomenal change in the man. Seven years ago, the elder Nicholas Malone had been a picture of health with a full head of hair and a steely disposition. He'd always looked twenty years younger than his actual age, but now he resembled a broken, little man.

"Sick? Oh, well. . ."

Nick helped him into a kitchen chair and waited till his grandfather caught his breath.

"Yes, I've been sick." He lifted his blue eyes. "I'm dying, son. I have cancer."

Nick was rendered speechless. "I. . .I didn't know," he said at last.

"I wanted to tell you in person, Nick. Not by letter. That's why I've been praying you'd return. There are a lot of things we need to say to each other before I go home to be with the Lord."

"You planning on going anytime soon?" he teased. He hoped the bit of levity would relieve some of the tension in the air and break down any existing barriers between them.

It worked. The old man chuckled. "At my age, it could happen in a moment. But the doctors have given me six months to a year."

"Mm. . ." Nick pulled out a chrome chair, padded in red vinyl, and sat down. "Well, I guess you're right about us having to do some talking. That's why I came."

His grandfather smiled. "I'm so glad. How long can you stay?"

"Just the weekend, I'm afraid."

"Have you graduated?"

Nick shook his head. "I'm a senior at Kent. Actually, I've been hopping back and forth between junior and senior status for years because I kept changing my major to avoid the draft. But I kind of ran out of options and it looks like I'll get my bachelor's degree in May whether I want to or not."

"I am very proud of you."

"For what?" Nick asked, grinning. "For managing to stay out of Vietnam or for earning my degree?"

"For the latter, son. A college degree. Your father would be proud, too. He had an education, you know. Smart man. . .smart man."

Nick nodded silently. All his life he'd been compared to his father and hadn't ever measured up. But maybe now Grandpa would accept him for who he was.

A rueful expression suddenly crossed the old man's face. "Your great-great-grandfather gave his life in this country's Civil War. . ."

Oh, here we go, Nick thought. "Well, I'm not giving mine in Vietnam!"

His grandfather lifted a hand with great effort. "I would never tell you to do such a thing. We all must choose which battles we fight in this life. I wanted to enlist in World War I, but your grandmother wouldn't hear of it.

She was a peaceful woman and couldn't understand such politics as war."

"Not many can, Grandpa. But I'll tell you what. . .if President Johnson enlists, so will I. Seems to me the guys who advocate all this violence ought to be out there in the trenches themselves."

The old man grunted out a reply, smiling. "In my grandfather's day, such leaders did fight. Look at Grant, Lee. . ."

"Ah, the good ol' days," Nick quipped. Standing, he glanced around the sparsely decorated kitchen. It hadn't changed much. "Got anything to eat? I'm starved."

"Help yourself, son."

"Thanks."

Nick scrounged through the fridge and the cupboards, and finding nothing of great interest, he settled for a peanut butter and jelly sandwich. Then, after helping his grandfather to the front room and into an easy chair, Nick ate while the old man dozed. Minutes later, he took his plate to the kitchen and, reentering the living room, observed his grandfather staring at the far wall.

"You okay, Grandpa?"

Turning his head, he smiled. "Leah Somerville painted that picture. It's Laurelwood, her childhood home in Pennsylvania," he said, referring to the object of his scrutiny. "Leah was my grandmother."

"Yeah, I know. . ."

Nick looked at the painting, and a sense of melancholy enveloped him. How many times had he become entranced by the portrait? As a boy, he used to imagine entering the pastoral scene, walking up to the house, opening the door, and there would be his mother, waiting for him with opened arms.

Home.

He'd never had one.

"Leah's husband, my grandfather, was Blake Nicholas Malone, the man killed in the Civil War."

Nick tore his gaze from the painting. "I hope you're not trying to make me feel guilty for deferring my enlistment or something."

"Oh, no," said the old man. "Nothing of the sort. I'm just remembering." He smiled. "It's what I do best these days."

Nick relaxed, perceiving his grandfather spoke the truth and didn't have any hidden agenda behind his words.

"Did you know, son, that my mother gave the painting to Betsy and me as a wedding present? Betsy and I. . . we brought it to Ohio with us back in 1899."

"I know, Grandpa. I've heard the story a kazillion times. But it's funny you should mention wedding presents," Nick said, seating himself on the brown-and-orange printed sofa, "because I just happen to be getting married."

"Oh?" Curiosity crossed the old man's face. "To whom? When?"

"To Raine Bartley and. . .soon."

"Raine?" He frowned. "Odd name."

"Not really. Her full name is Amy Lorraine, but she likes to be called Raine."

"I see. And you met this young lady at college?"

Again, Nick nodded.

"Is that why you came home today? To invite me to your wedding?"

"Sort of. . .I don't know." Nick glanced at his hands resting on his blue-jeaned clad knees. "See, I'm at a benchmark in my life. I'll graduate soon, and with any luck, I'll be able to teach at the university while I get my masters. With even more luck I won't get drafted." He paused. "My number's up, but I don't intend on reporting for duty. I'm getting married and. . .well, that's the reason I'm here. I wanted to find out what went wrong between us so it does not happen to me and my. . .son or daughter." Looking into his grandfather's moist eyes, he added, "Raine's pregnant."

"Mm. . ." His grandfather turned away and, for a long instant, Nick wondered if he drifted back to sleep. But then he asked, "Do you love her?"

"Yes."

"Does she love you?"

"Yes."

"You sure?"

Nick grinned as his grandfather's gaze moved back to him. "I'm as sure of Raine's love for me as I am of the flowers in springtime."

"And you're poetic, too."

He laughed. "Too? What else am I, Grandpa?"

The dying man sobered. "You're lost, son. You need to get saved."

⌇

"You are not marrying that long-haired hippy freak!" Geoff Bartley bellowed while his wife cowered at his side.

"Like, don't freak out, Dad. We're adults. We can discuss this."

"There's nothing to discuss."

"But I thought you liked Nick. You met him last year

and then invited him to come for Christmas."

Her father took a deep breath, his face losing some of its angry redness. "I was being polite, Amy, that's all."

She winced at the use of her given name. Ever since her sixteenth birthday, she'd insisted upon being called "Raine." She'd decided upon the nickname after writing a song she titled, "Can't Control the Rain." And then it occurred to her—rain. Amy Lorraine. Raine. And she, like the elements, would not be controlled! She had her own mind, she'd make her own choices, and she promptly changed the song to "Can't Control the Raine." She then explained her position to her family, friends, and teachers, who complied with her newest request—all but her father, who still stubbornly referred to her as Amy.

"Dad, I'm going to marry Nick, and you can't stop me."

"Oh, yes, I can."

Raine stood from where she'd been sitting in her parents' den. "No, you can't."

He stood as well. "Yes, I most certainly can!"

From out of the corner of her eye, Raine saw her mother lift a trembling hand to her mouth in the manner of any good docile doormat. The sight caused her to stand her ground all the more firmly.

She glared at her father, thinking that despite their differences, they were a lot alike. Chestnut-brown hair, hazel eyes, and a do-or-die willfulness that had caused them many a face-off.

Like this one.

"I'm going to marry Nick, Dad," Raine repeated.

"Then I'm going to stop paying your tuition," her father countered.

"Fine." Raine said. She'd anticipated it. "After this semester I'm dropping out for a while anyway."

Her mother gasped, which earned her a cold stare from Raine's father. Then he returned his gaze to Raine. "And just why are you dropping out, young lady?"

"Because I'm pregnant."

His eyes grew wide. "You're what?!"

"Pregnant, Dad. You know. . .as in expecting a baby." There! The bomb had been successfully dropped.

From her banished little corner, Raine's mother began to weep softly.

"Oh, hush!" Raine's father snapped. "Tears won't solve anything." He looked back at Raine. "If that's the only reason you want to get married, there are other ways to remedy the situation."

"I've considered them. But I want to marry Nick."

"Amy, you don't even know your own mind. How could you? You're twenty years old. A babe in the woods—and you've got your whole life ahead of you. Finish college. Get your degree. Teach music, just as you planned. Forget about setting up housekeeping." He inched closer. "Amy, I know a doctor who will—"

"Forget it, Dad." Raine crossed her arms stubbornly. The argument was growing dull. "I'm marrying Nick," she said for the umpteenth time. "What other threats are you going to hurl my way?"

"Threats?" her father asked, wearing an incredulous expression. "Why, I never make threats."

"Yeah, whatever." Raine turned to her mother, her heart breaking. Just once she'd love to see the woman tell her husband off. "Mom, are you all right?"

She nodded.

"I didn't mean to hurt you, Mom. Really."

"Well, you have," her father interrupted. "Just look at her. She's crying because of you, Amy! You've shamed your mother. She'll be humiliated now. . .won't even be able to set foot inside the grocery store because of your promiscuity."

Raine nearly laughed. "Save the guilt trip. I'm still marrying Nick."

He fell silent for several long moments. "If you marry that. . .that draft-dodging loser," he stated at last, "you'll never be welcome in this house again."

"Geoff, no!" her mother piped up.

Raine smiled. *Go, Mom!*

"You stay out of this," he said, pointing a long, accusatory finger at her.

Raine's mother recoiled obediently.

To Raine, he added, "Marry that man and I will disown you. No daughter of mine will marry an *artist.*" The word rolled off his tongue like "rapist" or "fascist."

"Dad," Raine replied at last, "if you can disown me just because I love Nick and want to marry him, then so be it."

With that she grabbed her wool poncho and woven shoulder bag and left the house.

Chapter 3

N ick, you're back!"

"Alive and in the flesh." He chuckled and, much to his delight, Raine threw her arms around his neck and hugged him tightly where they stood in the doorway of her little apartment. "That's quite a welcome," he said at last, smiling down into her hazel eyes.

"Come on in. How did your weekend go?"

"Not bad." He stepped into Raine's living room and took off his jacket while she closed the door behind him. "My grandfather was happy to see me—said he'd been praying I'd come home. Man, we got along better than I ever dreamed possible. He's changed. But dig this," Nick added solemnly, "he's got cancer and isn't expected to live through the year."

Raine grimaced. "Wow—what a bummer."

Nick nodded. "Yeah, except he's not depressed, and that surprised me. He's really into the Jesus thing and that keeps his spirits up."

"Did you tell him about us?" Raine asked, flipping her long, wavy, molasses-brown hair over a slender shoulder.

Nick nodded. "He asked if we loved each other, and I told him we did. Then he started telling me how I've got to repent of my sin and get saved. Born again."

"That's wild!"

"Really. Although, he didn't say it in a condemning or judgmental way." Nick shook his head, still marveling at the conversation. "But that's what he said."

"So what did you say?"

"I told him I wasn't ready for religion, although my grandfather insisted it's not about religion, but a relationship with the Lord Jesus Christ. And would you believe, Raine, that my grandfather admitted he's been a Christian for most of his life? But he said he didn't act like much of one when I was growing up because of his bitterness against God for allowing my parents to die, then my grandmother. Grandpa actually apologized for neglecting me and for not being more a part of my life."

"Wow." Raine plopped down on the couch, folding her legs under her. "That's far out!"

Nick sat beside her. "It blew my mind." He put his arm around Raine and pulled her close to him. "Grandpa wants to meet you."

"Really?" She smiled, and a little dimple winked from her left cheek. "So all's forgiven between you and your grandfather?"

"Yeah, I guess so. I mean, it doesn't make much sense to stay angry at him, seeing he's dying and everything."

"Hm. . ." Raine turned momentarily pensive. "So, like, death is really manipulative. You know, you find out you're going to die and you use it to make people do what you want. Controlling."

"Maybe for some people," Nick agreed. "But with Grandpa. . .well, Raine, he didn't know I was coming. It's not as if he had time to plot and plan."

"Oh, right. Good point." She nodded, looking contemplative once more. "I just don't trust the older generation. They don't understand us."

"We don't understand them either, I guess. And speaking of misunderstanding. . .how did it go with your folks?"

Raine released a weary breath. "It was a bad scene. . . as usual. I walked out when my father threatened to disown me. I hitchhiked back to campus."

"From Akron? I wish you would have called me."

"It's not that far."

"Hitchhiking's dangerous." He sighed. "Man, I knew I should have gone with you."

"You couldn't have done anything. And, man, I just have to liberate my poor mother! She looks so hopeless and pitiful."

Nick didn't know what to say, so he said nothing. He'd seen firsthand how Amelia Bartley groveled around her husband. However, when he wasn't around, she seemed to be a nice lady.

"You'd better not do that to me," Raine threatened.

"Do what?"

"Treat me like a doormat."

"No way, Raine. This is me, remember?"

She gave him a satisfied smile before snuggling in next to him.

"My grandfather says we should get married at his church."

"Church? But I wanted to get married this summer in

a garden, flowers all around us, and in my hair. . ."

"And a baby sticking out a foot in front of your wedding dress."

She groaned. "I forgot about that. But so what?"

Nick shrugged. "I just think we should get married as soon as possible. Grandpa agreed."

"Ganging up on me, huh?"

He grinned mischievously in reply. Then, thinking it over, his amusement subsided. "Raine, maybe I should try to talk to your father. Reason with him."

"It won't do a lick of good. Oh, don't mind him, Nick. He'll come around. He always does."

Nick knew better than to argue with Raine about her father. "Okay. . .if you say so."

***

Two weeks later, Nick drove Raine out to meet his grandfather. The elderly man seemed pleased to see them, and he gave Raine a warm embrace.

"Such a lovely girl," he said, shuffling his way back into the house while holding on tightly to Nick's arm.

"Yeah, she's not too bad." The glib remark earned Nick an elbow in the ribs and one of Raine's pointed stares. But he laughed them off.

Once inside the living room, Nick seated his grandfather before settling in beside Raine on the sofa. They exchanged pleasantries, and the older man inquired about Raine's family background and education. He mentioned her unusual name, and she explained how she'd acquired it. Then the topic shifted to their wedding plans.

"Grandpa, will your pastor marry Raine and me this weekend?" Nick asked forthrightly. "I know it's short notice and everything, but Raine can't come up with the rent for her apartment for next month. I can pay it. . .if I move in with her."

"Except Nick doesn't want to shack up," Raine added. "He's into this 'till death do us part' thing, and there's no talking him out of it."

"Do you want to talk him out of it?" the old man asked.

"Not anymore." Raine turned her eyes on Nick, and his heart beat a little faster. "We're in love."

They gazed longingly at each other until Nick's grandfather cleared his throat. "I suppose I could telephone Pastor Jim. He's our associate pastor. Nice fellow. Young. You'll like him."

With painstaking effort, the aging man rose from his chair and walked into the kitchen where a black phone hung on the wall near the refrigerator. Nick heard him placing the call, and with each whir of the rotary dial, his anticipation soared. He gazed up at the painting perched above the mantel and smiled. Maybe he would belong to a real family after all. His own.

⚭

Raine watched through wary eyes as the man introduced as Pastor Jim stepped into the house with his wife, Moira. They looked like part of the now-generation, but were they really? Raine continued to scrutinize the couple as Nick led Jim and his wife farther into the living room, explaining that his grandfather was in bed resting.

"No problem," the pastor said, helping his wife out of her coat and handing it to Nick. "I understand it's you two we came to talk with, not your grandfather."

Nick nodded, hanging the wraps in the closet.

Crossing the room, he settled onto the arm of the same upholstered chair in which Raine sat, while the pastor and Moira made themselves comfortable on the sofa.

"Why don't you tell me a little about yourselves," Pastor Jim suggested, raking a hand through his collar-length black hair. His dark eyes narrowed in a kind of interested scrutiny. "Nick, you go first."

"Sure. I'm going to graduate from Kent State in May, I belong to the SDS, and I want to marry Raine. Plain and simple." He paused. "Have we met? You look familiar."

The pastor shook his head. "I don't believe so."

"Um, there's more to you than that, Nick," Raine interjected. "I'll tell them if you won't."

He shrugged.

"Nick's a talented artist," she announced to their guests.

"And Raine's a gifted musician," Nick countered.

"Sounds like a match made in heaven," Moira said, smiling. She wore her dark-brown hair like Raine wore hers—long and parted down the middle, but that's where the similarities ended. Moira's eyes were a deep brown, and she was soft and plump-looking in her blue jeans and multicolored pullover sweater.

"What are your church backgrounds?" the pastor inquired.

"I seldom went to church," Nick said. "And if I did attend, it was on holidays with friends. My grandfather wasn't into the religion thing back then."

"Do you have a relationship with the Lord Jesus Christ?"

Nick shook his head. "How can you have a relationship with Someone who died nearly two thousand years ago?"

The pastor smiled. "I'll explain that in a minute. Raine? What about your church background?"

She shrugged. "I was raised in your typical old church. My father forced my brother, sister, and me to go every Sunday. He was an usher and on the financial board, and he'd sit in the pew looking so holy, it made me sick. My father, like most every other churchgoer, was a fake, and I saw through his facade. Dig it, how can a man worship God on Sunday morning and walk all over his wife on Sunday afternoon? Fake, man. Totally fake!"

"Hm. . .I assume you don't know the Lord Jesus either. Is that correct?"

She nodded, albeit uncomfortably. "Hey, what's this got to do with performing a marriage ceremony, anyway?"

Pastor Jim smiled warmly. "My first concern is for your souls."

"Our souls are cool," Raine said. "And didn't you hear? God is dead."

Jim's countenance darkened. "It's a popular saying, Raine, but don't believe the lie. God is not dead. He changed my life."

"Don't trust anyone over thirty," she replied, giving Nick a furtive glance.

"Well, I'm twenty-nine and three-quarters, so you can trust me," he declared with a disarming smile. "Can I tell you how I came to know the Lord Jesus?"

"Whatever turns you on," Raine said, feeling cynical. "But you won't get me to convert."

"Hear me out before you make any decisions, okay?" She agreed, and Nick nodded.

"I used to work with the underground, helping guys

defect to Canada instead of going off to Nam. But then one day I got this feeling my efforts weren't changing anything. As many men as I helped escape, the same number enlisted or reported for the draft.

"Discouraged, I went out drinking one night, and outside the bar, some guy handed me a little pamphlet about spiritual battles in high places. It explained that Jesus Christ is the Almighty Warrior and Victor and that to be on His side, one must be born again. I believed, and my faith changed my life. I was overwhelmed with joy, and a total sense of peace filled my spirit when I understood that God's always in control.

"Some time later, as I got into reading the Bible, I realized a real war raged around me—one that claimed men's souls, not just their lives—and I wanted to do something about it.

"Then I got drafted, but I didn't dodge it. I reported, feeling like a hypocrite because I persuaded hundreds not to go, and yet I knew I had to." Pastor Jim smiled broadly. "Turns out I flunked my physical and couldn't enter the army. Praise the Lord! But I'm a soldier just the same. A soldier in God's army."

"A lot of guys aren't that lucky," Raine said, still wary of the pastor. "They have to go to Nam and fight with real bullets, real grenades, real bombs."

"True, but if they're born again the Bible way, they'll never die—even if they're killed in the rice paddies. And every death is appointed by the Alpha and Omega, the Beginning and the End, the Almighty Creator of the Universe. God isn't surprised each time a man is killed on the battlefield. Oh, now, I'm not trying to minimize the horrors of war. The boys in Nam see things no human being should ever have to encounter. But let's face it, we're all going to die sometime, whether in the United States or in Vietnam. The question is, where will *you* live for eternity? It's a decision. It's a choice."

"I'm just going to be out there," Raine said, thinking of the stars, moon, and vast nothingness above them. "Jesus Christ belongs to the older generation—the one that started the war in Vietnam—not to me and mine. We're into peace and love."

"Well, actually," Moira said, leaning forward and wearing a kind expression, "Jesus *is* peace and love. He doesn't just advocate it. And when He was here on earth, Jesus Christ was totally radical. He turned the world upside down with what people in His day viewed as fanatical views. I mean, Jesus claimed He was the Son of God. He said He was perfect. He called the Pharisees hypocrites and threw the money changers out of the temple. He unapologetically healed a man on the Sabbath—something unheard of. No one did anything on the Sabbath, but Jesus faced His critics undaunted. Still, there were those who doubted Him. So the Lord performed miracles. He raised a man from the dead, walked on water, healed the sick, cast out demons. Yet, many would not believe He was who He said—the perfect Son of God."

"And many others," Pastor Jim added, "followed Him because they thought He'd be the one to overthrow the Roman government, when in actuality, Christ's secret ambition was to die a cruel death on the cross for the sake of humanity. But He didn't stay dead. God, the Father raised Him up on the third day, and now Jesus Christ lives and reigns forever at His side in heaven."

"Isn't that far out!" Moira asked, smiling broadly. "And what love—He gave His life so others can be set free if they'll only believe."

"Free?" Raine asked, lifting a curious brow.

"Free," Moira replied. "Jesus said if we continue in His Word, we're His disciples and we'll know the truth, and the truth will set us free."

Raine thought it made sense. The truth setting people free. Upon further consideration, she decided she rather liked the idea of a radical Jesus who wanted to change the world. The Jesus whom Pastor Jim and Moira spoke of died for a cause He believed in. That was cool.

Peering up at Nick, Raine saw the contemplative expression on his face and decided he, too, was giving the matter serious thought.

Pastor Jim leaned forward and handed them each a small New Testament. "It's all in there. Everything we just told you about Jesus Christ. Read it for yourselves."

"I will," Raine promised, watching Nick pocket his.

"So. . . ," Pastor Jim said, clapping his hands together, then rubbing them in a conspiratorial manner, "what about this wedding?"

Nick explained the situation and Raine's condition and a date was set. The following afternoon.

"Seems a bit hasty," Pastor Jim admitted, "but considering the circumstances, I think it's best. I don't want you two falling into more sin—"

"Sin?" Raine shook her head. "No, Nick and I love each other. That's not sin."

The pastor gave her a caring smile. "I understand, but

the Bible calls a physical relationship before marriage sin. Now, Raine, I'm not trying to condemn you, so don't roll your eyes at me like that." He chuckled lightly at her adverse reaction to his statement. "We all sin, and that's why we all need a Savior—Jesus Christ."

"Admitting one's sin is a hard thing," Moira said. "All my life I was considered a 'good girl,' by parents and teachers alike. I had a difficult time understanding I was a sinner. But I was. . .and still am."

"We'll always have that old sin nature," Pastor Jim continued. "The difference is some are sinners saved by grace and some aren't. Does that make sense?"

"Sort of," Raine replied hesitantly. "I guess I have a lot to think about." She looked at Nick. "And we've got a wedding to plan!"

"Right."

"We'll leave and give you two time to prepare for tomorrow," the pastor said.

Nick retrieved their coats and saw them out the door.

"What do you think?" Raine asked skeptically. "I'm not sure if I like that couple or not."

"I know what you mean, but he's a pastor. I suppose he's obligated to preach to us about sin and everything." Nick frowned, looking pensive. "But I know I've seen that guy somewhere before. I've been trying to place him and I'm almost sure he's the one who spoke at the Haunted House a couple of weeks ago. Remember, Raine? The man I told you about with the conservative viewpoints. I liked what he had to say."

Nick paused, pacing the living room carpet. "I wish I could remember the guy's name. . ." Another pause for deliberation, then Nick snapped his fingers. "Stoddard. Yeah, that's it. I'll have to ask my grandfather about Pastor Jim's last name."

"Whatever," Raine said disinterestedly. "Now, are you going to marry me tomorrow afternoon or not?"

Nick smiled. "I am." Stepping forward, he wrapped his arms around Raine's waist, pulled her close, and kissed her. "I'm the luckiest man alive."

Nicholas Parker Malone and Amy Lorraine Bartley were married on Sunday, March 2, 1969—the same day Soviet and Communist Chinese forces battled on the Manchurian border. Many were killed on both sides.

Chapter 4

"Hey, it looks like Raine—except there's not a cloud in the April sky." Jennifer Thompson giggled at her pun and then pushed her short, auburn hair off her face.

"You're such a comedian," Raine quipped good-naturedly. Then she burst into a grin. "So, how are you, Jen?"

"Fine. I'm gearing up for finals next month and hoping I'll pass every one. How are you? How's married life?"

Raine smiled. "It's groovy." She fell into step beside Jen, and together, they crossed the Kent State campus. Spring was in the air. A fresh, crisp scent wafted on the light breeze, and tiny buds could be seen on the trees.

"How are you feeling these days?"

"Oh. . ." Raine shrugged. "I feel. . .fat." She and Jen shared a laugh, before Raine added, "I'm almost five months along now, and I'm actually looking forward to having this baby and being a mother."

"Wow. So what are you and Nick going to do once he graduates?"

"We're moving in with his grandfather. He's dying of

cancer and Nick feels he should be with him. They weren't close during Nick's childhood, but in the past few months, they've reconciled." Raine gave Jen a smile. "Truthfully, I rather like the old guy."

They chatted a bit more and then, reaching the student union, they parted ways. Raine ambled the rest of the way back to her apartment alone. Nick was teaching his art class, and she had some studying to do.

Nick. He'd changed since their wedding day, and Raine didn't know what to make of it. She recalled how he'd come home several nights ago, informing her of his disillusionment with SDS, and Raine knew it stemmed from his budding relationship with Pastor Jim Stoddard. Yet she could understand where they both were coming from. The organization had become almost Marxist in its philosophy, and instead of promoting peace, it advocated violence in order to get its voice heard above the political din. Moreover, four SDS leaders had recently been charged with inciting to riot, which started several destructive protests on campus, and Nick didn't want anything to do with it. Raine couldn't blame him.

But what about making a difference in the world? What about the crusade to end the Vietnam War?

Man, I hope Nick's not becoming part of the establishment, Raine mused as she picked up the mail and unlocked their apartment door. Inside, his belongings combined with hers crowded the tiny place. She set her backpack on the sofa and flipped through the envelopes. A letter from her mother surfaced, and Raine quickly tore it open.

My dearest Raine,

Raine smiled, glad her mother had used the name she preferred.

> *I detest the rift in this family caused by your disagreement with your father, but I feel helpless to repair it. You are my beloved youngest daughter, yet he is my husband and I am resigned to his wishes. He has told everyone at church that as far as he's concerned you are dead. It does not seem as though he will change his mind about disinheriting you, and my heart breaks with his stubbornness. Please forgive him, Raine. Don't let bitterness destroy your life. Be happy with Nick. But my darling, I must tell you good-bye for as long as your father wishes the abyss between us to exist. It is with tears filled with pain that I write these words. I love you, Raine. You are my flesh and blood; however, I am bound by my marriage vows to love, honor, and obey. . . .*

"What a joke!" Raine muttered, tossing the letter onto the kitchen counter. Swallowing her tears, she collected her wits, telling herself she should have expected as much. Except she had really thought her father would have a change of heart. And she'd never anticipated her mother's defection. . .but again, she should have prepared herself for it. "Typical," Raine muttered.

She unzipped her backpack and pulled out her music theory text. Collapsing onto the sofa, she tried to forget her turbulent family affairs and concentrate on studying.

And that's how Nick found her when he arrived home.

"Hiya," he said, sauntering to the sofa and leaning over to place a kiss on Raine's neck.

"Buzz off, Nick. Can't you see I'm busy?"

He brought his chin back, surprised by her sharp tone. "You're usually not too busy for a kiss, even when you're studying, but, hey, that's cool."

Perplexed and feeling more than a little hurt, he set his book bag down and entered the kitchen. Raine had said she'd do some grocery shopping today, but the cupboards and fridge looked as bare as they had this morning. He glanced over at her, scowling into her textbook. No way would he ask her about some dinner.

"I'm, um, going to the student union for something to eat," he announced quickly, heading for the door.

"Wait, Nick."

Her voice had softened, and as he paused in the doorjamb, he turned and watched her rise from the sofa, her hazel eyes pooling with unshed emotion.

"I'm sorry," she sniffed. "Don't go."

His confusion heightened, but he closed the door again. "What gives, Raine?" She wasn't a woman easily given to tears, and Nick felt somewhat alarmed by what he saw. "Is it the baby? Something wrong?"

She shook her head and wiped away an errant tear. "It's my mother. Here, look at this." Raine crossed the small room and plucked the letter off the counter. Handing it to Nick, she added, "I don't know what's the matter with me lately. It's like my feelings have become all wishy-washy. I'm angry, then I cry. . . . Oh, Nick, what's happening to me? I used to be so. . .practical."

He grinned wryly, taking the proffered letter. "Hormones, baby. Pastor Jim says Moira has awful mood swings—and she's expecting their fifth child!"

Raine sniffed again. "Yeah, well, I guess my mother's letter set me off this time. I'm sorry for snapping."

Leaning forward, Nick kissed her tenderly before glancing at the note in his hand. After reading it, he could understand why Raine was upset.

"Man, I feel like this is all my fault," Nick said.

"Yours? No way. Don't go riding on some guilt trip. It's my dad's fault. . .and my mother's for not standing up to him all these years." Raine closed the distance between them, wrapped her arms around his waist, and rested her cheek against his chest. "It was bound to happen sooner or later, Nick. Maybe my father has wanted to disown me since I was old enough to talk back."

"I'll give him a phone call."

"Don't waste your breath. It won't do any good."

"Maybe he'll come around. . .like Grandpa did."

"Yeah, maybe in twenty years."

Nick draped his arm around her shoulders, hugging her to him. He touched his lips to her forehead. "We've got each other," he whispered. "And you're all I'll ever need."

Raine lifted her gaze as more tears filled her eyes. "I love you, Nick. . .but just look at me. I'm an emotional mess."

"You're a beautiful mess." He chuckled lightly as she swallowed the last of her tears and looked at him askance.

"A beautiful. . .mess?"

"Guess I'm no poet, eh?"

Raine shook her head, smiling. "Stick to painting."

"Okay, but I can cook, too. Let me prove it. I'll go to the grocery store and pick up a few things, and I'll create the best meal you've ever tasted, Raine. What are you hungry for?"

A thoughtful expression crossed her delicate features, and then she laughed softly, the dimple in her cheek winking at him. "It might sound weird, but I've been dying for a helping of meatloaf for two weeks."

Nick wrinkled his nose. "Meatloaf?" It wasn't one of his favorite dishes.

"Please. . . ?"

One glance at her pleading greenish-brown eyes and he acquiesced at once. "Sure. Meatloaf it is."

"And chocolate ice cream."

Nick frowned. "You mean, like, in the meatloaf? I've heard of strange cravings before, but—"

"No, silly. For dessert." She giggled.

"Oh, right. Chocolate ice cream. Right."

Raine laughed again, and Nick left the apartment. His love for his new wife swelled in his heart as he congratulated himself on making her happy just now. He thought he'd do just about anything for her. Seeing Raine smile made it all worthwhile.

Graduation day came and went in a whirl of events. But the very next morning, Nick loaded up his blue Volkswagen bus, stuffing in every last item from his and Raine's apartment. And then they hit the road.

"I don't feel like a student anymore," Raine remarked, when they drove away from the campus. "My life is totally different from my single friends' now that I'm married and expecting a baby."

"Do you regret it?" Nick asked.

She glanced at him in mild surprise. "No, of course I don't regret it. I love you, Nick. What would I do without you?"

He looked pleased by her reply, and Raine wondered why he always seemed so insecure about her feelings for him. She did the best she could to assure him she'd never change her mind—she'd never leave him. But Raine struggled with her own emotional ups and downs lately, and it wasn't always easy to be the strong, confident wife Nick seemed to need.

"Hey, Raine," he said, pulling her from her reverie, "did you hear what happened in California a few days ago?"

"No, what?"

"Well, students on the Berkeley campus were joined by some street people and other revolutionaries and they staged a major protest outside People's Park."

"People's Park?"

"Yeah. It's a site the university had decided to build dormitories on, but the kids took it over and renamed it. I can't believe you haven't heard about this."

Raine shook her head. "I've been busy packing. Guess I'm out of touch."

"Well, that's okay," Nick encouraged her, "I'm glad to bring you up to date."

"So, what happened?"

"The university called the police and they put up a huge fence to keep everyone out, but that started a huge riot. Police used tear gas and the works. Finally the national guard was called in and they sprayed the protestors with the same stuff used against the Vietcong over in Nam."

"Oh, wow!" Raine couldn't believe it.

"All in all, nine hundred arrests were made, two hundred suffered injuries, and one death was reported."

"Man, the revolution is, like, happening!"

"No, Raine, nothing's happening," Nick stated flatly, "because revolutionary methods aren't bringing about change. We can't be fooled. Violence breeds violence, and death is death, whether people die protesting the war or fighting in it." He paused for a long, pensive moment. "Sometimes all this rioting and destruction blows my mind. It's wrong. The radicals are wrong!"

Raine studied her husband's profile as he sat behind the wheel of the VW. He wore an intense expression, the one she found so utterly attractive, yet his cause had shifted. He no longer sided with SDS and the radicals who promoted the coming revolution; instead he took a stand against them. It confused Raine. It worried Raine.

"Nick, don't turn into my old man, that's all I've got to say!"

"What are you talking about?"

"You. You're becoming part of the establishment."

"No, I'm not. I'm just somewhere in the middle, balancing in between. I mean, look, Raine, I've got to work and support you and our kid, right? Well, that alone makes me seem 'establishment.' But I'm just being responsible. And I can't very well defend an organization that's advocating violence. . .even if it furthers the same cause I support."

"Yeah, well, that makes sense. . .I guess. Oh, Nick, you're messing with my mind!"

He laughed. "No, Raine," he said, throwing her a heart-melting smile, "I think we're both just growing up."

Chapter 5

R aine watched the uneven rise and fall of the old man's chest, certain that the next breath he took would be his last. Two months had gone by since they'd moved in with him, and Grandpa had surpassed his six-month life expectancy; however, Raine doubted he'd live till Christmas. He was sure to die any day now. He looked so worn and depleted.

She shifted her weight on the sofa, trying to make her rapidly growing body as comfortable as possible, and glanced around the living room. The wall clock, the framed photograph of Nick's grandparents on their fiftieth wedding anniversary, a childhood portrait of Nick's father. . .the collection caused Raine to feel lonely and incomplete.

She sighed, wishing Nick would hurry up and get back from his visit with the Stoddards. Pastor Jim was scheduled to speak tomorrow night at a nearby college, and Nick had volunteered to help prepare the presentation on the necessity of non-violent anti-war demonstrations. Raine yawned just thinking about it. Lately, the subject bored her. She couldn't get into it. Besides, someone needed to stay home with Grandpa, and she actually enjoyed taking care of him.

She looked down at her watch. Almost time for his nightly pain medication.

Situating herself once more, she allowed her gaze to roam over the various knickknacks in the two matching, glass-encased curio cabinets before it came to rest on the painting hanging proudly above the mantel. It depicted a serene panorama complete with an old-fashioned-looking house and some outbuildings. Was it a farm?

"My grandmother painted that picture," the old man fairly croaked.

Raine jolted. "I thought you were sleeping."

"I woke up and saw you admiring the painting."

"Yes. . ."

"The homestead was called Laurelwood, and the original home stood in Pennsylvania. But my grandfather, Blake Malone, had an identical house constructed in Eau Claire, Wisconsin, where he owned a lumber mill."

"He appreciated the architecture that much, huh?"

"Oh, no, my dear," the old man said with a trembling smile. "My grandmother was so lonesome for her home in Pennsylvania, that my grandfather built her a replica."

"Wow. . .he must have loved her a lot."

"He did."

Raine smiled. "So your grandparents fell in love and lived happily ever after. That's really beautiful, man."

"Well, not quite. They had only been married a few years when Blake enlisted in Colonel Hans Christian Heg's 15th Wisconsin Infantry. My grandfather died a hero's death at the Battle of Chickamauga in September of 1863. Leah was expecting her third child at the time."

"How incredibly sad." For a moment Raine couldn't breathe. Tears stung the backs of her eyes. "Poor Leah, losing the man she loved."

"She never remarried either, even as young as she was when he died. Leah remained faithful to Blake's memory."

Raine sniffed. "Oh, now, Grandpa, don't make me cry. I practically sob over everything these days!" She swatted a tear as it made its escape down her cheek.

He chuckled, a dry, rasping sound. "My Betsy was that way, too."

As Raine fought for composure, she realized she was hearing history firsthand. . .well almost firsthand. Close enough. "Grandpa," she said, rising from the sofa in one quick motion, "don't say another word. I want to get some paper and write down what you're telling me."

The old man looked pleased. "In the desk drawer, dear. There's paper in the desk drawer. . .and while you're up, bring me my pills."

Raine accumulated Grandpa's medicine, a glass of water, a tablet of paper, and a pen. The old man swallowed the prescribed drugs while Raine quickly documented the story he'd just told her about Blake Malone's death in the Civil War.

"Tell me some more, Grandpa," she said once he settled back in his chair.

"You're a charming young lady."

Raine felt her cheeks warm at the compliment. "I think you're the first person over thirty to say such a thing. My father disowned me, that's how 'charming' he finds me!"

"He'll be sorry," the old man replied. "I spent so many

years feeling angry and bitter over my circumstances, that it nearly cost me my grandson. I was so blind, stubborn. . . ignorant."

"Don't get uptight about it, Grandpa. That's in the past. As for my dad. . .well, he'll probably soften up. He can never stay mad at me for very long."

"I hope not."

"Now, tell me more about the Malone family."

His gaze narrowed as he studied the painting. "Leah stayed in Wisconsin and my parents inherited the house. I was raised there. But, after I married Betsy, we moved to Ohio because I wanted to farm. It was an adjustment. . . for the both of us."

"Nick said you owned the land all around this subdivision."

"That's right. Sold it for a pretty penny, too. But my money didn't take away the pain of losing my son and wife. They meant everything to me." He paused. "I think that's why God took them."

Raine frowned, confused. "Why would God do that? Pastor Jim says God is good and full of love."

"Yes, but He is also a jealous God. To my shame, I can honestly say that I loved my family more than I loved my Lord."

"That sort of scares me," Raine admitted, wondering if God would send a bolt from out of the blue in her direction.

The old man merely grinned. "The fear of the Lord is the beginning of wisdom, my dear. Now, about the painting, Betsy and I received it as a wedding gift from my parents back in 1899. . . ."

Raine wrote furiously for the next hour. She wouldn't have guessed the dying man had the strength or gumption to chatter on the way he did. As she listened, however, she learned more about her husband and acquired a new appreciation of him. Moreover, she began feeling connected to him and the rest of the Malones.

"Nick was a smart lad," Grandpa recounted, going off on another of his rabbit trails, "and he had a smart mouth to match, not to mention a knack of getting himself into all kinds of scrapes. At eighty-one years old, I neither had the patience nor the will to tolerate an adolescent. Course, that wasn't Nick's fault. . . ."

The old man paused, wearing a rueful expression, and gradually his breathing slowed. Raine waited for him to continue, but after several minutes ticked by, she realized he'd fallen asleep. Looking down at the papers in her lap, she began thinking over everything she'd written and wondered what the future held for her and Nick. . .as a family.

Family. She'd taken hers for granted over the years. Certainly her parents weren't without their problems, but they were still her parents, and as odd as it seemed, she missed them.

Standing, Raine stretched her back and patted her protruding belly affectionately before walking into the kitchen. She poured herself a glass of water and stared at the telephone, wondering if she ought to call. Perhaps she could effectively reason with her father if they weren't glaring at each other.

She lifted the receiver and dialed the familiar number. She listened to it ring at the other end while her heart pounded anxiously.

"Bartley residence."

Raine paused. The words seemed stuck in her throat.

"Hello? Someone there?"

"Dad?"

Silence.

"Dad, it's me. Will you talk to me?"

"What do you need, money?"

"No."

"What then?"

"Nothing. I don't need anything. I just. . .well, I wanted to say I'm. . ." Raine swallowed hard. "I'm sorry."

Her father laughed, and Raine cringed at its bitter sound. "Marriage isn't what you thought, huh? That long-haired hippy dumped you already. Where are you, some bus depot?"

"No, Dad. Marriage is cool. Nick's great. I guess. . . well, I'm getting into the family thing, that's all. I thought maybe we could talk."

"Don't call here anymore. Got it?"

"But, Dad—"

The decisive click in her ear caused Raine a moment of heart-wrenching sorrow.

"Who's on the line?"

She turned suddenly to find Nick standing at the doorway. His face was tanned from doing yard work earlier in the day, and his shoulder-length blond hair shone like brass beneath the fluorescent kitchen bulb. "I didn't hear you come in."

"I just got here."

Raine nodded and hung up the receiver. "I called home and tried to talk with my father. You know, I think he might have taken me back if I'd said my marriage wasn't working out or I needed something. . .like his money. I don't think he can stand it that I'm not dependent on him anymore. I mean, even my older brother, the big ROTC freak, relies on Dad for everything."

Nick walked slowly toward her. Reaching out a hand, he stroked her cheek. "Want me to try?"

Raine shrugged. "Sure, except it won't help." Closing her eyes, she leaned into his caress. "I missed you tonight, but your grandfather and I had a great time rapping about the Malone family history."

"Groovy," Nick replied, sounding distracted.

Opening her eyes, Raine met his gaze and hoped the longing she saw in it would dissipate so they could discuss the foremost issue on her heart. Family.

"I wrote down everything your grandfather said. You know, so we can share it with our kids. . .their heritage. . . Nick, are you listening?"

"Yeah." He gathered her into his arms and nibbled at her neck.

Raine pushed at his chest. "Could we, like, have a conversation here?"

He snapped to attention. "Sure."

"I recorded your family history. Isn't that cool?"

"That's out of sight, baby," he replied, doing his best to look interested.

"It got me thinking about the whole family thing, Nick, and I felt this overwhelming urge to call my folks."

"Hm. . .but your dad didn't have an open mind, I take it."

"Are you kidding? My dad's mind is as closed as East Germany."

Chuckling, he released her. "Let me try talking to him."

"All right, but it's at your own risk."

Raine recited the phone number and watched Nick dial it. Then she stood beside him, waiting nervously.

"Yes. . .Mr. Bartley? It's Nick Malone."

Raine placed a hand over her mouth and watched in disappointment as Nick attempted to reason with an irrational man.

"Mr. Bartley, I'm not deaf," he stated hotly. "Stop shouting." Nick held the phone away from his ear, and Raine heard her father curse.

"Hang up, Nick," she insisted in a hushed tone. "You don't have to put up with that abuse."

Despite her request, he tried once more. "Mr. Bartley, listen for a minute, will you? Man!" Nick finally slammed the receiver into its cradle. "Raine, I love you, but your dad is one. . ." He caught himself.

"Say it, Nick. You'll feel better. Call him every name you can think of."

He shook his head. "No, that won't solve anything."

"Want me to do it for you? It'd make me feel better." She smiled at him, and at last, he chuckled.

"You're beautiful, know that?"

Before a glib retort could even take shape in her head, Nick leaned forward and pressed his lips against hers in a sweet kiss. As it deepened, Raine slipped her arms around his neck, reveling in the fact that her husband cherished her even if her father felt quite the opposite.

"I love you," she murmured against his mouth.

"Mm. . .I love you, too."

Grandpa's hoarse voice suddenly wafted in from the living room. "Would one of you two *lovebirds* mind helping an old man to his bed?"

Reluctantly, Nick disengaged himself from Raine's embrace, and she saw a moment's frustration flicker in his teal-blue eyes. "Coming, Grandpa." To Raine, he whispered, "Nothing's wrong with his hearing, that's for sure!"

She laughed. "I'll take care of him tonight," she offered. "I don't mind, and I can see you're tired."

"I won't argue."

"And while I'm getting Grandpa settled, you can read my notes. They're on the sofa."

At Nick's look of resignation, Raine strolled into the living room and assisted the old man up from his recliner.

"You're a darling girl," he told her.

"And you're a darling old man," she returned.

"I'm ninety-one, you know."

"Yeah, I heard that rumor." Raine sent a wink in Nick's direction.

"Too bad you're not seventy years older," the elderly man stated with a twinkle in his liquid blue eyes.

Raine inhaled sharply before expelling a surprised laugh. Seeing Nick's wide-eyed expression, she burst into hysterics. "Why, Mr. Malone," she said at last, feigning indignation, "I'm a married woman, you know!"

"I know, I know. . ."

He chuckled, sputtered, and coughed the rest of the way down the hall to his bedroom. There, Raine helped him out of his bathrobe and hung it on the hook on back of the door. Clad in his pajamas, he painstakingly maneuvered his frail body onto the double bed. Raine covered him with the quilt and placed a kiss on his forehead.

"G'night, Grandpa."

He squeezed his eyes shut and the expression on his face registered the agony he felt as the cancer coursed through his already ravaged body. Then, slowly, his features relaxed. He sighed. "Goodnight, Betsy."

Startled, Raine brought her chin back. Betsy? His wife? She shook her head and readied an explanation but thought better of it. What could it possibly hurt if she allowed this dying man to believe his beloved wife had tended to his most basic needs? Besides, she reasoned as she switched off the lamp beside his bed, he'd most likely become confused between his pain medication and all the reminiscing.

The matter settled in her own mind, Raine crept out of the room and silently closed the door behind her.

Chapter 6

R aine, wake up. . .Raine?"

She opened sleepy eyes and found Nick leaning over her, giving her shoulder a mild shake.

"Raine, wake up."

"I'm awake. What time is it?"

"Six o'clock."

"In the morning?"

He nodded.

"It's too early to wake up," she protested, rolling over onto her side.

"Raine, it's Grandpa."

Concerned now, she turned over and sat up. "What about him?"

Nick swallowed hard. "He's dead."

"What?"

Solemnly, he nodded. "I got up a few minutes ago to get something to drink and for whatever reason I decided to check on him." He paused, looking both sad and scared. "That's when I found him. Must have died in his sleep."

"Oh, Nick. . ." Raine gulped down the onset of sorrow welling inside her. "He was so talkative last night when he told me all about the Malone family. . ."

"I know. . ." Nick paused. "What do I do now, Raine? I mean, about Grandpa's body?"

She shrugged. "I don't know."

"Who do I call?"

"Beats me." She thought it over anyway. "How about the doctor?"

"What's he going to do?"

Again, Raine shrugged helplessly. "Didn't Grandpa leave some instructions?"

"Yeah, but they're all about his funeral wishes, his will, and the lawyers. He's got it written down and in a lockbox in his room. He gave me the key." Nick's voice broke. "Raine, he's dead. Dead!"

Kneeling on the bedcovers, she put a consoling arm around him and kissed the top of his head.

"Man, six months ago, I couldn't have cared less if Grandpa died. Now I feel like I lost a friend or something."

Raine's vision blurred with unshed emotion. "I know what you mean," she said, sniffling.

Nick brought his equally moist gaze to hers. For long moments they stared at each other before their tears fell freely.

"Stupid old man," Nick muttered, wiping his eyes. "I hated him when I was growing up. When I came to see him last February for the first time in years, it was to con-front him, not befriend him."

"But aren't you glad you did?" Raine asked softly.

"Yeah," he admitted, smiling in spite of himself. "Grandpa knew he hadn't done a good job raising me, and he felt sorry about it. . .and now I *know* he was sorry about it." Nick paused and put his fingers in Raine's long, thick hair, gently combing it back off her face. "What was it that Moira Stoddard once said? 'The truth will set you free?' Well, I guess by reconciling with my grandfather, I learned the truth. I won't have to spend the rest of my life wondering if he ever. . .loved me. I know he did."

Touched by the sentiment, Raine could only nod a reply.

"Maybe I'll call Jim. He can tell me what to do next. What do you think?"

"Good idea."

Taking her hand, Nick helped her off the bed and together they walked to the kitchen telephone. As he dialed the Stoddards' number, Raine felt the baby move within her womb. She cast her gaze down the hallway, toward Grandpa's bedroom, and marveled at the irony. She carried life in this room, but death lay in the next.

Raine shook her head, dispelling the heavy thoughts, yet she'd always been a deep thinker. More so since her pregnancy. She smirked inwardly, recalling what her father used to say: "Amy, that's your problem. . .you think too much!"

"Sorry to wake you up, Jim," Nick said into the telephone receiver, "but I thought you should know. . . Grandpa died."

Raine moved to the sink and filled the percolator with water. Opening the cupboard, she found the coffee and added the grounds before plugging it in. Pivoting, she watched Nick hang up the phone.

"Jim's on his way over and he suggested I call an ambulance." He smiled, looking chagrined. "I suppose if

I hadn't freaked out after finding Grandpa dead a few minutes ago, I would have come to that conclusion myself."

Raine gave him a weak grin, and Nick placed the next phone call. After requesting an ambulance and giving their address, he set the receiver back in its cradle. Facing Raine once more, a sober expression crossed his features.

"Do you think we should go in there and. . .well, say good-bye before the ambulance gets here?"

"Go ahead if it'll make you feel better," Raine said, "but I want to remember your grandfather the way he was last night. Alive."

Nick nodded thoughtfully.

"Besides," she added, "if what Jim says is true, Grandpa's not in there anymore, so it's too late to say good-bye." She shuddered. "Man, I'm getting bad vibes. I've never had to deal with death before."

"I have," Nick replied stoically. "And it's dark and lonely—at least it is for those of us left behind."

"And those who have passed away. . . ? "

She didn't expect an answer, but Nick replied just the same.

"I'll bet Grandpa's found eternal peace. My parents, too. My grandfather told me they were Christians. I suppose it's not dark and lonely for them."

"So you think there's something to it, huh? Religion?"

"Maybe," he said with a hint of a smile tugging at the corners of his lips. "I mean it sounds right when I listen to Jim talk about being born again, but I'm just not completely convinced. How can there be only one way to heaven when the world is full of so many different beliefs? When I asked Jim that question, he said various religions exist because man corrupted the truth of the Bible."

"Yeah, and you sound just like Pastor Jim," Raine quipped.

He gave her a furtive glance, then strode purposefully toward their room, where he quickly dressed. Raine followed and pulled on a bathrobe, covering her long nightshirt.

Shortly thereafter, the ambulance arrived.

While Nick led the attendants to his grandfather's room, Raine poured herself a cup of coffee and walked out to the backyard patio. Why did she feel so surprised at Grandpa's passing? She'd known it was coming. However, it almost seemed as though she'd secretly hoped he would conquer the inevitable.

Death.

It happened to everyone.

There was no escaping it.

Raine lifted her tearful gaze to the azure August sky. "God, if You're really up there," she prayed mournfully, "would You show me the truth about death, so the truth will set me free?"

The elder Nicholas Parker Malone was laid to rest on August 17, 1969—the last day of the Woodstock Music and Art Fair on Max Yasgur's farm in New York. A reported 450,000 young people attended, tripping out on drugs while listening to the non-stop music. It was also the same day Hurricane Camille blew her fury through Louisiana, Mississippi, and Alabama. Thousands of residents fled to safety, but many others paid no heed to the storm warnings and stayed in Camille's destructive path. Consequently, some four hundred people were killed.

Days later, Raine and Nick sat in the living room of Grandpa's house with the Stoddards, discussing a gamut of topics, including the funeral, Woodstock, and the storm whose aftermath was still being televised.

"Part of me wished I could have been at that concert," Raine stated. "I can really groove to Jefferson Airplane; Blood, Sweat, & Tears; and Joan Baez. But the other part of me is glad I missed it. I mean, when I saw pictures on TV of the twenty-mile-long traffic jam, the field of mud, and the piles of garbage everyone left behind, I was disappointed with my generation."

Nick agreed. "I heard a report that said the drug use was phenomenal. Those kids didn't have their heads together for four days."

"Wow." The pastor shook his head in wonder. "Sounds like Satan is having a great time altering the states of those young people's minds. Makes me almost wish Hurricane Camille would have hit that part of New York and forestalled the rock 'n' roll, drugs, and indiscriminate sex. No doubt there are damaged lives out there today because of that concert."

"Think so?" Raine asked. She didn't see how—unless someone took an overdose.

Jim nodded. "I just wish more young people would listen to God like they listen to tripped-out rock stars."

"You've got a point there," Nick said, looking thoughtful.

"You know," Moira said gently, "Jim mentioned the

recent hurricane, and I can see a spiritual comparison between it and so many of our generation losing their way. It's as if God gives all of us a storm warning, just like the residents in the South received—except God's warning is in the Bible. He says, 'If thou shalt confess with thy mouth the Lord Jesus, and shalt believe in thine heart that God hath raised him from the dead, thou shalt be saved.' And that's saved from eternal death. But those who don't listen to God's forecast are going to be like the people who were killed by the hurricane—the ones who perished."

"Wow, Moira, that's really heavy," Raine replied, feeling somewhat impressed by the woman's analogy. Since Grandpa's death, she had gotten to know Moira Stoddard better and decided the woman was cool, even if she did quote the Bible all the time. There was a genuineness about her, and she had a love for their generation which Raine admired. The fact that they were both expecting babies gave them something in common.

"Do you believe it, Raine?" Moira asked. "Do you believe what I just said about God's warning to mankind?"

"Sort of. I don't know. . . ."

Beside her on the couch, Nick nodded thoughtfully. "Religion is one heavy trip, man."

"Doesn't have to be," Jim observed. "It's the indecision that's weighing you down."

"Indecision? Hm. . .maybe you're right."

Raine stood. "Who wants more lemonade?"

No one replied affirmatively, so she strode into the kitchen and refilled her own glass. When she returned to the living room, Nick was handing Jim some papers.

"Looks like Grandpa left everything to me—all except

for an allotted amount he wanted to go to the church."

Nodding, the pastor scrutinized the legal forms. "What are you going to do? Sell the place?"

"No. Raine and I think we'll stay. Might as well, seeing as we need a home in which to raise our family."

"Good." Jim smiled, looking pleased. "I've been praying you'd stick around."

"I'm going to do some job hunting, but it's nice to know we've got some dough to fall back on for a while."

"You'll need it for hospital expenses," Moira stated knowingly.

"No way," Raine interjected, reclaiming her place on the sofa beside Nick. "I'm not delivering my baby in a hospital with all those cold, indifferent doctors and nurses. I'm giving birth at home. Here. And Nick is going to be present for the whole thing. I mean, this is his kid, too."

"Yeah," he agreed, "I don't want to be banished to some impersonal waiting room while Raine has the baby."

"Well, I suggest you two have a backup plan," Jim said. "Just in case something goes wrong."

"I'm perfectly healthy," Raine insisted. "What could possibly go wrong?"

Chapter 7

As the summer months reached an end, Raine found herself spending more and more time with Moira Stoddard. Nick had found a factory job soon after his grandfather's death, and when he left each morning, Raine felt alone and out of touch with the world. But the Stoddards' lively household cured her melancholy. Their four children, two boys and two girls, had energy enough to power the State of Ohio, and Moira was relieved when Levi and Dinah, the two oldest, were back in school.

But now Raine's baby was almost two weeks overdue.

"Man, I wish this kid would hurry up and come!" she lamented in the Stoddards' kitchen while Moira started supper.

"I wish you'd see a doctor," her friend retorted, throwing a long thatch of dark-brown hair over her shoulder.

Raine gave her a hooded glance before breaking into a smile. "You're such a little mother. But I'm a big girl, and I say no doctors!"

Moira shrugged as she stood at the counter, chopping an onion for the casserole.

"I'm healthy," Raine insisted, feeling as though she had to win Moira to her side. "And both Nick and I have been reading all the prenatal and delivery books available."

"I know. You've told me before."

"Oh, but I didn't tell you this part," Raine added enthusiastically. "Nick met a doctor on the assembly line at work who told him there's nothing to delivering a baby and he wrote out detailed instructions for him. . .us."

Moira raised a skeptical brow. "If he's such a good doctor, why is he working at a factory?"

"He hated conforming to hospital rules. Everything's money, you know? This guy just loves people."

Again, Moira shrugged out a reply, and Raine could tell she didn't approve.

"Hey, can I help you do something?"

"No," Moira replied. "Everything's cool."

"Are you sure you don't mind that Nick and I stay for dinner?"

"I would not have asked if I minded, silly," Moira said with a little laugh, her deep brown eyes twinkling amusedly.

Raine smiled. "Good. Then I'll just sit here and concentrate on having this baby." She paused before adding, "Mind power, you know?"

"How 'bout God power instead?"

Raine didn't reply, but stood and stretched her aching back. She allowed her gaze to rove over the green-and-yellow flowered paper on the kitchen walls and the white lacy curtains. In the corner by one of the windows, a brown macramé hanger dangled from a hook in the ceiling and cradled a potted leafy plant. Raine wanted to change the subject but knew it wouldn't do any good. As a pastor's wife, Moira took the role seriously and she could preach as well as her husband if afforded the opportunity.

"Raine, what's stopping you from accepting Christ?"

"I don't know," she replied honestly. "Maybe it's my church background and the hypocrisy I saw growing up. I just don't want to become one of *them.*"

"I can understand that reasoning. I hope I never become a hypocrite. But I wish you wouldn't let things people have done in the past stand in the way of your relationship with the Savior. He's trustworthy."

Raine watched as Moira stirred the onion into the ground beef before slicing a green pepper. Nibbling her lower lip in consternation, she sensed that what Moira and Jim said about the Bible was the truth. On the other hand, she was scared—scared that conforming to Christianity would put an end to her individuality.

"Moira, let me ask you something," Raine hedged. "Since becoming a believer, are you more of your own person?"

"No. I belong to the Lord, not myself."

"See! No way, man. I don't want to be in that kind of bondage!"

"Are you in bondage married to Nick?"

Raine thought it over. "No, but he's like I am. We respect each other's space and accept one another for who we are."

"So does the Lord Jesus. He didn't create mankind to be puppets, He created them to reflect the many unique facets of His glory. It's not bondage to belong to Him. It's a pleasure." Moira paused before adding, "And I think if you'd stop and be honest with yourself for a moment, you'd agree, otherwise, you wouldn't be hanging out with me as much as you do. I've got something you want, Raine."

Folding her arms stubbornly, Raine walked to the screen door where she spied the two youngest Stoddard children playing on their backyard swing set. Moira was right; she did have something Raine wanted. It was that warm, peaceful ambience that enveloped her each time she entered her friend's home. Raine had begun to wonder if her own gloomy feelings were attributable to Grandpa's dying in their house—as if death still prevailed. It was one of the reasons she'd decided to give birth to her baby there. She wanted to, literally, bring life back into the place. Conversely, a vibrancy abounded here at the Stoddards'.

She turned from the doorway just as Moira slipped the casserole into the oven. She coveted the other woman's sunny disposition. True, she wasn't perfect. Raine had seen her impatience with the children at times. But even so, there was an undercurrent of love that surged from Moira to the kids and from Moira to Jim. And yes, Raine wanted that for her family. . .love. Peace.

"You know," she said at long last, "maybe it is time I got born again."

Raine wanted to laugh at Moira's shocked expression. She recovered quickly, however, and waved her into the living room.

"Let's pray right now."

Together they knelt near the sofa, and after taking Raine's hands, Moira led her in a simple prayer:

"Dear God, I'm confessing with my mouth that I am a lost sinner and that Jesus Christ died for my sins. I'm now asking the Lord Jesus to come into my heart and save me. I accept Him as my Savior and pray this in His holy name. Amen."

"Did you mean it, Raine? What you just prayed?"

"Of course I did."

"Then you just got saved!" Moira raised her hands and lifted her gaze. "Thank You, Lord!" she cried happily.

Raine smiled and glanced around. "So where's the earthquake and the thunderbolt?" she teased.

Moira laughed merrily. "I don't know about that, but I do know the angels are rejoicing in heaven right now."

And deep within her heart of hearts, Raine rejoiced too.

Nick arrived from work, and Jim came home shortly thereafter. Moira served the casserole, and Raine decided their dinner proved little better than a circus, what with the kids' boisterous clambering around the table.

After finishing the meal, the children were promptly scooted outside with a Popsicle. Raine helped Moira wash dishes, and once the kitchen looked orderly, they joined the men on the patio.

"Moira has been needling me all night to tell you guys something," Raine announced, feeling more than a little embarrassed, though she couldn't imagine why.

From the cushioned lawn chair, Nick glanced at her expectantly. Jim, too, gave her his attention.

"I converted today. I'm a Christian."

Jim jumped to his feet. "All right! Out of sight!" he

cheered, causing Raine to break into a fit of laughter.

Nick stood and gave her a hug. "I got saved too," he whispered. "Happened a few days after Grandpa died."

Raine pulled back, frowning. "Why didn't you tell me?" She couldn't help feeling somewhat betrayed. She and Nick never kept secrets from each other.

"I didn't want you to feel you had to become a Christian just because I did," Nick said, his teal-blue eyes pleading for understanding. "I wanted you to feel free to accept the Lord all on your own. But I've been praying for you every day since my conversion."

"You have?"

He nodded.

Raine shrugged in acquiescence. She believed him and could hardly be angry with him when he'd only been thinking of her welfare. And he *prayed* for her? Far out!

Nick smiled in obvious understanding. Then he looked down at Raine's extended abdomen. "Man," he said, "it's like there's a basketball between us."

"I know the feeling," the pastor interjected with a little laugh.

The street lights cast long shadows onto the pavement as Nick and Raine drove home later that night. The neighborhood seemed strangely silent. No kids riding their bikes. No teenagers blaring rock 'n' roll from car radios as they cruised by. Nick grinned, thinking, *Oh, yeah, school's in session again and they've all got homework!* He couldn't say he minded the quiet, it would just take some getting used to.

They entered the house, and Raine began talking at

once. "Maybe if I paint in here. . .wouldn't that brighten things up?"

Nick nodded.

"And I could wallpaper the kitchen with a sunny design. Cheery, you know?"

"That's cool."

He followed Raine down the hallway to the third bedroom of the house which housed the crib, changing table, small white dresser, and rocking chair.

"Do you think we'll have a boy or girl?"

Nick chuckled. "Raine, you ask me that at least ten times a day. I don't know what we're having."

"Which do you want?"

"Either. . .I don't care. I told you before."

She spun on her heel and threw her arms around his neck. "I love you."

"I love you, too." He kissed her, then added, "Seeing you so happy makes me happy."

"I'm totally happy," she insisted, her hazel eyes smiling into his. "I've got the most wonderful husband in the whole world."

Nick kissed her once more, enjoying the taste of her lips, the way her body, heavy with child, felt in his arms. The pastoral scene his great-great-grandmother painted so long ago flittered through his mind. Home. Home at last. . .with a family of his own.

Raine pushed away. "I have to use the bathroom," she whispered, looking embarrassed.

Nick chuckled softly. In this late stage of her pregnancy, Raine had to do that a lot. While she ambled down the hallway in one direction, he went in the other.

Entering the living room, he turned on the television set.

"Nick. . . ?"

"Yeah?" he replied distractedly, changing channels.

"Nick, come here quick!"

Instantly, he forgot the TV and rushed toward the bathroom. Raine stood at the door. A large, wet stain soaked the legs of her maternity pants.

"My bag of waters just broke," she said smiling. "Looks like we're going to have a baby tonight."

"Really?" Nick's mind reeled. "Okay, don't panic."

She laughed. "I'm not."

He shook his head. "No, I meant *me!*" He paced several steps. "Okay, what do I do first?"

"Get the bed ready," Raine prompted. "Remember? The sterile sheets and stuff I prepared?"

"Oh, right."

Nick ran through the house, gathering the necessary materials, then pulled the sheets off their bed before quickly remaking it. His heart hammered anxiously the entire time.

Meanwhile, Raine had changed into a large night shirt. She looked relaxed, confident, and extremely pleased their child was finally making its entrance into the world.

"If it's a girl, I want to name her Betsy," Raine said, climbing into bed. "After your grandmother."

"Fine," Nick replied nervously. "Are you feeling okay?"

"I'm feeling great. If it's a boy, I want to name him Nicholas Parker—after Grandpa and you, of course. We'll call him Nicky. Isn't that cute?"

Nick wiped the perspiration from his brow. "I hated

it when people called me Nicky."

Raine laughed, and then a contraction hit. She squeezed her eyes closed as an expression of anguish crossed her face.

"Maybe I'd better call an ambulance," Nick said. "I don't think I can handle this."

"Forget the ambulance. I'm fine," she insisted. "It's just going to hurt for a while until I get the urge to push. That's what Moira told me, and she ought to know!"

"Raine, I've got bad vibes about this home delivery thing."

"Here comes another contraction," she announced, ignoring his comment. "That was fast. The closer they are together, the sooner the baby will come."

Against his better judgement, Nick waited it out, sitting beside Raine in bed and timing her contractions. It seemed to take forever, and he occasionally dozed. Finally, six hours later, at three in the morning, she felt the urge to push.

"Get ready, Nick," she panted.

"Maybe I should call the ambulance now."

"No, the worst is over. Our baby is about to be born. Do you have the camera ready?"

"Yeah, but taking a picture is the last thing I feel like doing."

"Well, I certainly can't take one. . .I'm sort of busy." She attempted a laugh before bearing down and moaning with exertion.

At last a slippery, bluish-gray human being emerged, letting out an immediate cry that surprised both parents.

"Crying means the baby's breathing," Raine said,

collapsing against the pillows. "What is it?"

"Huh?" Nick was trying desperately to determine what to do next.

"Nick, is it a boy or a girl?"

"Oh. . ." He checked, then smiled at Raine. "It's a girl."

"Betsy," Raine murmured with a sweetly. "Can I hold her?"

"Um, yeah. . .but first let me figure out what's supposed to happen here first."

Raine, who had read every childbirth book in the public library, walked him through the final steps and delivered the placenta.

"See, wasn't that simple?" she asked as Nick placed their child in her arms.

"Next kid you have in the hospital," he muttered, glad the event was over.

Raine shrugged off the retort. "Take a picture," she urged him.

"All right."

Nick grabbed the camera, focused the lens, and snapped several shots. He had to admit, Raine looked beautiful, even after nearly eight hours of labor. Her chestnut-colored hair framed her delicate facial features while adoring hazel eyes looked at their daughter.

"You'll make a great mother," Nick said smiling at the two most important females in his life.

"Thanks."

Raine began to nurse the baby while Nick dallied at the bedside for a few minutes, watching in awe. The miracle of a new life. He felt overwhelmed by it. If he'd ever doubted the existence of God, he didn't anymore. Only an Almighty Creator could engineer such an intricacy as life.

Standing, he finally disposed of the soiled sheets. In the kitchen, he stretched and made a pot of coffee before preparing to phone his boss and tell him he wouldn't be in to work.

"Nick? Nick, come here I need you!"

The urgency in Raine's voice brought him quickly back into the bedroom.

"Nick, I'm not feeling so good," Raine said. "Take the baby. . . ."

Seeing her ashen face, Nick took the now-sleeping child and set her beside Raine.

"Nick. . ." She held out her hand.

He took it, noticing it felt ice-cold. "Raine, what's wrong?"

A throaty moan escaped her lips and her eyes rolled back before she lost consciousness. Nick rushed to the kitchen and phoned the ambulance, wishing he'd done so hours ago. Once he felt sure medical personnel were on their way, he returned to the bedroom. Raine lay listlessly against the pillows, looking deathly pale. Frightened, Nick sat on the bed and gathered her into his arms. She was cold. So cold. . . .

"Raine, open your eyes, baby." He gently patted her face. "Raine, please. . .please!"

Chapter 8

I'm sorry, Mr. Malone," the doctor stated gravely, "we did our best."

Standing in a small, private waiting area of the emergency room, Nick struggled to comprehend the words. "Raine. . . ? "

"Mr. Malone, your wife bled to death after giving birth. Apparently part of the placenta detached and—"

"No!" Nick cried, as if the doctor had any say over life and death. "No, it can't be true!"

"Easy, now, son, I know this is difficult news."

"No!" Nick shook his head. "I want to see her."

"Very well." The doctor sighed wearily. "Come with me."

Nick followed the man through a set of double doors and into a draped room where Raine's lifeless body lay on the sheeted gurney. He closed his eyes against the horror before him. Raine. His precious Raine. Dead.

"No, God, no! Oh, God. . ." The prayerful words caught in his throat as tears fell from his eyes.

"There is some good news," the doctor said. "Your baby daughter is very healthy. She's almost ten pounds, and twenty inches long."

In all his writhing sorrow, Nick could scarcely think of the child. Raine. His beautiful Raine. Gone forever.

The doctor cleared his throat. "Son, is there someone we can call for you? Someone who can come and drive you home?"

"No, there's no one. I have no one. . . ."

"Oh, now, everyone has *someone*," the doctor stated.

"Not me. . . Raine's all I had. . . ."

Slowly, he walked to her bedside and, lifting her motionless hand, he held it in both of his and wept. How long he stood there, he couldn't say. It seemed as if time had no bearing. He felt suspended between reality and the hereafter. Part of him wished he could die with Raine, and part him was already dead.

"Mr. Malone," a soft-spoken nurse said, pulling him from his trance-like state. "Mr. Malone, we need to take care of your wife's body now. I'm sorry, but it's time. . . ."

Logic somehow registered in his hazy brain, and Nick nodded.

"Your daughter is in the nursery on the fourth floor if you'd like to see her."

Again, a nod.

"Is there a funeral home that you'd like to use?"

Nick remembered the one Jim Stoddard had suggested when his grandfather died and he gave the nurse its name. Then, almost reluctantly, he left the emergency room, but he didn't go up to the nursery. He left the hospital and walked through town like a man tripping on drugs, seeing no one, hearing nothing, only aware of himself and the intense pain and incredible sense of loss ravaging his very soul.

Finally as evening began settling around him, Nick felt someone tap his shoulder.

"Huh?" He looked up and saw a policeman eyeing him speculatively.

"The park closes at seven," he said.

Suddenly aware of his surroundings, Nick nodded in acquiescence. "Right. I'll leave."

"If it was up to me, I'd close this park down completely so you hippies couldn't cause so much trouble. Anti-war demonstrations and equal rights protests. . . bah! You're a lot of troublemakers, that's what I say. Now get outa here!"

Nick barely heard the tirade as he left the premises. He walked in the direction of home but didn't feel up to facing it alone, so he ambled over to the Stoddards' place.

Jim answered his knock at the front door. "Hey, man, where've you been? Nick? What's wrong, pal?"

Nick entered the house, and Jim closed the door behind him. "Raine's dead," he blurted out as another onset of tears fairly gushed from his eyes.

Moira came running from the kitchen. "What? What's going on? Did Raine have the baby?"

With painstaking effort, Nick relayed the events, the birth of little Betsy and then Raine's sudden death. Moira covered her mouth, looking horrified before she, too, burst into tears. Jim, misty-eyed as well, slung a brotherly arm around Nick's shoulders.

"I feel like it's my fault," Nick choked. "I must have done something wrong."

"Don't blame yourself," Jim said.

"God. . .why did He let this happen?"

Jim shook his head, looking uncertain. "I don't know. I don't have all the answers. But I do know this: We have to trust God regardless."

Nick thought that was easy for Jim to say since his wife was standing right there, alive and healthy.

"Where's the baby?" Moira asked, her voice thick with sorrow.

"Still at the hospital," Nick replied, collapsing onto the sofa. "I don't know what to do with her." He lifted his hands helplessly. "I don't know the first thing about taking care of a baby!"

"We'll help you."

"You've got your hands full, Moira," Nick replied.

"What about Raine's parents?" Jim asked.

"No way. I wouldn't dream of letting them take care of my kid."

"Do they know? About Raine?"

Nick shook his head. "On the way over here I wondered if you'd agree to make the call for me, Jim. I mean, Raine's old man hates my guts. He's not going to listen to anything I have to say."

"Sure, I'll call her parents for you."

"And the funeral arrangements. . .man, I don't think I can handle them."

"I'll take care of everything, Nick," Moira said.

He sighed, feeling as though his load had lightened somewhat. However, he didn't think the excruciating ache in his heart would ever go away.

Almost exactly one month after burying his grandfather,

Nick buried his wife. Raine's parents never came to the funeral, her father maintaining his daughter had died the day she married "that no good hippy." Nick wasn't surprised.

Cradling his daughter, whom he named Betsy Raine, he listened to Jim read from the Bible at the graveside service: "The LORD is my shepherd; I shall not want. He maketh me to lie down in green pastures; he leadeth me beside the still waters. He restoreth my soul; he leadeth me in the paths of righteousness for his name's sake. Yea, though I walk through the valley of the shadow of death, I will fear no evil; for thou art with me; thy rod and thy staff they comfort me. . . ."

Nick wished this were all a bad dream. He wished he'd awaken and find Raine sleeping beside him in their bed. Gazing down at Betsy, he wondered how he'd ever take care of her. For now, Moira was feeding her bottled infant formula and changing her diapers. But how could he see to her needs and work a job to support them financially too?

As the days progressed, Nick realized the desperateness of his situation. He sat in the living room of his grandfather's home and gazed at the pastoral scene his great-great-grandmother had painted while, down the hall in her bedroom, Betsy screamed her head off. He'd fed her, burped her, changed her. . .what more could he do?

Nick sighed. His deep sense of loss overshadowed everyday life, weighing him down with an indescribable hopelessness. He missed Raine terribly. The baby's incessant cries were getting on his nerves. It suddenly occurred to him that, perhaps, this was how his grandfather had felt. Maybe he'd been so overcome with insurmountable grief that he hadn't been capable of raising a child.

Nick realized it was true enough of himself.

Standing, he walked to the kitchen and dialed the Stoddards' number. "Moira? It's Nick. Can you take care of Betsy again tonight? She won't stop crying." He sighed with relief. "Thanks."

Nick hung up, then strode purposefully into the baby's room, where she lay wailing in her white crib. He tried to shut her cries out of his mind as he packed her things. Finally, he lifted Betsy out of her little white crib, wrapped her in a blanket, and set her in the infant seat Moira had lent him. Outside, he strapped her into the VW's backseat, listening to her bawl all the way to the Stoddards' house. When he arrived, she suddenly quieted and Nick realized she had fallen asleep.

"Thanks a lot, kid," he muttered facetiously, carrying her to the front door.

Moira didn't say a word about the baby's change in disposition, but took Betsy into her arms and carried her off to the cradle which she'd set up in the master bedroom.

I'm a lousy father, Nick lamented inwardly, watching her go.

Turning on his heel, he let himself out of the house. Jim hadn't gotten home from his work at the church yet, and it smelled like Moira was in the process of cooking supper. Nick didn't want to get in the way. Bad enough he'd burdened them with his daughter.

Back at home, it was as quiet as a tomb. Nick wrestled with his circumstances, hating them, cursing them, but knowing there was only one thing he could do.

He'd have to give Betsy up for adoption.

The thought rankled him, saddened him, yet it seemed the only solution.

"Lord, God, I want her to have a home," he said, his voice echoing like thunder as it filled the empty living room. He gazed at the painting, walking slowly toward it, then took it down from its perch. "Home," he said, his tears spilling on the canvas. "A home with parents who'll love her and cherish her the way Raine—" Nick swallowed his abysmal sorrow. "The way Raine and I planned to."

His decision made, he put the painting into his VW and packed the rest of Betsy's meager belongings before driving back over to the Stoddards' place.

Jim's old '58 Chevy sat in the driveway, indicating that he'd arrived home from work. And as usual, he insisted Nick stay for supper.

He didn't argue. It beat being alone.

After they'd eaten and Moira had left to help the kids with their homework, Nick sprung the news on Jim.

"I've decided to give Betsy up for adoption."

Jim winced. "Are you sure, Nick? Things'll get better as she gets older."

Nick shook his head. "No they won't. I can't work and raise a daughter. I'll have to find babysitters—"

"Moira can watch her."

"Moira is busy taking care of your four. . .with another on the way. No. It won't work."

"Nick, this is your daughter. You can't give her away. Think about it."

"I have. And it's for the best," Nick argued. "Look, I love that little girl more than words can say, but I'm not capable of raising her properly, and I can't impose on you and Moira forever. I don't want to give her up. . . ." Nick paused, fighting for control over his emotions. "I hate the thought of giving her away, but in my heart, I feel Betsy deserves a real home with a mom and dad who'll treasure her." He paused, tears filling his eyes. "Don't you know a nice Christian couple who want a child?"

Jim looked resigned to Nick's idea. "Yeah, I do. In fact, our entire church family has been praying with these two because she can't have children and they desperately want a baby."

"Great. But don't tell me who they are. And don't tell them about me. I don't want Betsy knowing she was adopted. Just take her to them. I trust your judgment. Tell them I love her. I'll always love her because she's my little girl, but I can't take care of her. I've tried for the past couple weeks."

"I know you have." Jim paused, wearing a sober expression. "But have you prayed about this Nick?"

"Praying doesn't come easily for me right now. But I know in my heart that I'm doing the right thing. I don't want her to grow up like I did, feeling unloved and unwanted." He hesitated momentarily. "But there is one condition to the adoption, besides keeping the adoption secret. . . ."

Nick rose from the chair he'd been sitting in, walked out to the VW, and retrieved the painting. Carrying the cumbersome object into the house, he set it against the far wall.

"This has to go with Betsy. You don't need to know why and neither do her adoptive parents, it just has to go with her. Make sure you tell the couple who take her."

"I will."

Jim looked misty-eyed as he gazed first at the painting and then at Nick. "And what will you do? Where will you go?"

Pensively, Nick stared at his ancestral work of art. "I've thought about that, too, Jim. I've thought about it a lot." He turned to his friend. "I'm going to enlist."

"What? You can't be serious!"

Nick held up a forestalling hand. "My number is up, and I don't have the courage to go back to Kent. Not without Raine. The memories there would kill me."

"But you don't believe in war. Why enlist? Wait until they draft you anyway."

Nick shook his head. "I don't know what I believe anymore, and I want out of Ohio. The fact is, I want out of life."

"Oh, I get it. This is some backward suicide attempt, huh?"

"Maybe. Call it whatever you want." Nick narrowed his gaze. "But if what you've been preaching is the truth, Pastor," he said emphatically, "then I've got no control over whether I get blown away in Nam or live for another fifty miserable years. God has an appointed time for me to die. Am I right?"

Jim nodded, albeit grudgingly. "You're right."

Closing the distance between himself and his friend, Nick placed his hands on Jim's shoulders. "Pray for me, man."

"I've never stopped."

ω

Nearly a week later, Nick walked slowly down the

sidewalk, making his way to the recruiting office. He'd called a realtor that morning and put his house up for sale. He'd begun to pack his and Raine's belongings, as well as Grandpa's, deciding to store anything worth keeping and sell the rest.

Glancing around him, Nick realized it was the peak of the fall season. Leaves were dancing on treetops in colors of red, orange, and gold. They were dying on the October wind and swirling to the ground, collectively covering lawns in blankets of autumn brown.

Soon it'd be Thanksgiving. Christmas. Winter. Spring. Summer. Nick couldn't imagine facing the seasons without Raine.

Nick passed by storefronts, some of them still familiar from his teenage days. He crossed the street by the grade school and took a shortcut through the city park. When he reached the other side, he spied a group of hippies sitting in a circle on the pavement outside the army recruiting office. One of them strummed a guitar and sang along with the others. As he neared, Nick recognized the melody before he even heard the words. It was the song Raine used to sing. "Where Have All the Flowers Gone?" except, he quickly noticed, the singers were on the fourth verse:

And where have all the soldiers gone, long time passing?
Where have all the soldiers gone, long time ago?
Where have all the soldiers gone?
Gone to graveyards every one!
When will they ever learn, when will they ever learn?

For a moment, Nick's breath caught in his throat, and he felt like he should be there with the kids, singing and protesting the war in a nonviolent way. But he knew he wasn't one of them anymore because he just didn't care. His grief had somehow given way to apathy.

He stepped up to the door and opened it as the final verse of the song filled his ears.

And where have all the graveyards gone?
Gone to flowers, every one!
When will they ever learn, oh when will they
    ever learn?

Grinning bitterly at the irony, though tears filled his eyes, Nick entered the office and enlisted with the United States Army.

ANDREA BOESHAAR

Andrea was born and raised in Milwaukee, Wisconsin. Married for twenty years, she and her husband Daniel have three sons. Andrea has been writing for over thirteen years, but writing exclusively for the Christian market for six. Writing is something she loves to share, as well as, help others develop. Andrea recently quit her job to stay home, take care of her family, and write. She has authored seven Heartsong Presents titles.

As far as her writing success is concerned, Andrea gives the glory to the Lord Jesus. Her writing, she feels, is a gift of God in that He has provided an "outlet" for her imagination. Andrea wants her writing to be an evangelistic tool, but she also hopes that it edifies and encourages other Christians in their daily walk with Him.

Going Home Again

by Yvonne Lehman

Dedication

Dedicated to the opportunity-givers:
Andrea, Tracie, and Becky

Chapter 1

Late June 1994, Eau Claire, Wisconsin

Nick Malone had never read one of Thomas Wolfe's books, but he'd heard the words, "You can't go home again," attributed to that writer. He knew it was true. He'd tried it. After Nam, he'd found the old dilapidated house, the replica of Laurelwood, where his grandmother had grown up. He'd bought the house, renovated it, and lived in it for the past twenty years.

It was part of his heritage, but it turned out to be just a house.

He couldn't go back and recapture a childhood he couldn't even remember.

And he couldn't go back and change the past. It was over. Done! He'd accepted it. Until Mary stirred it up. Mary—whom he'd hired to be his housekeeper, not his commanding officer.

"You've shut yourself off from the world, Nick," she said, when they sat on the porch after supper, drinking lemonade.

Nick wasn't one to argue, except with his dog after he

chewed up another slipper. But he couldn't let Mary's remark pass. He'd pretended so long, he'd almost convinced himself. He taught history and art in high school, taught twelve-year-old boys in Sunday school for the past fifteen years, and he'd been a Boy Scout leader for the past five. "You know what I do, Mary. How can you say I'm shut off from the world?"

"I know you're busy, Nick. So am I," she said in that matter-of-fact way of hers. "But I lost my husband six years ago. I recognize emptiness and loneliness when I see it."

He almost regretted the hurt in her eyes when he said, "My life is just the way I want it, Mary. I'm almost fifty. Too old to change."

She gripped the arms of the rocking chair and pulled herself up. "I'm forty-five this month. But I don't intend to ever be too old to change." She picked up the glasses sitting on the banister, stepped around the hound dog, and headed for the screen door.

Something about her manner prevented his saying, "I didn't finish my lemonade."

She came out, carrying her purse, heading for the front steps. "Good-bye, Nick."

Did she say "Good-bye," or "Goodnight"?

"Mary?"

Stopping at the steps, she reached out and laid her hand against the white post. But she didn't turn.

"Mary, could we. . .talk?"

She moved down to the first step, still holding on to the post. "We talk about everything, Nick, except us."

Nick swallowed hard. He'd never seen this side of

Mary. Her voice has become as leaden as the sky since the sun had dropped below the horizon. He stopped his rocking and leaned forward.

"You know there can't be any us, Mary. Not the way you mean."

She walked down to the bottom step before she turned. "Is it because of them?"

Nick knew what she meant. When anybody asked, he'd told them he lost his wife and baby years ago. When they said, "I'm sorry," Nick acknowledged with a nod, but no words. He couldn't talk about it. He stood then, stepped over his dog, and held onto the banister with white knuckles, staring at Mary.

A knowledge, quick as lightning, seared his brain.

If he didn't call her back, she'd be gone for good. He'd never see her again except when he sat in the congregation looking at her singing in the choir. She was a determined woman. That was obvious after her husband died, leaving her with unexpected debts. She'd run the mission program at church and volunteered at the hospital, but she'd never worked for pay. Mary, who lived in a nicer house than most at church, put a notice on the bulletin board asking to clean houses.

Nick was staring at Mary but seeing the past five years flash before his eyes. He'd hired Mary soon after he started helping with Scouts. Sometimes he'd let them meet on his land, go fishing in the pond, run and play over his acreage. He even taught them how to plow up the land and grow vegetables. That's when he decided he could use a woman around to straighten up the house, cook a little, freeze and can the vegetables.

He'd thought maybe they could help each other out. But she'd gone far beyond the call of duty. She cooked and cleaned, took care of him when he had the flu, fed him chicken soup to cure his colds. They'd prayed together when he was concerned about one of his church boys or a Scout. She held his hand when his Lab died. She laughed when a little spotted hound had wandered into the yard with its ears dragging the ground. "Hi, Friend," he'd said to the little tail-wagger. The dog stayed, and so did the name.

The dog, named "Friend," was company.

But Mary had been a real friend.

She'd been good for his ego too. He acted like it wasn't true when she said he had beautiful green-blue eyes. He'd pretended to laugh it off when he mentioned he had more gray hair than blond and she said he was a handsome man.

He'd tried not to notice that she was a fine looking woman. Now, allowing himself to really look at her, as if for the first time, he saw that her beautiful smile had vanished from her pretty round race, surrounded by soft brown curls. Her dark brown eyes were swimming.

He owed her. . .something.

When he said nothing, she said everything. "I love you, Nick. But I can't wait around forever over a lost cause."

"Mary." His voice was gravel. His eyes were hot with over twenty-years worth of unshed tears. "I've nothing to offer a woman."

"You have a heart, Nick."

With hunched shoulders and a bent head, he denied that. "Oh, honey. It's busted." He bit on his lower lip to stop its trembling. Then he trembled all over.

He felt her arms around his back.

He turned, and she held him while he sobbed. She didn't say a word. A long time later he realized he had a woman in his arms—for the first time in twenty-five years, he had a woman in his arms. His hand was against her soft brown curls. Slowly, his hands moved to his shoulders and he stepped back. Her face looked as washed as his felt. "Mary," he said. "Let's talk about. . .us."

"First," she said softly, "you have to talk about them."

He did. They sat in the chairs on the porch, in the dark. He told her the whole sad story. He'd been a part of the hippy culture, fallen in love with a dynamic girl named Raine. They'd been in love and lived by their own rules. After she got pregnant they married. She died giving birth to his child.

The hardest part was telling about giving his baby girl away. "I had nobody," he said. "I couldn't take care of her. I wanted her to have the loving childhood I had missed."

Now that Nick had started talking about it, he couldn't seem to stop. He'd been a young Christian without family and without hope. He hadn't learned much about trusting God in those days. So he'd joined the war he had protested, hoping someone would do what he was too cowardly to do himself—take his life.

It turned out differently than he'd ever expected. When it looked like he might die any minute, he discovered he didn't want that. He had no reason to live and didn't want to die. Yet, he fluctuated between telling God to go ahead and take his life and then the next prayer would be for protection.

While he was fighting and begging, Nick debated with the Lord, kind of like what he envisioned about the biblical account of Jacob wrestling with the angel of God all night. Finally, Nick had surrendered to God and told Him that He could use his life in any way He saw fit. Nick couldn't stand any more grief over losing his wife and baby. He couldn't take anymore of watching his buddies being blown apart and people killing each other for no good reason that he could find.

He'd had enough of being angry, enough of being scared, enough of running from God. *Get me out of this, Lord, and I'll live for you*, he managed to think while numb from doing what he was trained to do and sick to death of it.

Nick was aware of the saying, "There are no atheists in foxholes," and realized the truth of it. When you stared death in the face daily, you couldn't escape the question of what comes next. He'd had to admit to himself that even if he didn't always like what God allowed, God's love for him was constant. And he knew it wasn't God warring in Vietnam; that was man's doings.

I want to be a peacemaker, he'd decided. After the war was over, he hadn't forgotten his commitment to the Lord. And the Lord was faithful in beginning a healing process for Nick.

"I've accepted Raine's death," Nick said now to Mary. "But I've always wondered about my little girl. I was a brand-new Christian back then. If I'd had more experience with the Lord, maybe I could have found a way to keep my little girl. Church people would have helped me. But I didn't know. At least I had the presence of mind to give her to Pastor Jim. I trusted him to see to it that she'd be in a good home and raised right," he said, talking past the ache in his throat. "Losing her was the hardest part."

"I know," Mary said. "I had a stillborn baby and could not have any other children. I know what it's like to have a child and never be able to touch him, to hold him, to watch him grow. The Lord gives us strength to get through those times, Nick. He brings joy into our lives in other ways. But I don't think we can ever stop thinking about them, asking once in a while, "What if it had been different?"

Hearing the tears in her voice, he reached for her hand.

He hadn't thought a woman could ever get to his heartstrings again, after he lost Raine.

Raine had stormed into his life.

Mary had tiptoed into his heart.

Chapter 2

Second week in July, 1994 — Carbondale, Illinois

Tina Robinson Abbot was as excited as the children —maybe more so. She'd sent notes home so parents would know her plans and have the children prepared accordingly. Shortly before eleven o'clock, she and her workers led the barefoot children, dressed in old clothes, out onto the velvety green lawn at the side of the church.

They had practiced, but this was the real thing, and they all anticipated the week's grand finale, just as many of them had the previous week, when watching the Fourth-of-July fireworks over Crab Orchard Lake. They were prepared for the perfect ending to a week's study of Noah.

"Okay, it's almost time. Now, remember," Tina warned, "no snickering, or he will suspect."

They all nodded and quickly took their places, making a big circle. John, a helper during summer break from college, put a big cardboard box in the center of the circle, then hid behind a high boxwood shrub at the side of the building. Tina looked around at the circle of children, sitting cross-legged beneath a clear blue sky with the hot sun about to toast them all. "Okay, ready?"

"Ready!" they screamed. Tina laughed and put her finger to her lips as she hurried up the steps to find Noah, who was being kept occupied by her preacher-dad.

"It's time," she called, walking up to them in the hall-way. There stood Brent Abbot in a choir robe. She'd insisted he wear walking shorts and T-shirt underneath.

Brent grimaced, asking Pastor Daniel Robinson, "Why do I let your daughter talk me into these things?"

"Because you love me?" Tina teased.

"Could be," Brent teased back, grinning with a hint of mischief in his eyes.

She glanced at her dad, his face wearing a broad smile. He winked at her approvingly. Tina felt so blessed, never failing to realize she was loved by the two most wonderful men in the world.

"But now," she said, "it's time for Noah to make an appearance. I mean, what's a flood without the main character? They've really looked forward to this, Brent. So, just go to the center of the circle and read this poem about the biblical account of Noah. That simple."

Rather than react to that doubtful look on his face, she took his hand, leading his sandaled feet along the hallway, through the doorway, down the steps, and across the lawn. Several stifled giggles could be heard as the two of them made their way to the center and stood beside the box.

"I'd like to introduce you to Mr. Noah," Tina said, as straight-faced as possible. "We've gotten all the animals into the ark this week, and now it's time you heard the story straight from—" She grinned as her eyes met Brent's. His warning glance meant, "Don't say, 'from the horse's mouth.' "

"Straight from the mouth of Mr. Noah himself." Putting her hands together, Tina started the welcoming applause, then made her way to a spot within the circle.

Tina sat watching her handsome husband, with his brown hair touched by the golden sun and his deep blue eyes alive with warmth and caring as he related to the children. They all sat with their eyes riveted to Brent as he read, in his resonant voice, the dramatic poem about the flood.

The air literally crackled with anticipation as Brent read the last line. "And the rains came tumbling down!"

"What?" Brent exclaimed and jumped, hearing the sound like growling and scraping beneath the box, just before it flew up into the air and rolled on it's side, revealing the whirling sprinkler now turning and spewing streams of water all over him like a cloudburst. The children jumped up, singing about the "floody, floody" and things getting mighty "muddy, muddy." Brent stood, wide-eyed, open-mouthed, totally drenched.

The children and their teachers all held hands, sopping wet, singing about the animals coming two by two, then lifted their hands high, shouting, "Noah, Noah."

As Tina had expected, Brent began to laugh, tossed the robe aside and joined in the circling and singing. The children were following him and his antics now. Yes, they needed the example of a fun-loving Christian man who could be the brunt of a harmless prank.

John turned off the water and the "dry" workers herded

in the happy, laughing children to dry off and get changed. Brent retrieved the robe and wrung it out, then gave Tina a wicked look. "I rearranged my schedule for this?"

"And this," she said, looking up into his face, knowing he would plant a kiss on her lips.

He did. "It was worth it," he said. "I wish I could reciprocate, but I just don't have your creative mind."

"That's why we complement each other so well."

"I know," he said lovingly. "I'd be some ol' stuffed shirt without you."

"Oh, but I love what your shirt is stuffed with—pecs, and biceps, and broad shoulders." She traced a line across his chest with her fingers.

"You better stop it," he warned. "We're in public, you know."

"We're married," she quipped, with a mischievous look in her teal eyes. He picked a blade of grass off the robe and let it fall onto her chestnut-colored hair that curled as it dried beneath the hot rays of the midday sun, then held her hand as they filed in behind the children.

We're married, she never ceased to think in wonder. She'd taken seriously her mom and dad's admonition for her to complete her education before marrying. But that was before Brent Abbot joined the church and stood at the front to be welcomed by members. She shook his hand, looked into his eyes, and forgot everything except the awareness, *That's the man for me.*

Brent, twenty-eight at the time, was a mite more reticent. He told her later, that he "hoped" she was the woman God had picked out for him. Soon afterward, he had acknowledged he couldn't imagine living his life with anyone else. To her great surprise, her overly protective parents agreed to her pleadings to let them marry in July after she graduated from college.

She felt like the entire three years they'd been married had been a honeymoon. Brent was her fulfillment. And now that she'd earned her master's degree in education and he was "over the hill, past thirty," she was going to surprise him with an announcement that would mean the world to him. Just thinking about it made joybumps form on her arms.

When they would celebrate their third wedding anniversary next week, she would tell him, "Brent, I'm ready to start a family."

Daniel Robinson had watched from a window, knowing the lawn would never be the same, but what was grass compared with little children learning about the Bible and having fun? There was no comparison. Grass could be replaced. His daughter, the beautiful Tina, was one of a kind and irreplaceable. *Oh God, thank You for her. Thank You for giving her to me and Rosa. And now for giving her a fine husband like Brent.* Daniel thanked God everyday for Tina and all the joy she had brought into his and Rosa's lives.

She had been a light in their dark world of despair so long ago. Shortly after they'd been married for a year and were expecting their first child, it was discovered that Rosa had a goiter, caused by a thyroid condition. She refused medication that might harm the unborn child. She miscarried in her fifth month. Her goiter had enlarged to the point of making swallowing and breathing difficult. The radiation treatment would prevent her from ever having a healthy child.

Daniel had already felt the call to go into the ministry. He'd already enrolled in seminary, and Rosa had been as excited as he to think of serving the Lord in such a special way. Their future was all mapped out. Then it was like having the rug pulled out from under them. They tried not to, but they couldn't help questioning why God had let it happen. That had been like a trial by fire, and although they were grieving, they knew what to do. They took it to the Lord in prayer and renewed their vow to serve Him.

During that time of despair, Pastor Jim told them about a two-week-old baby whose mother had died and whose father couldn't take care of her. The baby had no relatives. She needed a home and someone to love her.

Both Daniel and Rosa were fearful when they went to the adoption agency that day. They mustn't try and replace the child they lost. But the moment they looked at that adorable little baby with its fist in its mouth and beautiful round face and a head full of curly blond fuzz, they both had known this was not a replacement for any child. She was her own little person and seemed to be God's gift to them.

As plans for the adoption proceeded, they were told that the birth father had named the child Betsy Raine. They weren't given a last name. Rosa had searched her baby-naming book and looked up with a light in her eyes, telling him that "Betsy" meant "devoted to God."

"Bettina is a derivation of Betsy," she'd said. "Could we name her that? In a way it's keeping the name her birth father gave her, and yet it's our own name for her too. She's such a tiny little thing. Bettina seems to suit her."

So she became Bettina Raine Robinson.

Daniel and Rosa never saw the birth father and didn't know his name. But he had made two requests when he turned over the baby to Pastor Jim. He'd wanted the painting of the homestead that had been passed down from generation to generation to go with the baby. And he did not want his little girl to ever know she was adopted.

Daniel smiled now, remembering. Tina had never replaced the little baby they lost. That one was with her heavenly Father, waiting to show them around heaven someday. Tina was winding her way around their heartstrings daily, bringing more joy than they could ever have imagined.

Daniel hadn't cared for the request that Tina not be told she was adopted. He must set the example of being upright and honest on every level. But in the early years he'd wanted to abide by the wishes of the natural father.

Then the years passed, and it seemed best not to say anything. It should have been done early, if at all. And besides, she was his and Rosa's daughter in every way. Later, they felt they could not shock her with information like that. It didn't seem right.

They'd hoped and prayed some man would not show up on their doorstep someday, claiming his rights as a birth father and tearing their world apart. He hadn't.

When Tina was very young, she'd been told that the painting had been handed down, generation after generation, and she'd accepted that. As she grew older, she asked once who had painted it, and they could honestly say they didn't know. She'd kept it stored away in a big box in the basement, where she put a lot of paintings when she was taking art classes. When she married Brent and moved into his apartment, she'd left the paintings behind. She'd probably forgotten them.

Tina was twenty-five now and married.

There seemed to be no reason for concern about the past. She was theirs in every way that mattered. Daniel strongly believed in the saying, "If it ain't broke, don't fix it."

He and Rosa considered Tina their little miracle child. The secret of how they came to have her was like those paintings—stored away because they weren't relevant anymore.

Chapter 3

Early the next morning, Daniel Robinson punched the blinking button on line two. "Good morning," he said cheerily. "Pastor Robinson here." Smiling, he leaned back in his swivel chair, and turned toward the window, glad for a chance to look out at the pleasant summer morning awash with golden sunshine and a clear blue sky.

"Good morning," the caller said politely. "I wasn't sure anyone would be there on a Saturday morning, but thought I'd give it a try."

"Oh, yes," Daniel said, trying to place the caller's voice, but being unable to. "We're making sure everything's ready for Bible school commencement Sunday night."

The caller cleared his throat. "Is Jim Stoddard still the pastor there?"

Daniel's smile vanished. He'd thought everybody around there knew that Pastor Jim had suffered a stroke several weeks ago. Maybe this was a former member, checking to see if such a rumor were true. "Pastor Jim has had some health problems lately," he began, trying to soften the blow to the unsuspecting caller. "He had a stroke that the doctor explained as 'expressive aphasia.' He's coming along fine, out of the hospital now, and is in therapy at the rehab center to regain some of the motor skills he lost."

"I'm sorry to hear that," he heard at the other end of the line.

"Yes, we all are. I'm taking over the pastoral duties temporarily until Jim can return. Could I help you with anything?"

"No. I need to talk with him. Can he have visitors?"

"He has limited visitation," Daniel said, smiling to himself at that. It seemed the entire church membership wanted to go and see Jim. "I've never before known of a man who had a visitors' waiting list."

"Yes, I can imagine," the caller said, "if he's like he was when I knew him. He could persuade a lamppost to come to church. And if it didn't, he'd stand and preach to it."

Daniel laughed lightly. "That's Jim all right," he agreed.

"Could you give me directions to the rehab center? I'm from out of town—"

"Out of town?" Daniel asked.

"Yes, I knew Pastor Jim twenty-five years ago."

"You must be a former member of his church?"

The caller hesitated. "No, not really. But I thought a lot of him. I'd just like to see him, talk to him."

Daniel swiveled around, away from the window. "In case you don't get in to see him, could I give him a message for you?

"Thank you, no. It's a personal matter."

Out of town? Twenty-five years ago? A personal matter? Maybe he should have asked what the caller wanted and then have told him that Pastor Jim was unavailable. *No, I'm a Christian. A pastor. I can't go around trying to think of how to manipulate a situation. God, forgive me.*

Finally, it registered that the caller had asked for directions again. "Or I could manage to find it. What's the name of the rehab center?"

"Where are you, sir?" Daniel asked.

The caller named a motel on the outskirts of Carbondale. Daniel gave him directions.

"I'll go on out there and see if I can visit with him," the man said.

Daniel stared at the phone he'd just hung up. *What do I do? First thing, I'd better pray.*

Lord, I don't know what's going on here. Maybe nothing. You know I've felt this way before. Mainly, when my Tina was a little girl and the church would have visitors from Ohio. I always wondered, are they here because of friendship with Jim, or are they here to try and tear mine and Rosa's hearts out? I put it in Your hands, Lord. Then I take it back. Well, I'm trying to give it over to You again. I need Your peace.

Daniel drummed on the telephone receiver with his fingers. The man had said he wasn't a former member of Jim's church. He'd just known Jim years ago. And it would be foolish of Daniel to go out there and check it out.

But wasn't it his responsibility to make sure somebody from the past didn't come around making the situation worse for Jim? Sure it was! And he also had a responsibility to offer hospitality to someone from out of town if they needed it. Brent took Mondays off and worked half a day every other Saturday. Daniel was pretty sure this was his day to work. He'd call and ask if Brent could go to the center. Glancing at the wall clock, he saw that it wasn't even ten o'clock when the secretary put him through to his son-in-law.

Brent was always pleased when Daniel asked a favor of him. It wasn't easy walking in the shadow of such a giant of a Christian as Pastor Daniel Robinson. Daniel had told him point-blank when he came to pick up Tina on the first date, "We raised that girl to be a certain way for over twenty years, and we don't expect anybody to come along and change her. You do, and you answer to me."

That night, he hadn't felt like Dr. Brent Abbot, a grown man who'd recently been taken in as a partner in the career of his choice. Instead, he felt like a high school boy asking a girl out on a date for the first time. He'd have been trembling in his boots if he hadn't been wearing dress shoes.

Pastor Daniel had put the fear of the Lord in him. Mainly, Brent had been afraid he couldn't come up to the standards of Daniel Robinson. When he'd said as much, Tina had laughed it off. "Don't worry about being like my dad," she said. "You couldn't anyway. He's perfect for a dad. But if I wanted to spend the rest of my life with a man like him, I'd be home tonight instead of out with you."

That made sense. But Brent didn't want to disappoint either Tina or her parents. So when Daniel said there was a man from out of town going to visit Jim and he'd appreciate Brent's going out there and meeting the visitor, seeing if there was anything the man needed, Brent was more than glad to do it.

Shortly after 12:30, he walked into the church office where Daniel was talking with one of the deacons. "Oh, here's my favorite son-in-law," Daniel said, motioning for Brent to take a seat.

The deacon laughed and said he needed to get back to the speaker system.

Brent grinned and sat. Daniel often referred to him as his favorite son-in-law, when in fact he was Daniel's only son-in-law.

"You must have left your office early," Daniel surmised.

"My last appointment was cancelled," Brent explained. "The man called my secretary and said he'd misread the ad in the phone book. He thought we were Abbot, Collins, Christian: Counselors. He found out we're Abbot, Collins: Christian Counselors."

The two laughed. Brent shook his head. "He wasn't looking for a Christian counselor."

"That's probably what he needs," Daniel said.

Brent nodded.

Daniel sighed. "Any change with Jim?"

Brent noticed the tired lines around Daniel's eyes. Since Pastor Jim's stroke, Daniel was holding down two jobs—his own as associate pastor, plus preaching every Sunday. Brent regretted having to say that he hadn't noticed any improvement in Jim from the last time he'd seen him, two days ago. He had been improving daily.

"After the visitor left, the nurse told me that Jim had seemed sort of dazed, staring like he didn't really know the man. He didn't say one coherent word, and his hand shook so much he couldn't even point to the yes and no words on his writing pad."

"Did the nurse think it was the man who upset Jim, or is this just a bad day for him?" Daniel asked, concern in his voice.

"She didn't say. But Jim's had out-of-town visitors before, and it didn't seem to bother him."

Seeing Daniel run both hands through his gray-sprinkled brown hair, Brent added, "The nurse didn't seem too concerned. She acted as if a slight regression at times is normal."

"You talked to the man?" Daniel asked.

"After the visit," Brent said. "He didn't have any family with him. Said he was from Wisconsin. Been driving for two days and got in late last night. He looked tired."

Daniel leaned back in his chair. "Did he say why he came to see Jim?"

"He gave me the impression that Jim had witnessed to him when he was a hippy in Ohio. Now he wants Jim to know that work wasn't in vain and that he is still living his life for the Lord."

"A hippy in Ohio," Daniel said reflectively. "I knew a few hippies in Ohio twenty-five years ago."

Brent laughed. "I'm not sure what hippies looked like back then. But this man was tall, average build, looked in good shape for a man at least in his mid-forties. His hair was light. Looked like a mix of gray and blond. I don't know what color of eyes he had. But they weren't dark. Not like yours." He shrugged. "There was nothing particularly outstanding about him. I guess you'd say he's average."

Daniel chuckled. "Doesn't sound like any hippy I ever knew. What's his name?"

Brent thought. He often used word association to

remember names. Nicholas, as in Jolly ol' Saint. The last name was like that fighting fellow in the movies—Stallone. "Nick Malone," Brent said. "Do you know him?"

"The name doesn't ring a bell," Daniel said.

The name doesn't ring a bell, Daniel was telling himself, even as Brent was leaving the office. But other things did—twenty-five years ago in Ohio. Light hair, light eyes, like Tina's. All that rang bells—a memory bell, a warning bell, an alarm bell.

I'm jumping to conclusions, Daniel told himself. *I felt this way many times in the past. Whenever anyone visited the church from Ohio, where Pastor Jim used to preach. Where Daniel had lived before going to seminary.* He'd always wondered, *Have they changed their minds?* Did they discover they couldn't live without this most precious child in the world? Had they come to claim her, to disrupt her life, to tear their hearts out?

Oh, ye of little faith.

Daniel slumped into his chair. *Yes, Lord. I'm a weak, scared mortal. I know what Your Word says. I know You're in control. But I also know You work in mysterious ways. And I know You have a refining fire. I know I have to trust You. I'm trusting You, Lord. Now, make me mean it.*

Daniel pushed away stabs of concern that something might happen that would disrupt his daughter's life, shatter her world as she knows it. It just wouldn't be right for her to discover she'd been adopted, after twenty-five years of her believing he and Rosa were her biological parents.

But he mustn't imagine things. He'd done so in the past, but none of his fears had materialized. He was just tired and letting his imagination run away from him.

After all, Daniel had many people come to him or write letters of appreciation for the Christian influence he'd been in their lives. Sometimes it took them ten, fifteen years or so to realize it. This Nick was just one of those appreciative ones. Jim had changed many lives when he involved himself in the hippy culture. A grown man who could look back and see the difference in his life since coming to the Lord would want to thank Jim.

That was it. If Jim hadn't asked Daniel to come and serve as his associate pastor fifteen years ago, Daniel would be writing a letter or coming to Jim and telling him how much he appreciated what he'd done for him in Ohio.

There was nothing to fear.

Chapter 4

The last thing Nick wanted to do was cause anybody any problems. That's why he'd kept all this to himself for so many years. After Nam, he had gone back to Ohio where he'd lived with his grandfather. He'd gone out to the old house, and other people were living in it. He'd stood in front of the big house where Raine's parents had lived and wondered if they were sorry they had disowned her. Would they have felt differently if they'd known she had a baby? He decided they wouldn't have. How could anybody want their grandchild when they'd disowned their own flesh and blood?

Was he any better, by giving his daughter away? But he'd meant it for good. Could he have found a way? He couldn't answer. But back then he'd wanted to know that Pastor Jim had found her a good home. He'd gone to the church where Pastor Jim preached and was told he'd left that church a year before. Nick took that as his answer. He needed to let things be. What could he have done for a little girl anyway? He still had so many things to learn about his spiritual walk with the Lord. So he decided the best thing to do was to bury the past, go to

Wisconsin, and start over.

He'd buried the past all right. The trouble was, he knew where it was buried. Right there in his heart, and he took it out and looked at it many, many times, usually at night, lying in that bed with nothing but empty sheets beside him. He'd long for his wife, and he'd start thinking about the day he'd told his little girl what he was going to do. He'd fed her a bottle for the last time. Held her in his arms for the last time. He kept telling her he was doing what was best for her, and he'd wiped away the tears that fell on his little girl's face.

That night he'd taken her over to Pastor Jim's house, hating himself for what he was about to do, yet knowing he had no other choice. He loved his baby daughter, but as distraught as he was over losing Raine, he knew giving Betsy up for adoption was the best thing for her.

He didn't know how he got back to his apartment. Didn't know how he saw to do it because the storm in front of his eyes couldn't be cleared away with windshield wipers. Finally, he made it inside and to his bed. He'd never ached like that, even when he'd had the flu. Nothing eased the heartache. There was just a big, hard, aching throb in his chest until that night in Nam when he finally surrendered his grief to the Lord and God began to heal the wound.

A few times after that, Nick had examined the scar. A few times after that, he'd taken back the memory.

Lying there, in a motel room in Carbondale, Illinois, was one of those times. He remembered it all, and his pillow became sopping wet.

"You have to ease your mind that she's all right,"

Mary had said, and it was something Nick had wanted to hear. He'd wanted somebody to make him find out. Mary had said his mind would never be free to start a life with her until the past was finally settled. He had to at least see Pastor Jim.

So he'd tried.

But Pastor Jim was mute. Pastor Jim couldn't speak or write a word.

Was that God's way of saying Nick should never have come? Did Pastor Jim have to suffer because Nick Malone was still making mistakes? *Oh God, don't let that happen. Punish me, if You must. Don't let anyone suffer because of me. I'll leave, Lord. I'll go back where I should have stayed. And if that's not good enough for Mary, then I'll just live the kind of life I've lived for the past twenty years. It'll be lonely in a lot of ways, but I've done it before. And You know what I've wanted most in my life is for my little girl to have the good life I wasn't able to give her. I should have trusted You, instead of coming all this way—for nothing.*

Lord, You know, giving up my daughter was the hardest thing I've ever done in my life.

Now, I'm giving her up to You again. I don't know why I let Mary talk me into this. That's not true. I do know. I wanted to do it. I've wanted to do it for twenty years. It's done. And I've learned nothing except it was a mistake. Maybe that's what I needed to learn.

Nick watched a Sunday morning worship service on TV while eating a muffin and drinking coffee he'd purchased from the restaurant next to the motel. He appreciated the invitation that the young man named Brent had given for him to attend his church. But Nick didn't feel like being in a crowd. He'd have to smile and shake hands and answer questions. That wasn't his mission here. He'd already decided he didn't really have a mission here. This was a mistake. He'd try once more to see Jim, then he'd go home.

"This is Nick Malone," he said, when a woman answered the phone at the rehab center. "I visited Pastor Jim yesterday. I'm from out of town and wondered if I might see him today?"

"I'm sorry, sir. But Sunday visitation is limited to his family members. Hold on a moment, please." Soon she spoke again. "We could let you visit for a short while Monday morning at 10:30."

"I'll be there." But after hanging up, Nick didn't feel right about this.

He felt like he hadn't been hearing the Lord very well lately. Not about Mary, not about Jim, not about his little girl. All that must have been his own desires, not the Lord's. But he'd stay around another day. He'd already seen Jim once. It shouldn't hurt to see him again, and it wouldn't be as much a surprise to Jim this time. He felt like he'd shocked Jim when he visited him yesterday. He didn't want to cause anybody any trouble.

And too, he couldn't expect Jim to suddenly recuperate as if he'd never had a stroke. He couldn't expect the man to start talking or be able to write him a letter on that pad where he hadn't been able to write a word yesterday.

Suddenly, Nick had an idea. He looked at the business card that the Christian counselor had given him the day before. When he thought church would be over and people would have time to get home, he dialed the home phone number listed on the card.

"May I speak with Brent Abbot, please," he asked when a woman with a pleasant voice answered the phone.

On Monday morning , Nick got his things together and put them in his car. He checked out of the motel and bought a manila envelope that the clerk got from the office. He was waiting for Brent at the rehab center when the younger man arrived.

"Good to see you again," Brent said, shaking Nick's hand.

"Thanks for agreeing to be with me when I visit Jim. I think I might have shocked him on Saturday. It's kind of you to agree to visit with me."

"Glad to do it," Brent said. "I don't work on Mondays, so it's no problem."

"I've decided to go back to Wisconsin after seeing Jim," Nick said. "I wonder if you'd do me a favor?"

"If I can," Brent replied.

"You said that the doctors expect Jim to recuperate." When Brent nodded, Nick continued. "Would you keep this for him?" He held out the manila envelope, and Brent took it. "There's a letter and a picture in there, along with an address and phone number where I can be reached in Wisconsin. When you think Pastor Jim is able to understand or maybe respond in some way, you might give it to him."

"Yes, I could do that. But would you mind telling me if it's something that might upset him?"

"I don't think so," Nick replied. "If he didn't recognize me on Saturday, this might surprise him into remembering. But the option of responding is up to him. You're welcome to take a look at what's in there and decide when you think is the right time to show it to him."

The nurse came out of Jim's room. "You may go in now. We were so pleased with the way he related to his relatives yesterday. All his vital signs are good." She was all smiles. "Well, you'll see."

"Wonderful," Brent said. He glanced at Nick. "Shall we go in?"

Nick gestured for Brent to go first, then followed him in.

Jim was sitting in his wheelchair near a window where he could look out. Nick thought he looked better. His eyes moved from Nick to Brent and turned from friendly to troubled, as if wondering who Nick was. His gaze lowered to the notepad on his lap.

Brent went over and put his hand on Jim's shoulder. "How are you today?" he asked.

Jim slowly closed his eyes and opened them again, indicating he understood the question perfectly and was fine, considering the circumstances.

"You remember Nick. He came to see you Saturday."

Nick pulled a chair up near Jim and sat, not wanting to tower over the man. At first he thought Jim was reaching for his pencil, then realized he was trying to move his arm toward him. Was he trying to shake his hand? Did that mean he remembered him? Maybe. Nick stepped over and took the trembling hand in both of his, wanting to caress that hand, to still its trembling, to make it strong like it was when he'd held his little girl, promising to find her a good home. But Nick had no power to do such.

Jim looked into his eyes, and Nick thought they were moist. Jim's partial smile moved on one side of his face only. Rather than make an emotional scene and begin asking questions that would only upset them all, Nick carefully led Jim's hand back to the arm of the wheelchair that he'd been grasping when they walked in.

Brent took the towel that lay next to the notepad and blotted away the drool caused by the half smile and undecipherable sound Jim had made. "Can you talk to us today, Jim?" he asked, leaning back against the wide windowsill.

Slowly, with shaky fingers, Jim pointed to "No."

Brent made a friendly laugh. "Too much company yesterday, huh?"

Again, the partial smile and lowering of his eyes, without attempting to write anything.

"Do you know me, Pastor Jim?" Nick asked and Jim pointed to "Yes."

Nick couldn't resist asking, "Is there anything you can tell me?"

Jim's finger, without much shaking at all, moved immediately to "No."

"Then I should leave," Nick said. "I hope I haven't upset you or caused any trouble."

When he said that, Jim's finger again pointed to "No." His eyes met Nick's with a steady stare that seemed to say, "Then why are you here?" But he moved his arm toward Nick again.

Nick didn't shake his hand this time. He leaned over and hugged him. "I won't try to contact you again. I just want to thank you for all you've done for me." He kissed the side of Jim's face and quickly left the room.

Nick heard Brent tell Jim he'd be right back, then he followed Nick outside the room.

"It was nice meeting you, Nick. You have a safe trip going back."

"Thanks," Nick said, shaking his hand. "You've been very kind." He glanced at the envelope that Brent still held. "Feel free to read the letter and if you don't mind, you might just let me know about Pastor Jim's condition." Nick walked away, feeling the eyes of Brent Abbot staring into his back.

I'm going back to my house, kept running through Nick's mind as he drove his car out toward the highways that would lead him back to Wisconsin. It reminded him of when he went back after Nam. He'd gone back wondering what his life would be like. Would he be able to live the Christian life? Could he live without Raine and without his baby girl?

He had.

This time, he was still without Raine and without his little girl. But he knew what he was going back to. He was going back to the life the Lord had laid out for him. His house, his Sunday school class of boys, and his Scout troop. This trip to Illinois hadn't cleared his mind. He hadn't settled anything. He hadn't let it go. So he wasn't ready for Mary.

She'd know it without his saying so. She'd come to know him.

He had no idea if he'd just keep driving until he couldn't drive anymore or if he'd stop somewhere for the night. It didn't matter. The scar on his heart was bothering him. But he'd call a few hours before reaching Eau Claire.

Mary would say, "Did you find out anything?"

He'd say, "No."

She'd say, "I'll have something here for you to eat."

He'd say, "Thanks."

Then she'd say, "Good-bye, Nick."

He wouldn't be able to say anything more because there wouldn't be any need for it. And when he went to church, he'd know she was sitting in the choir. But he wouldn't have to look. No, he just wouldn't look.

Chapter 5

Brent knew there must be something very important in that manila envelope for Nick to have made a trip all the way from Wisconsin, stuck around Illinois for a few days, and then driven back. Since he didn't work on Mondays, he took the envelope to the apartment.

Tina wasn't back yet. She'd told him she planned to go to the church to pack up Noah's ark animals. He laid the envelope on the coffee table and called Pastor Daniel to give a report on Jim.

"The nurse said Jim was a lot better yesterday," he said when connected to Daniel. "He looked good today, but I got the feeling he could have communicated more but didn't care to. Still, he had a good visit with Nick, the man from Wisconsin."

"They communicated?"

"Yes and no," Brent said, with a short laugh. "Jim seemed to know Nick. He shook his hand and indicated he remembered him. But the visit was brief."

"So the man's gone," Daniel said.

Brent detected a note of relief in Daniel's voice.

"He's gone," Brent said.

"Thanks, Brent, for going out there. I'm covered up here."

"I know. And Jim knows too, Daniel."

"Thanks. Uh, Brent, Tina's here packing up the animals. And Rosa said she's inviting you and Tina over for supper tonight."

"That sounds appetizing." They both laughed lightly before hanging up. Tina's ineptness in the kitchen was a standing joke. Nobody minded though. Her expertise lay in other areas. Everyone at the Bible school commencement, who'd gone down to the fellowship hall, had "oohed" and "aahed" over the animals she'd drawn and cut out from cardboard for Noah's ark and had the children paint. The parents had been as delighted as the children to see colorful birds, two of every kind, hanging from the ceiling and the huge, multi-colored rainbow spread across one wall.

Smiling, just thinking about how empty his life was before Tina came into it, Brent felt that overwhelming sense of gratitude to God for choosing her for him.

He picked up the envelope, thinking about filing it away until Jim showed more improvement. Holding it in midair, he thought of Nick's telling him to look at it and decide when Jim should see it. Maybe it was something that would be helpful to Jim now. It wasn't as though he was looking into someone else's business, although that was included in his line of work. Besides, Nick had asked him to do this.

Brent sat on the couch, opened the envelope, took out the first page and began to read.

Dear Pastor Jim,

Please forgive me if my visit caused you any concern at all. Perhaps I shouldn't have come. You see, all these years, I've kept my past to myself, perhaps even reveling in my own grief. I've met a woman now who says I have to settle this once and for all in my mind or I'll never be free to love and build a life as I should. She thinks I've built my life on failures of the past. I'm a little old to start over, but she says it's never too late.

I don't even know if you remember me. But I don't suppose too many people came to you with a request like mine, twenty-five years ago. Just in case, I'm Nick Malone. I had long blond hair, down to my shoulders back then. Through you and Moira, my wife Raine and I became believers. But we hadn't been Christians for very long before Raine died in childbirth. I wasn't equipped to care for our baby girl, so I asked you to find a home for her while I went off and enlisted in the army.

There was nothing like my experience in Vietnam, facing horror and death every day, to draw me closer to our Lord, and I'm still following Him today. I know you'd want to know that. I teach history and art in high school, teach a group of boys in Sunday school, and hope to help spare them from taking the route I took away from God. You need to know this, so you know that I'm not trying to make trouble for anybody.

I just wanted you to know that about me. I guess you've wondered. And I wanted to ask if you

*know that my little girl is all right. I'm not asking
for names or places. I have no right to ask that. And
it would be too great a temptation to know. I might
give in to a weak moment and make a call or drive
by her house if I knew.*

*I'm sorry you've had a stroke and can't speak.
But I'm pleased to know the doctors say your condition is temporary. I'll be praying for you. I've
included a picture that may help you remember what
I'm referring to. This picture is like the painting I
asked you to keep with my daughter when I gave her
up for adoption.*

*I'm living in Eau Claire, Wisconsin, now. If
you ever want to talk to me, or see me, just write to
me or call the number listed below. If you don't want
to tell me anything, I understand. Already, I'm
starting to think I shouldn't have come here with the
intention of asking such questions anyway.*

*If you think it best not to contact me, I under-
stand that too.*

*May God restore you to complete health is my
prayer.*

Your brother in Christ,
Nick

Brent read over the parts about the little girl. It was too
vague for him to understand. He supposed Nick and his
wife had divorced and the wife had custody. Nick must
have thought he wouldn't return from Vietnam and
wanted his child to have something of his past, a painting that had meant something to him. Maybe Nick's wife

had remarried by the time Nick returned, and he thought it best not to disrupt their family.

Brent sighed. Maybe the picture would shed some light on the matter. He pulled it out of the envelope and turned it right side up. That looked familiar. Well, he supposed it should. It was a picture of an old-style white frame house of years ago. There were still a few of them around when you drove out into the country. In fact, it was similar to houses in Wilmot, Ohio, that some of the Amish lived in that he and Tina had seen when they'd driven up to Ohio to visit her dad's parents. Nick had said he knew Jim in Ohio.

He stacked the two sheets of paper together and started to return them to the envelope. Something stopped him. He looked at the picture again. He'd seen that exact house somewhere. Wait! Looking back at the letter again, he read that Nick said the picture was like the painting he'd left with his little girl. Brent's eyes grew wide with shock as he stared at the picture, read the letter again, and returned to the picture.

The realization came that it wasn't the house that was so familiar. It was the picture itself. He was recognizing a painting. Maybe he was mistaken. Of course he was mistaken. He'd go with his original thought, that it was similar to the Amish houses in Ohio. After all, he could have seen that exact house, or one just like it.

Brent got up and put the envelope in his small file cabinet where he kept a few things he didn't want at the office. He felt strange doing it, but locked the cabinet and put the key in his pocket. He'd fasten it to his key chain later.

And he'd put the envelope out of his mind until Jim improved. After all, the contents of it were for Pastor Jim, not for Brent Abbot to worry about.

～

"I appreciate your helping me, Mom," Tina said to Rosa on Tuesday morning at church as they stacked and packed cardboard birds that the janitor had taken down from the ceiling.

"Oh, honey, I'm glad to. You'd think I'd be used to your creativity, but it never ceases to amaze me. This Noah's ark theme was absolutely marvelous. You have a way of pleasing children and adults."

Tina smiled. She never ceased to be pleased with her mom's compliments. "Well," she admitted, "I'm not creative in the kitchen like you."

"That comes from the Italian side of my family," Rosa said, "but your creativity is expressed in such innovate ways." She studied a colorful parrot, shook her head as if she couldn't understand such talent, then put it in the box.

"Speaking of family," Tina said coyly. "I think I'm ready to start one."

Rosa's mouth flew open in surprise. Then she went over and hugged Tina. "Oh, honey, that's so wonderful."

"Now don't jump the gun," Tina said, laughing. "I'm not pregnant yet."

"Oh, but it's so exciting, just thinking about having a little baby in the family. I still have the bassinet I used for you when you were a baby." Rosa closed up the bird box and taped it, now that all the birds were in.

"Now, don't you breathe a word about this to dad or Brent. I'm going to surprise Brent by telling him when we celebrate our anniversary. He's going to be thrilled." A disturbing thought came into Tina's mind. "Mom," she asked suddenly, "you don't think I'll have trouble getting pregnant like you did, do you?"

Seeing her mother's troubled expression, Tina almost wished she hadn't asked. She knew her mother didn't like to talk about those early years of marriage when she had health problems and difficulty getting pregnant. After a moment of concentration, her mom spoke again.

"A thyroid condition that went undetected for a long time was the cause of my problem, Tina," Rosa explained. "You don't have that condition. You shouldn't have a thing to worry about." She shoved the box aside. "Now are we still going to go out for lunch?"

Tina loved it. Going out with her mom and talking about babies as if she were already pregnant. Then they stopped at a fast food place, ate a salad, and talked primarily about Tina and Brent's plans for celebrating their third wedding anniversary.

They planned to take one of the tents from church that the youth used when they went on camping trips. "We'll stay at Oak Point Campground at Lake Glendale. We'll laze around, enjoy nature, do some hiking and sightseeing. On Sunday morning we'll invite other campers to join us in an open-air worship service if they want to. Brent's taking a CD player and tapes. On Sunday afternoon we're going to Garden of the Gods. Then Sunday night, voila! I'll drop the bomb on him." She spread her hands as her mother laughed, delighted.

"Oh, honey, it sounds like a perfect way to celebrate."

"It will be. Oh, he'll like that shirt I got him, but

telling him I'm ready for that family is going to blow him away. And we have just about enough money saved for a down payment on a house."

Rosa reached over and laid her hand on Tina's. "You're one happy girl, aren't you?"

"Oh, Mom," she said, her eyes shining. "I love Brent so much it scares me. And he loves me. It's so beautiful." A troubled thought crossed her mind. "That won't change when we have a baby, will it?"

"Oh, yes," Rosa said immediately. "Your love will just grow stronger and deeper." She nodded meaningfully, her dark eyes moist.

Chapter 6

Brent tried to forget it, but couldn't. He'd have to check it out to prove to himself that the picture was not the same as the painting. On Wednesday morning, he slipped the manila envelope out of the file drawer and put it in the glove compartment of his car. His last appointment ended at 3:30, but instead of staying to look over any files, he called Tina.

"Hi, hon," he said, when Tina answered the ringing phone. "I can leave a little early today and wondered if you'd like for me to stop by and get some tomatoes from your mom."

"You must have read my mind," she said, making him smile as she went on to say she planned to fry catfish and make slaw. "Tomatoes will be the perfect side dish. Hurry home."

He said he would. He didn't like being less than completely honest. This was the first time he'd ever told Tina one thing while his intentions were something different. He tried to justify it to himself by the mental reminder that he was going for tomatoes. And too, whatever Nick had said to him, or given to him, was of a confidential nature. He was bound legally and ethically to adhere to the standard of confidentiality.

It was a hot day, and Rosa had the house closed up and the air-conditioner going. But she came to the door immediately when he rang the bell. "Come on in, Brent. Tina called and said you were coming by for some tomatoes."

"If you haven't given them all away by now," he said, smiling. If ever there was a giving woman, it was Rosa. The Robinsons didn't have time to do any gardening, but Rosa always had her tomato patch.

"Oh, no," Rosa said. "There's some out there that need picking. You're welcome to all you want."

"Thanks. Want me to pick all the ripe ones?"

"That would help," she said. "It's my day to take supper to the Craigs. And I'm anxious to see that little baby." She gave him a wistful look. "There's nothing like having a little baby in your arms."

"I get your point, Rosa." It was no secret she looked forward to having grandchildren.

"Well, I'm going on," she said. "Just make sure the door's locked when you leave."

"Oh, by the way," Brent said. "You still have those old paintings of Tina's?"

She was thoughtful. "I'm trying to remember where they are. In the basement somewhere. Seems like Daniel stored them. Probably on that back table. You can look."

"Thanks," he said.

After Rosa left, Brent took the envelope out of his glove compartment and went to the basement. He ripped the tape off a huge box and sure enough, there were the paintings he'd seen when he and Tina were dating. Some of them were painted while she was taking college art classes.

He pulled out the painting with the picture. There was a difference in texture and color. The old one was done in oils on canvas. The picture was sketched with colored pencils and without as much detail. There were some slight differences in the size of the trees at the front corners of the house and in the background. There was a slight difference in the terrain and amount of flowers in the yard. The sky was bluer in the present picture.

Brent stared, sighing heavily. There was no denying those were the same kinds of trees, the same kinds of flowers. There was no mistaking that the same house and the same barn were in the painting and the picture. The two chimneys on the roof were in identical spots on both. The details of the picture and painting even stopped at the same spot at the end of the canvas and edge of the paper.

For a long time, Brent went over every detail, trying to find a discrepancy. He was unable to. Whomever drew that picture knew this painting backwards, forwards, inside and out.

What could it mean?

When Brent walked into the apartment, Tina rushed to meet him. "Where are the tomatoes?"

"Tomatoes?" He hit his forehead with the heel of his hand. "I can't believe this. I forgot them."

"You left them in the car?"

"No. I. . ." He hedged. Another half-truth. "Your mom said I could pick them. She had to leave and told me to make sure the door was locked. She left. I made sure the door was locked and I left. Where's my brain?"

"Who cares?" she said. "As long as that handsome head of yours lies on my pillow, it doesn't have to have a brain." She came closer and lifted her face to his. "I can hardly wait to celebrate our anniversary," she said.

"I didn't think we needed an occasion to celebrate our love," he said, pulling her close.

She raised her arms to around his neck and tiptoed so her lips could meet his. He bent his head and accommodated her waiting lips. "I love you, Tina," he said, between kisses.

"I love you too," she said dreamily as she snuggled close to his chest. He never wanted anything to spoil this perfect love they had for each other.

—❦—

Later that night, Brent awoke, staring toward the ceiling in the dark. The questions came again. What did the identical picture and painting mean? Why were they alike? Who was Nick Malone, really? What was his relationship with Jim? And why had Daniel been so concerned? Why had Jim seemed to have a slight relapse and not been able to say or write a word to Nick?

Okay, Brent told himself. *I'm going to see where my instincts lead me. I'm in the business of doing that. I'll analyze this from that point of view.*

Brent went over it, step-by-step, in his mind. Jim had been shocked to see this man from the past, whom he hadn't seen in twenty-five years. He was either shocked into a slight regression, or he pretended he couldn't speak or write. Daniel had been concerned. No! Daniel had been fearful about the man from the past. Daniel and Jim knew a man twenty-five years ago that meant something to their lives. Apparently, it was something unpleasant. Or at least, secretive.

Now, the painting. Tina had a painting that she'd told him had been handed down from generation to generation in her family. That's all she knew of it, and she'd said her parents hadn't known its origin. But now a man comes along who apparently knows all about it.

And the most puzzling part was Nick's wanting to know that his little girl was all right. What about his little girl? What did she have to do with the painting?

Brent sat up on the side of the bed, staring toward the faint glow of moonlight from around the window blind. But no ray of light was shed on his questioning mind. If he let his imagination go where it would, he came to a shocking conclusion. He didn't want to think it. But the only thing that made any sense was that Rosa had been pregnant with another man's baby and married Daniel. The other man was Nick. He'd known about it, and of course Daniel had known about it.

Brent didn't want to think that. But people weren't perfect. Not even Christians and pastors. Brent himself had done a lot of things that weren't pleasing to the Lord. It didn't mean you couldn't get forgiveness, learn from your mistakes, and go on to live a Christian life. And he knew there couldn't be any better people than Daniel and Rosa Robinson. But this was something he'd rather not know.

Yet Brent knew Rosa and Daniel both had talked about being raised in Christian homes. Nick had written that he wasn't an active Christian back then. Maybe he had forced Rosa.

Brent leaned his elbows on his legs and held his face in his hands. But that would mean Daniel was not Tina's biological father. Children didn't have to look like their parents, but they generally did. Both Daniel and Rosa had dark hair, dark eyes, olive skin. Tina was fair with chestnut-colored hair and blue-green eyes—like Nick's.

While everything seemed to fit, there were still things that didn't fit. The painting indicated his reasoning might be correct, but at the same time seemed to argue against it. Why would a young man who had forced a girl give a family painting to Pastor Jim? Wouldn't Jim have had Nick arrested if such were the circumstances? And wouldn't Daniel have told him if he were not Tina's biological father?

"What's wrong, Brent?" Tina asked, propping up.

"Nothing, honey. I'm just having a little trouble sleeping. Sorry I woke you." He lay back down, kissed her lightly, and curled around her. *Lord*, he prayed, *forgive me for letting my imagination go wild and thinking such things about Rosa, Nick, Jim, Daniel, and. . .my wife. There has to be another explanation. Guide me to handle this in the right way.*

⚘

Tina felt certain the weekend change of pace was just what Brent needed to get his mind off the problems of his clients. He'd been lost in his thoughts many times during the week, hadn't slept well, and often looked concerned. On Saturday morning when they arrived at the campground in the Shawnee National Forest, she knew she was right. After getting the tent set up with the help of a couple guys camping nearby, she and Brent ate a picnic lunch she'd packed, then hiked off to enjoy the panoramic scenery. Beneath a clear blue sky, they climbed tall rock formations and looked down upon gently flowing rivers and streams. In the afternoon they swam in Lake Glendale and strolled along the beach while an orange sun dipped behind the forested hills, leaving behind its golden imprint on the sky.

They roasted hot dogs over a fire ring and watched the moon rise in a darkening sky. A night alone in a tent with only the sound of small animals scurrying about and insects singing was a perfect ending to a day spent with the man she loved. Tina was about to tell him so when she heard a snort and looked to see that Brent was sound asleep, breathing deep through parted lips.

She smiled, turned out the lantern and snuggled close. The day had been perfect. Tomorrow would be even better. Someday, they'd bring their children out here and teach them about nature and all of God's beautiful creation put here for their care and enjoyment. Brent had been willing to start a family right away after they married, but he'd been so sweet to say he wanted to wait until she was ready. Her last coherent thought was, *Brent is going to be so pleased when I tell him I'm ready to start a family.*

Chapter 7

Tina couldn't recall ever having seen a more perfect day. She and Brent had awakened early after sleeping all night long with her having opened her eyes only once during the night, feeling a gust of wind rock the tent slightly, but fallen right back to sleep in her husband's arms. It seemed the morning was made just for campers to enjoy. After breakfast and a worship time with two families who joined them, Tina and Brent packed up their equipment and headed for Garden of the Gods.

The two of them hiked much of the eight miles of winding trails until Tina found the perfect spot to view Camel Rock from a distance, back at the edge of some giant oaks. The morning was cool, a welcome relief from a week of temperatures in the nineties. Patches of deep blue sky peeked through a layer of cotton ball clouds, providing the perfect topping above the landscape of lush green forested hills and towering rock formations.

Brent sat beside her, with his feet crossed at the ankles, his forearms resting on his knees, and his fingers entwined as he gazed out reflectively at the panoramic view. He was trim and lean in his walking shorts and knit shirt.

Glancing over, she smiled and leaned toward him, puckering her lips for a kiss, to which he quickly responded, then resumed his reflective gaze. She didn't think she would have the patience to just sit while someone else did their thing. But Brent was special that way, so unselfish and patient.

"I really enjoy this, Tina," he said. "You know, we plan outings that are inexpensive since we're saving for a down payment on a house. But the beauty of it is reason enough to be here."

Tina smiled. "I agree. Why go to the desert when we have the world's biggest camel right at our back door?"

"Well, I considered going somewhere when I had to walk over and around all those animals you had in the apartment," Brent jested.

She wrinkled her nose and poked him on the arm and he grinned. Oh, it felt so good to be loved.

After a long while of sketching, she shook her hand that was beginning to feel a little stiff. "Okay. I've done Camel Rock." She laughed, adding, "Without the people." A couple were sitting on the camel's head, stuck out over the treetops. A group stood on each of the camel's humps. "And I sketched Anvil Rock and the Tower of Babel."

"These would be good teaching aids for children," Brent commented. "Teach them the Bible stories, then bring them out here on a field trip and see if they can pick out the camel, the tower, and. . .uh oh."

"What?" Tina said, glancing at him, wondering what was wrong.

"You're sketching Noah's Ark now. And look at that sky. Grey clouds are rolling in and I have a feeling I might get drenched again."

Tina's glance at the sky revealed he was right. She laughed. "I'll hurry." She almost blurted out that Noah's Ark might be the perfect motif for their baby's nursery. She could paint the sky, clouds, sun, and birds on the ceiling. Oh, but she would tell him about it later. Feeling her hair lift with a sudden breeze, she did only a preliminary sketch and closed the pad. "Ready," she said.

***

"Ready," Tina said aloud to herself, looking at her reflection in the mirror. She'd asked Brent to drop her off at the apartment before returning the tent and camping supplies to the church, then she'd jumped into the shower and was now wearing the teal-colored dress that Brent always admired, saying it enhanced the color of her eyes. "This night just has to be perfect," she added, touching her freshly washed hair.

Hearing him at the door, Tina rushed into the living room.

"What's going on here?" Brent said, with a twinkle in his eyes, indicating he was pleased.

Tina smiled. "Just wait 'til you taste the dinner I've planned for you."

Brent looked at the table, then beyond to the kitchen. "Well, something smells delicious," he said, coming closer to her.

She halted him with her hand. "I think that's my shampoo you're smelling. Now, let's do this right. Why don't you take your shower while I take care of the rest?"

While he showered, Tina set candles and wedding-present china on the table, along with cloth napkins. The doorbell rang and she welcomed the arrival of dinner she'd ordered from a nearby restaurant. She had their plates ready, candles casting a warm glow throughout the room and the lamps turned low.

When Brent walked into the dining area, he stopped short. "Am I in the right place?"

Tina grinned. "Don't tell me I don't know how to set a perfect meal on the table."

Brent smiled. His eyes met hers in a loving gaze. "This is fantastic. You are fantastic."

Tina laughed delightedly as she poured sparkling white grape juice in the long-stemmed glasses they'd used at their wedding and each year on their anniversary. After the delicious meal, Tina set the plates on the kitchen counter, poured more grape juice, and set a bowl of chocolate-covered cherries in the middle of the table. "Dessert," she said, then set a wrapped package in front of him.

Her present to him was a dress shirt, since he wore one almost every weekday and on Sundays. "Exactly what I wanted," he said.

Then Brent opened the apartment door, reached outside and brought in three beautiful red roses in a florist vase. "One for each wonderful year," he said, and then drew from his pocket a small box. Tina knew what would be in it. Her wedding present from him had been pearls and he said he would give her another pearl on each anniversary.

Tina opened the box and delighted in the lovely pearl, a beautiful expression of Brent's love. Now, for her special present to him. She gave him another wrapped present. She hugged her arms to herself, feeling delicious little shivers travel up her spine just thinking about having

Brent's baby. What a perfect expression of a married couple's love.

She watched as he unwrapped the book and read the title, *How To Be a Great Dad*.

His smile faded, and finally he looked across at her. "Are you trying to tell me something, Tina?"

"I am," she said, with a big smile. "This is my anniversary surprise for you. I think it's time we started a family."

She didn't think he'd be that surprised. After all, he'd always said for her just to let him know when she was ready to start a family. She went over to him, wanting him to take her in his arms and say that was a most wonderful anniversary present.

Instead, he caught her hands. "Tina. Let's talk about this."

"Talk?" she managed to ask. Why wasn't he ecstatically happy instead of looking concerned? She pulled her hands away from his. "What's there to talk about?"

"Let's celebrate our anniversary, but postpone the baby part for a little while—"

"Postone? Why, Brent? I finished my master's degree. Isn't that what we were waiting for before we started a family?"

"Yes, hon," Brent hedged, taking her hands in his. "And you know I want a family. It's just that so much is going on right now."

"Like what?"

"With Pastor Jim in rehab and our not know knowing what's going to happen is a strain on all of us. Is this any time to bring a grandchild in on your parents? Your dad's taken over the pastorate and is still doing his full-time job as associate. Your mom is helping Jim's wife."

Tina couldn't believe this. "I'm talking about having our baby, Brent. Yours and mine." She jumped up. "Are we to wait until the world's problems are solved?"

"Now, don't get upset."

"Well, you're not making any sense."

"I'm sorry. I know that. It's something I can't talk about right now. Please, give me a few days."

"A few days, Brent? You've already had three years." She shook her head. Her lips trembled. "What's the matter? Don't you like my looks anymore? Don't I please you? Don't you. . ." She sniffed. "Don't you. . .love me anymore?"

He reached for her, but she swatted at him and backed away. Hot tears began to scald her face.

Brent stood at the window watching lightning streak through the night sky while his wife tramped through the apartment in the most granny-looking gown she owned, blowing out candles, taking the sparkling grape juice and chocolate-covered cherries into the kitchen.

A little later he heard the clink of glasses and wondered if she'd broken the long-stemmed goblets. He could hear her mumbling things like, "I don't get it. What's our life all about? He pretended to want children when I wasn't ready. Now, I'm ready and he says no. I don't know him. I don't know him at all."

Brent stayed at the window, preferring to watch that storm instead of the one inside. He knew it wouldn't do any good to try and talk with her until she calmed down. And he knew how sensitive she was. That's part of what he loved about her.

He didn't see how he could hold his wife in his arms and agree to bring a child into the world with all these unanswered questions in his mind. Suppose she got pregnant and the answers to these questions caused a greater turmoil in her than they did in him? Was that the kind of situation in which a couple should start a family?

He didn't know what to do. A Christian counselor who couldn't even talk to his wife. But what could he say? There were questions that he dared not even think about, much deeper issues than those posed by a stranger who handed him an envelope with information in it that he couldn't. . .mustn't. . .ignore.

But how could he say to his wife, *Hey, honey, do you know anything about this painting that some man had twenty-five years ago in Ohio? A painting he wanted to go with the little girl he gave to Pastor Jim? Do you know why he drew a picture just like your painting? Do you know why this is significant to a man we've never seen? Do you know why it should mean something to Pastor Jim?*

Then another thought struck. *Do you know why your dad wanted me to go and check out that man? Why it disturbed Daniel Robinson so?*

No! Tina wouldn't have the answers any more than he did. One fact remained. There was a man who gave a painting and a little girl to Pastor Jim. Tina had that painting. Where was the little girl who was born in Ohio and would be twenty-five years old?

Where? Was she lying across the bed sobbing, feeling like her husband didn't love her anymore?

Chapter 8

S oon after Pastor Daniel reached the church office on Tuesday morning, Brent called and said he'd like to stop by on his lunch hour. Daniel was always receptive to seeing his son-in-law. A short while later, Rosa called.

"I called Tina this morning," Rosa told him in a troubled voice. "When I asked her how the weekend went, she started crying. Daniel, you know how the two of them have talked about starting a family. Well, now, Tina says Brent wants to wait longer."

That surprised Daniel. Several times Brent had mentioned that he was ready for a baby, anytime Tina was. "He's coming in later," Daniel said to his wife. "Maybe he wants to talk to me about it."

When Brent arrived around noon, he didn't look like a man who'd just had a weekend vacation. He looked tired and concerned.

"I intended to ask how your weekend went," he said, "but Rosa called Tina this morning. She's real upset, Brent."

Brent sighed heavily, as if carrying a burden. Seeing

his hesitancy, Daniel's voice was caring. "Brent, you're a part of my family now. You're like a son to me. I'm not taking Tina's side against yours. I just know how happy you two have been, and I'd like to see you get back to that. Now this might be just a spat. I don't want to interfere, but I'm here if you want to talk to me. Can you tell me what's wrong?"

Brent handed Daniel the envelope he'd brought with him. "Daniel, maybe you can tell me." Brent took a seat, watching as Daniel pulled out the letter and the picture.

Daniel stared at the picture in disbelief, swallowing hard. "What's this about?" he asked, afraid he knew. Hadn't he known something, deep inside, when he talked to the man on the phone?

"The letter explains it," Brent said.

Daniel read it. It was plain as day what it meant. "Did that man say anything to you?"

"No," Brent said. "He just gave me the envelope and permission to read the letter and decide if or when Jim could see it."

Daniel couldn't deny what the picture and letter meant. Fear struck in the middle of Daniel's heart. "Did you mention it to Tina?"

"No. I couldn't do that. I'm not sure what it means."

Daniel hated saying it, but after all these years, there was no need to confront Tina with something like this. "Well, Brent," he said, putting the letter and picture back into the envelope. "Let's just leave it that way."

"Leave it that way?" Brent queried, standing and placing his hands on the edge of the desk. "A man gave away his little girl and a painting went with her. My wife has the painting. Don't I have a right to know what that means? If it's something that's none of my business, okay. But it's already affecting my marriage, Daniel. I can't ignore this. There is a reason my wife has that painting. She told me that you and Rosa said it was hers, handed down through the generations. So you're aware of its history. Tina isn't just your daughter, Daniel. She's my wife."

Brent had never talked to him like that. But there'd never been a reason to. Suddenly, the roles were reversed. Brent was demanding that Daniel come up to a standard of behavior, rather than the other way around.

The truth shall make you free, said the Scriptures. Pastor Daniel could debate that meant the truth was Jesus. It is Jesus who makes one free from slavery to sin— a different matter. What would this truth do to Tina? Would it destroy her? She thought Brent didn't love her because he wanted to delay having a baby. What in the world would she think to learn her parents had kept this secret from her for twenty-five years? A secret kept by a man of God, a preacher, her dad, and her mom?

But at this point in her life, it was more important what Tina thought of her husband than what she thought of her mom and dad. He and Rosa wanted the best for their daughter. The best was a good marriage. Daniel knew he had no right to keep this from his son-in-law, who was understandably demanding answers.

"Sit down, Brent. Please." When he did, Daniel said, "I suppose you've figured out that I'm not. . ." Could he even say it? He had never said it to anyone. He had to say it. Brent knew. "I'm not Tina's biological father."

Brent nodded. "Nick Malone is. They have the same

hair, the same eyes, the same coloring." His eyes were troubled. "I suspected that. That's why I couldn't plan to start a family with something like this on my mind. I'm harboring a secret from my wife. Or if she knows, she's keeping a secret from me." His eyes bore into Daniel's. "She doesn't know, does she?"

"No. That's what the biological father wanted. I didn't know who he was. Pastor Jim said the father didn't want his daughter to know about him. He had two requests. One, that she not be told she was adopted. And two, that the painting of the old homeplace stay with her. We decided to honor those requests."

"How old was she when this happened?" Brent asked.

"Two weeks. Why do you look so puzzled, Brent?"

"I don't understand Nick's having that kind of control over the baby. Wouldn't Rosa have the legal issues on her side? I'm not trying to pry into your or her past. I'm just trying to understand this situation. You make it sound like Nick had custody or something."

"Well, yes," Daniel said. "He is the biological father."

Brent's eyes widened in surprise. He leaned forward. "Rosa isn't Tina's birth mother?"

"I thought you understood that. We adopted her, Brent." Daniel knew he'd have to tell the whole story, what little he knew of it. He'd been told the mother died shortly after Tina was born and of the father's two requests. When he finished, he had to ask, "This doesn't change your feelings for Tina, does it, Brent?"

Brent answered immediately. "This doesn't change who she is, what she is, or my love for her. I fell in love with Tina, not her heritage, whatever it might be."

Daniel believed that. Brent was a fine man. But he couldn't help but feel that Brent might not think as highly of him and Rosa, knowing they had kept this secret from their daughter and from him. It wasn't a sin to have kept this from her. They'd abided by her biological father's wishes. Everything they'd done for Tina was out of love for her.

"I don't know how you feel, Brent, but I don't see any purpose in shaking up Tina's life with this kind of information. Maybe we made a mistake not going against her biological father's wishes and telling her when she was growing up. But she has been our daughter legally and in every other way. She's a grown woman now. Why bring it up?"

"I understand your point of view," Brent said. "There's some logic to it. But if I keep this between you, Rosa, and myself, then I have a secret I keep from my wife. She's already upset because it seems I've changed my mind about having a family. Daniel, you say her mother died in childbirth. Is there some kind of heredity thing that would endanger Tina if she bore a child?"

Daniel slumped back against the chair and closed his eyes. "I don't know," he said miserably. He'd never thought of that.

"Can I take that chance with my wife? Can you take that chance with your daughter? Or do I just tell Tina I never want to have children? Do I destroy her love for me and our marriage? Are you asking me to live that way?"

Am I? Daniel asked himself. *Do I ask this admirable young man to bear a burden that isn't his? Do I cause him to be less than honest with his wife—my daughter? Am I not the one who has set a high standard of conduct for the man to whom I entrusted my daughter? Can I cause pain and suffering in their marriage because I'm afraid my daughter will lose respect for me if she learns I've kept this secret?*

The silence was interminable. Daniel felt Brent's eyes on him, waiting. They both wanted to do the right thing. But what was it?

Daniel stood. "Let me talk to Rosa about how we should handle this."

Brent reached for the envelope. Daniel put his hand on it. "This is my responsibility, not yours. I'll keep it, if you don't mind."

Daniel knew how to counsel other people and, as Brent did in his work, used Scripture to solve problems. But he didn't seem to have a specific passage for this issue. Or maybe it was easier to trust and have faith when the trial was on the other person's side instead of on your own. He could recall vast numbers of Scripture about faith, could quote them. One thing he must rely on. God said, "I will never fail you. I will never forsake you. All things work together for good to those who love the Lord."

He'd always believed those words. He'd relied on them, preached them. But never before had he had so much trouble applying them to his own life. He mustn't let fear replace faith. He dreaded facing Rosa with this. Maybe his mentor, Pastor Jim, could show him the best way to handle this situation.

Daniel left the church and drove to the rehab center, where a nurse was right beside Jim in the hallway. Jim was holding onto a railing along the wall, designed to assist patients in walking. Jim's right leg wasn't cooperating very well, but at least he was out of bed and out of the wheelchair. That looked like improvement.

The nurse smiled. "We're improving by leaps and bounds. We'll be back to our old self before you know it."

Normally, Daniel might have joked about the nurse's use of "we," as if she were the patient too. But this afternoon, he had more pressing matters on his mind than joking. "Room," Jim said, with the last part of the word muffled, but it was clear enough to be understandable.

"We're ready to go back to our room?" the nurse asked.

There was no misunderstanding Jim's nod.

After he was sitting in the wheelchair, in front of the window, Daniel drew up a chair in front of him. He didn't worry about the contents of the envelope being a shock to Jim. He'd already seen Nick. He'd already talked to the man. Daniel took out the picture and showed it to Jim, who gazed at it, then closed his eyes briefly, without attempting to speak.

"He left a letter for you. Would you like for me to read it to you?"

Jim's closing of his eyes indicated he would. Daniel read it, glancing at Jim occasionally, seeing his steady gaze as if he were trying to evaluate Daniel's response. After finishing the letter, Daniel told Jim how Brent had figured out the situation, the difficulty a secret like this was causing. "Do you know what Tina's mother died from?"

Jim's no was clear.

"What should I do, Jim? Do I tell Tina? Do I ignore Nick? What's this going to do to our family?"

Jim did and said exactly what Daniel expected.

Nothing! Daniel took Jim's hand in his. "Thanks for listening."

"You. . .do. . .ri. . .tin," Jim said, nodding.

"Will I do the right thing?" Daniel asked aloud, then realized how clearly Jim had spoken, and there was no drool to wipe away.

Jim said, "You." He pointed at Daniel. "Ball."

Daniel nodded and smiled. "Yes, the ball's in my court. Now what do I do with it?"

Jim replied what sounded like, "Play."

"Play?" Daniel asked.

Jim took his pencil and wrote, "P—R."

"Oh, I get it," Daniel said before Jim finished the word. "Pray. Good advice. That's what I'd tell someone else in this situation." He shook his bent head. "Jim, I'm a preacher. But I've never felt so inadequate. At a loss. . ."

Jim tugged on his arm, and Daniel lifted his gaze. Jim nodded and pointed to himself, then wrote, "Me too. Why me? Now I know."

Daniel nodded, understanding. Even Jim had doubts and questions sometimes. "Knowing you, I think you would act as a mediator between me and Nick in this situation if you could. But like you said, the ball's in my court. I'm the one who has to play it." He smiled wryly. "And pray."

Chapter 9

It seemed to Daniel that he spent the rest of the afternoon praying nonstop. When he arrived home, he had Rosa sit down with him, and he held her hands while he prayed for God's guidance and wisdom. Then he told Rosa everything he knew, from the time he talked with Nick on the phone, to Brent's question about how Tina's birth mother had died, and through his visit with Jim.

Rosa listened intently, then looked at the picture and read the letter. "Daniel," she said in that easy way of hers. "When that little girl was laid in my arms, she became mine. I don't know if this is possible, but I think I'm even closer to her than I would have been if she were my biological child. I've never for a moment taken her for granted. She has always been God's special miracle to both of us."

Daniel was nodding. When Tina was little, they'd talked about it a lot.

"But the only thing that ever worried me," Rosa added, "is that somehow, someway, Tina would stumble onto the fact that she was adopted. I wanted to abide by the biological father's request, but I didn't want her to find out unless you and I told her."

"I know." Daniel agreed with everything his wife said. "I don't want Tina to be hurt or disillusioned. If we tell her now that she's adopted, how will it affect her life? Will she forgive us?"

"If we don't tell her, Daniel, how will this affect her life with Brent? If he didn't know, it might be another matter. But you say he knows. I told you how excited Tina was about deciding to start a family. Now, her heart is crushed. Not because of Brent, but because of our secret. Ignoring this is not going to make it go away. If nothing else, we have to know why Tina's birth mother died in childbirth. We can't let this happen to our daughter."

Daniel knew Rosa was right. But he had to hear her side of it. Like he'd told Brent, communication was important in a relationship. And Rosa often made him see matters from a different viewpoint. That's exactly what she did with her next words: "There's something else, Daniel. You and I have been blessed with Tina for twenty-five years. Does this man not deserve some kind of blessing too? Can we not let him know his daughter had a good life and is happy—or at least *was* happy," she added with a poignant look.

"It's not that I don't want to share her," Daniel began.

"I know," Rosa said, smiling. "You're afraid she won't love and respect you anymore."

"Aren't you?" he asked.

Rosa nodded. "Concerned, yes. If we tell her, there may be a considerable adjustment period. But we'll get through it. I have faith in the kind of daughter we raised.

But what is most valuable—what Tina might lose or what she might gain?"

Daniel's questioning look encouraged Rosa to continue. "I've lost a lot in my life, Daniel. The worst time of my life was when I lost our baby and couldn't have more. Later, I lost my grandparents, then my own parents. But I had God and I had my husband to rely on. I honestly don't know how Tina will respond to you and me if we tell her she's adopted, but I know she has God in her life and I know she will turn to Brent. They will be her strength. Do we selfishly cling to our secret, or do we give our daughter the truth and allow it to make her free?"

Tina hated it! Not being able to make up with Brent because he wouldn't tell her what his problem was. He tried convincing her that it had nothing to do with a lack of love for her. She couldn't figure it out. Things got even more confusing when her mom called and said in a solemn voice that she wanted Tina and Brent to come over after supper.

"Mom," Tina answered. "Brent and I will solve our own problems."

"Honey, this is something your dad and I want to talk to you about."

"Okay," Tina said, without further questions. An eerie feeling crept over her. Something was wrong. And one look at Brent, who didn't meet her eyes, told her he knew what it was. Tina didn't ask. She didn't want to know that something awful was going on that she had to be told about in the presence of her husband and parents.

That feeling increased when Brent said, "I just want

you to remember that I love you, no matter what. Now, let's go pick up a milk shake or something and go to your parents' house."

How incredible, Tina thought a couple hours later. Twenty-five years, her entire life, changed in such a brief time. After asking her and Brent to sit together on the couch, her dad had started it by saying, "We love you, Tina. Don't ever doubt that. But there's something we have to tell you."

How familiar that sounded. When she was growing up and needed a spanking, her mom or dad would preface it with, "I love you and that's why I have to discipline you. I want you to grow up to be a good little girl." When she was older, and needed to be restricted, they would say, "I'm doing this because I love you and want you to learn a lesson from what you've done." And even in college, they'd say, "Because we love you we think it best you work during the summer and use some of that money for your education so you learn responsibility."

What had she done now that her dad had to preface his conversation with, "We love you"?

Her mom started then, retelling about the years of her miscarriage and thyroid condition that had been devastating and almost unbearable until Tina, their miracle child, came along. Tina had heard it before, but this time the story had a different twist. This time she learned that she hadn't grown in her mom's body, but she had come from the hands of Pastor Jim Stoddard, having been given to him by some man they referred to as her biological father.

It couldn't be true. But when she looked at the picture and read the letter, it was like looking at the box cover of the puzzle. Pieces were coming together. Over there were two people with dark hair and dark eyes. Here was a fair-skinned girl with chestnut hair and blue-green eyes. Their dispositions were mild. Hers was sensitive and impulsive.

"Why tell me now?" she asked.

Brent told her about confronting Daniel after seeing the picture and reading the letter. He even explained about looking at the paintings instead of picking tomatoes. He must have been as shocked as she. Her head turned quickly and she stared at him fearfully. "I'm not really the person you thought you married."

"That's right," he said seriously, and she felt a tremor go through her. Then he smiled, with a twinkle in his eyes, uncaring that her mom and dad were watching. "You get more interesting every day."

Then Daniel explained why Brent was so concerned. "He didn't want to keep a secret from you, Tina. And when I explained things to him, he was fearful because your birth mother died right after you were born. He was afraid that could happen with you."

Tina unclasped her fingers and moved them toward Brent. His was right there waiting to squeeze her hand affectionately and hold it in his. He hadn't stopped loving her. His attitude about waiting to start a family had been because he loved her so much.

After interminable silence, her dad said, "Honey, do you want to say anything, ask anything?"

Tina looked from one pair of questioning eyes to another. "I know what all of you have said. But I don't feel anything. Why don't I feel anything?"

"You haven't processed it yet," Brent said. "It isn't real to you."

She nodded.

She looked at the picture again. She read the letter again. A letter from her "real" father. Was this a dream? Or a nightmare? Some kind of joke? But no one was smiling. They were all looking at her like she might throw a tantrum or something. *Or are they looking at me like I'm a stranger?*

"Is that why I never really fit in? I mean, I don't look like you two at all. I don't think like you. I'm not really. . . made of you. None of your genes are in me. Suddenly, I feel like a stranger to myself. I know you people. But I don't know me."

Tina was working on a collage. Her mom and dad had so many extra prints that weren't in photo albums that Tina had no problem having them part with the pictures. Some she took from her own albums. No one asked why she was doing it. Brent thought perhaps she was trying to make sense of her life. Put all her life together as if the revelation of her adoption had scattered the pieces, like the puzzle he'd mentioned. Maybe she was trying to "know" herself.

He, Daniel, and Rosa were sort of tiptoeing around her. They were all doing the same things, saying the same things, but it was like walking a tightwire. When was Tina going to explode? Or was she escaping through keeping busy, looking over her life. Was she never going to share what she felt about being adopted? Or was she still in such shock she couldn't accept it? Was she in denial?

In his favor, Brent felt, was the fact that she had not turned from him. Their time together had changed, however. It was more intense, always serious, with none of her little playful antics or impulsiveness. Something was going on inside her, but he didn't press her about it. He'd recently harbored thoughts that he couldn't share. He would just be there, supporting her and loving her.

One bright spot in the waiting game was Jim's ability to go home. He would return to the rehab center for therapy a couple times a week, but his motor skills had improved to the point where he could walk, and most of his words were understandable. Brent and Daniel were encouraged when, after they told Jim what had transpired, he said that Tina was a smart girl. She would be fine; just give her time and don't push. "And," he said, adding his usual advice, "pray."

It was more than a week later that they were eating supper at Daniel and Rosa's house. The conversation was light and included their joy that Jim was making such great improvement. He might even be able to preach again in a few months, and Daniel's hectic pace would finally ease some.

Tina had brought her finished collage to show them after supper. It depicted many facets of her life, from infancy when Daniel was in seminary and they lived in a trailer, her early childhood in Ohio, the house where they'd lived, her at various ages and in activities like ballet, piano, swimming, and church. She included pictures of herself in kindergarten, grade school, high school, and college. A wedding picture showed her in her white gown with Brent in his tux. Daniel and Rosa Stood beside them, looking as happy as the bride and groom. The most recent was one that Brent had taken of her sitting on top of a boulder at Garden of the Gods, sketching Camel Rock.

They all praised the collage, wondering but not asking why she made it. Maybe it was for the child she hoped one day to have. Then Tina said, "I want to meet Nick."

Chapter 10

Nick was sitting alone on his porch, in the rocking chair, watching the day turn to night when the phone rang. He almost didn't answer it, but thought he might as well continue going through the motions of living, like he'd done for so many years. And now wasn't any different, except his food didn't taste as good and his laundry wasn't folded and he never dusted. Mary hadn't come to his house since he got back. She never would again. That was nipped in the bud before it ever got a chance to bloom.

This morning in church, he didn't look at her in the choir. He occasionally glanced at the preacher, but mostly he kept his eyes on the pink scalp showing through the thin gray hair of the woman sitting on the pew in front of him. While the choir sang their special, he closed his eyes, trying to block out any distractions.

"Hello," he said on the third ring, sounding as weary as he felt.

"Nick Malone?"

"Yes," he said. He'd heard that voice before but could not place it.

"Pastor Robinson here. I talked with you a couple weeks ago about Pastor Jim Stoddard."

Nick's first thought was that something had happened. "Is he all right?"

"Improving daily. He's going to be fine."

"I'm glad to hear it," Nick said. "I really appreciate your calling to let me know." But why was he calling? How did he get his name and number? Had Brent shared the letter with him? He supposed that was all right.

"I'm calling for another reason, Nick. Can you prove you are who you say you are?"

Nick gave a short laugh. "I have a driver's license and a Social Security number."

"No, I don't mean that. Your letter said you gave up your little girl to Pastor Jim twenty-five years ago."

"Did Jim not recognize me?" he asked.

"I think he did. But like you said, it's been twenty-five years. I don't want there to be any mistake here. Before we take this any further, I need to have proof that you're the one who put that baby in Pastor Jim's arms."

Take it any further? What did that mean? But this Pastor Robinson was talking about his little girl. Maybe he was checking this out for Pastor Jim, so he could let him know everything was fine with his little girl. "I have a couple of pictures of the baby and some notes her mother wrote about our family history before she died."

"I'm sorry to grill you like this, Nick. But I need to know how your wife died."

Even after so many years, Nick had difficulty talking about it. If the two of them had had more sense, Raine would have gone to a hospital and been fine. He'd have her. He'd have his little girl. "Raine had the baby at our home. She refused to go to a hospital. There were complications." His voice broke. "She lost so much blood. She. . .bled to death."

"I'm sorry I had to put you through this, but I had to know. Your little girl is grown now and planning to start a family. She needs to know there isn't something hereditary that might cause difficulty in childbirth."

"No, no there isn't. Raine was healthy. She was just like me at that time. Kind of hard-headed. But, Pastor Robinson. You must know something, since you're calling me."

Nick heard him take a deep breath before saying, "Nick, my wife and I adopted your little girl."

Nick dropped the phone and had to retrieve it. "I'm sorry. I dropped the phone. You and your wife? My little girl? Look, I didn't mean to upset anybody. I just wanted to know she was okay. I shouldn't have. Forgive me. I didn't mean to stir up any trouble."

When he stopped ranting, Daniel said simply, "She wants to meet you."

Nick was openly crying. He didn't know if it was from joy or regret that he'd maybe opened Pandora's box. "Do you mind? I mean, like I said. I didn't mean—"

The pastor interrupted. "Do you want to see her?"

"Could I?"

"I'll send you plane fare."

"Thank you for the offer," Nick said. "But I can handle that just fine."

"When can we expect you?"

Nick didn't have to wrestle with that question. "I'll take the next flight out."

Tina didn't know how she might feel, seeing a strange man that was supposed to be her biological father. But she had her support group gathered in her mom and dad's living room. Her parents were there, of course. Pastor Jim and his wife, Moira, came. Brent had gone to the airport to get Nick.

How they were able to talk about ordinary things, like Jim and Moira's family, Tina didn't know. Never had her mind seemed to be divided into two such distinct entities. Her heart almost beat out of her chest when Brent and Nick arrived.

Tina watched as Brent introduced Nick to her mom and dad. He was a good-looking man, but she thought he'd look more natural in casual clothes than the suit and tie he wore. He'd apparently dressed for the occasion, as had she. Instead of the usual shorts or jeans, she wore a summer dress.

Moira and Jim walked over to Nick, and they embraced for a long time, giving Tina the impression they had been good friends once. She noticed how Nick tried not to look at her, but his glances at her were as frequent as hers were at him. Finally, Brent brought Nick over to her.

Tina stood, staring into the blue-green eyes of the man who had given her away. "This is my wife, Bettina Raine Robinson Abbot," Brent said.

"You nut," she said, hitting Brent on the arm, then looking at the man again, extending her hand. "I'm Tina."

"I'm Nick," he said, taking her hand in his. The moment their hands touched, she saw his eyes change. They grew moist, and his chin trembled. But he smiled and said in an almost steady voice, "The last time I touched that hand it was about yea-big." He lifted his left hand, measuring about an inch with his thumb and forefinger. They all laughed lightly.

Just when she began to think he would never let go of her hand, he did and reached inside his jacket pocket. "I have some pictures here of when you were a baby." He turned to look at Daniel and Rosa. "If that's okay."

"There are no rules here tonight," Daniel said. "Tina wanted to meet you, and this is a time of complete honesty for us all."

Nick nodded and handed Tina some notes, along with the pictures. "Raine, your mother, wrote this. It's the Malone family history. My grandfather told it to her the day he died."

Tina took the pages and sat on the couch beside Brent to let him share in reading them. Nick sat in a chair almost opposite her, at the other side of the coffee table. The account was touching, the story of generations of a family united by its faith.

"Feel free to read it," Tina said and handed the letter to her mom. Like her dad said, there would be no secrets here tonight. Rosa read the story and passed it onto Moira, then stood and began asking what everyone wanted to drink. She had juice, lemonade, coffee, tea, and water. Everyone chose water.

"I'd like to hear about you and Raine, your relationship with the Stoddards and. . .myself when I was a baby," Tina said while Rosa passed around a silver tray on which sat crystal glasses of iced water and napkins.

She listened carefully as Nick and the Stoddards recalled those days. Still, after what seemed like hours of stories about people called her biological parents, Tina could not feel any connection with those early events. She liked this man. She liked his humility and his honesty about himself and the life he'd lived away from God and how he'd come to rely on the Lord. She believed he had truly grieved over giving her away. Although she had been conceived out of wedlock, she believed Raine and Nick had truly been committed to each other when they got married and that they'd continued to love each other until Raine's death. She believed his giving her away had not been an act of weakness, but one of inner strength. He had wanted the best for her.

Nick even talked about his chance with Mary that he'd messed up because he couldn't completely let go of the past. Then they began to catch up on the lives of the Stoddard children, now all grown, the youngest Tina's age.

Tina began to know Nick. She respected the fact that there seemed to be no pretense to him and that he wasn't trying to impress her or anyone. He was just baring his soul, trying to accommodate her desire to know about him.

When it seemed he'd finished with his story, she got up and retrieved the collage from behind the couch, then went over and showed it to him. She knelt beside him as he held it, and photo by photo, she explained her life to him. When she finished, she said, "You may keep it."

She had to look away from the wonder in his eyes as he said unbelievingly, "You mean it? It's for me?"

Tina returned to her place beside Brent and was grateful when he grasped her hand and held on tight. A night for honesty, her dad had said. What she would say would be said in front of all of them. She looked at her mom and dad. "Will it hurt you in any way if I were to include Nick somehow? You're my parents. Nothing can change that. Whatever I would have with him would be built starting from the present."

She had to stop and take a sip of water, then return the glass to the coffee table. All without removing that other hand from Brent's. Her parents had simply sat there, looking at her with the same expressions she'd known all her life—expressions of unconditional love.

"I do feel a special attachment to Nick, but I don't know him. I know he's blood related, and that means something. I don't mind that I didn't know him while growing up. But now that I do know him, I wouldn't feel right keeping my children from him. But if it would take anything from you, if you have any concern about that, then I don't want to do it. You're my family. God has given me the best parents a person could have. I don't want to give you a moment's hurt."

"Whatever you want," her dad said. Tina's mom looked at her with love-filled eyes. "Nobody can take away what we have, Tina," she said. "Nobody can erase the twenty-five years we've had together. You're your own person now. You're a married woman, about to start your own family. We'll always be a part of that. You are our legal daughter. You are our heart's daughter. But you have a blood-related parent. None of us can ignore it. I can't see that it would take from any of us for you to pursue a relationship with him, if that's what you want. We will support you in it."

Her mom looked at Nick then, still addressing her. "I

can't see that Nick would do any more than enrich your life. He can't force his way into your life, and I don't think he's trying to."

"No," Nick said, blinking back the moisture from his eyes.

"It's all your decision, daughter," her dad said. "Like we told you while you were growing up. You must make your own decisions about some things. If it's the right one, we will praise you. If it's the wrong one, we will be there helping you through it. You cannot lose the love we have for you. You're our daughter. Nothing can change that."

She went over and kissed them both.

Then she went over to Nick. He stood. "Nick," she said. "Nobody could have better parents than I have. No one could love me more, or have taken better care of me. I couldn't love anyone else more."

Nick's chin was trembling. "That's what I wanted for you."

She nodded, looking straight into Nick's eyes.

Nick was scared. What was she going to do?

Then she stretched out her arms. Nick glanced around. Nobody was protesting. They all had wet eyes. Or was that just a reflection of his own? They looked okay about it. If he embraced his little girl, if he held her in his arms, he might crush her. He might not be able to stand it.

But he did. With a sob he enveloped her in his arms.

"I'm glad to meet you, Dad," she said. After a long moment of a genuine hug she stepped back. She knew her face was as wet as his. "And I love you for what you've done for me." Tina's mother came over with tissues for them both and then took one for herself.

Tina returned to her seat. "Do you think you have a future with Mary?"

"If she'll have me," he said.

"Well," Tina said in that direct way that Raine had always had, "I already have parents. But I don't see any problem with our children having an extra set of grandparents. That is, if you think you're up to having chocolate-chip cookies on hand whenever they visit and being accepting of wet kisses, sticky fingers, and muddy feet."

"Yes, oh yes," Nick said immediately. "I mean, if it's all right with everybody."

He looked around. They all nodded and even smiled. Tina laughed. "I've already run this by everybody. They know it doesn't take anything from them."

Nick's laugh was one of joy. His little girl wanted him to be a part of her life. The feeling was overwhelming. His head bent and his shoulders began to shake. "I'm sorry," he said. "The saddest day of my life was when I laid my little girl in Pastor Jim's arms. The wound healed slowly. But there's always been the scar. There to haunt me, to taunt me, to make me question myself. God accepted me, but how could anyone else? Now, what I could never have hoped for has happened. I wanted my little girl to have the best life anyone could give you. You've done that. She's wonderful. I couldn't have done it. And now. . .this is the happiest day of my life. Heaven couldn't be any better."

His head bent. His shoulders shook. "I'm sorry," he said brokenly. "It's just that I feel the scar on my heart is fading." Wiping his face and forcing himself away from the strong emotions, he had to say one more thing. "Just tonight would be enough. To know my girl had a good life. But you're all offering so much more. Thank you. Thank you."

"I think we can thank our heavenly Father for this," Daniel said. "I've learned more in the past few days about how weak, how blind, how frail we human beings are than I learned in a lifetime. But I can see now that God has worked in this all along. I shouldn't have doubted. I shouldn't have feared. I'm a preacher, yes. But I am a frail human being, too."

Nick smiled through his tears. "Yes, but it's preachers like you and Pastor Jim who remind us of how God wants us to live. When we need it most, those words return to us."

Nick was overjoyed. His little girl was beautiful and wonderful and had a good life. He could see it with his own eyes. She couldn't be with finer people. She'd even said she loved him. She didn't hate him. She loved him for giving her away. And she wasn't being sarcastic. She wasn't being resentful. She was letting him know he had done the right thing and that she didn't hate him.

"I should go," Nick said, looking across to Daniel, afraid of what he might see in his eyes.

He saw only warmth and goodness. "No," Daniel said. "You're welcome here anytime Tina wants you here. You're part of the family. Whatever relationship she wants to have with you, we'll accept." He held out his hand. Nick went over and shook it, knowing Daniel was sealing his word with a handshake.

Chapter 11

Nick didn't think Daniel and Rosa would have asked if they hadn't been sincere, but he declined their invitation to stay at their home for the night. He called the airport and discovered he couldn't get a flight out before morning. He went home with Pastor Jim and Moira. That seemed right. There were still things he could tell Jim about his life, and he wanted to hear more about theirs.

Early the next morning, Brent came by and drove him to the airport. "Be seeing you," Brent said, as if he meant it.

As soon as he had his ticket, carrying his wrapped collage with him, Nick found a telephone and called Mary. "I met my daughter, Mary. She's beautiful and wonderful. I'll tell you all about it when I get home. Everything's okay, Mary."

"Maybe you can look at me again," Mary said.

"I can do better than that." He had to yell to be heard over the din in the airport. But he didn't care who heard. "I love you, Mary. Will you marry me?"

"I've waited a long time to hear you say that, Nick.

Yes. Oh, yes. I'll marry you."

"One other question, Mary. How do you feel about having grandchildren?"

"Nick. I thought I told you, I can't have children."

"Oh, that's all right, Mary. I have a daughter. And she wants to have children. And she wants us to be the grandparents."

Nick heard her sniff and then speak in a broken voice. "I would be honored, Nick, to be a grandmother to your daughter's children."

"Mary," he said. "It's almost time for my flight. I'm coming home, Mary. Coming home to you."

Walking away from the airport phone, Nick felt a lightness to his stride as he approached the boarding section. He laughed aloud. He couldn't help it. Thomas Wolfe might be famous, but he didn't know what he was talking about when he said you couldn't go home again.

Home is where the heart is.

Nick's scar was gone, and his heart could now belong to Mary.

Yes, indeed. Nick Malone was finally going home again.

When Tina arrived home from a friend's bridal shower at church late that evening, Brent wasn't in the living room. She followed the sound of soft music to the bedroom and gasped at the sight. There stood Brent, smiling at her in the glow of candlelight. Over against one wall stood the bassinet that had been stored in her parents' basement for many years. Now it was draped with a delicate white skirt that reached to the floor.

"What?" she whispered, walking closer to the bassinet, staring at the painting above it. "The painting of Laurelwood," she said, touching it gently with her fingertips. For the first time in her life she felt a connection to it.

"I didn't goof, did I, Tina?" Brent asked carefully.

She could only shake her head. Finally, she turned to him with tear-filled eyes. "Nothing could please me more. How did you ever think of doing this?"

He grinned. "I love the way you often surprise me, Tina. I thought I would try it for once. Come over here."

She followed him to the bedside table. On it were the long-stemmed glasses in front of a bottle of sparkling white grape juice and a small bowl of chocolate-covered cherries. She looked at him with love and wonder, hoping she knew what it meant.

"What I'm trying to tell you, Tina," he said seriously, "is that I'm ready to start a family any time you are."

"Here's your answer," she said softly, lifting her face for a kiss and circling his neck with loving arms.

After a long moment, Tina drew back. "I'd like to make a toast," she said. Brent poured the juice into the glasses. She walked toward the bassinet and lifted the glass toward the painting. "To all the generations who have gone before us, and those yet to come," she said, "who have and will have the love for God and home, symbolized in the lovely painting of Laurelwood."

YVONNE LEHMAN

As an award-winning novelist from Black Mountain, North Carolina, in the heart of North Carolina's Smoky Mountains, Yvonne Lehman has written several novels for Barbour Publishing's Heartsong Presents line. Her titles include *Southern Gentleman, Mountain Man,* which won a National Reader's Choice Award sponsored by a chapter of Romance Writers of America, *After the Storm,* and *Call of the Mountain.* Yvonne has published more than two dozen novels, including books in the Bethany House "White Dove" series for young adults. In addition to being an inspirational romance writer, she is also the founder of the Blue Ridge Christian Writers' Conference, a wife, mother, and grandmother.

A Letter to Our Readers

Dear Readers:

In order that we might better contribute to your reading enjoyment, we would appreciate your taking a few minutes to respond to the following questions. When completed, please return to the following: Fiction Editor, Barbour Publishing, Inc., P.O. Box 719, Uhrichsville, OH 44683.

1. Did you enjoy reading *The Painting?*
   ❑ Very much, I would like to see more books like this.
   ❑ Moderately—I would have enjoyed it more if _____
   _____
   _____

2. What influenced your decision to purchase this book?
   (Check those that apply.)
   ❑ Cover   ❑ Back cover copy   ❑ Title   ❑ Price
   ❑ Friends   ❑ Publicity   ❑ Other _____

3. Which story was your favorite?
   ❑ *Where the Heart Is*   ❑ *New Beginnings*
   ❑ *Turbulent Times*   ❑ *Going Home Again*

4. Please check your age range:
   ❑ Under 18   ❑ 18–24   ❑ 25–34
   ❑ 35–45   ❑ 46–55   ❑ Over 55 _____

5. How many hours per week do you read? _____

Name _____

Occupation _____

Address _____

City _____ State _____ Zip _____

If you enjoyed

The Painting

then read:

Frontiers

Four Inspirational Love Stories
from America's Frontier by Colleen Reece

Flower of Seattle
Flower of the West
Flower of the North
Flower of Alaska

_H_EARTSONG ♥ PRESENTS

Love Stories
Are Rated G!

That's for godly, gratifying, and of course, great! If you love a thrilling love
story, but don't appreciate the sordidness of some popular paperback
romances, **Heartsong Presents** is for you. In fact, **Heartsong Presents** is the
only inspirational romance book club, the only one featuring love stories
where Christian faith is the primary ingredient in a marriage relationship.

Sign up today to receive your first set of four, never-before-published
Christian romances. Send no money now; you will receive a bill with the first
shipment. You may cancel at any time without obligation, and if you aren't
completely satisfied with any selection, you may return the books for an
immediate refund!

Imagine. . .four new romances every four weeks—two historical, two
contemporary—with men and women like you who long to meet the one God
has chosen as the love of their lives. . .all for the low price of $9.97 postpaid.

To join, simply complete the coupon below and mail to the address provided. **Heartsong Presents** romances are rated G for another reason: They'll
arrive Godspeed!

YES!   Sign me up for Hearts♥ng!

NEW MEMBERSHIPS WILL BE SHIPPED IMMEDIATELY!
Send no money now. We'll bill you only $9.97 postpaid with your first
shipment of four books. Or for faster action, call toll free 1-800-847-8270.

NAME _____

ADDRESS_____

CITY_____ STATE_____ ZIP_____

MAIL TO: HEARTSONG PRESENTS, P.O. Box 719, Uhrichsville, Ohio 44683

YES1-99